PRAISE FOR BARBARA WOOD

"A master storyteller. She never fails to leave the reader enthralled."
—Elizabeth Forsythe Hailey, author of *A Woman of Independent Means*

"Barbara Wood is an entertainer."
—*Washington Post Book World*

"An accomplished storyteller."
—John Jakes, *New York Times* bestselling author

"Wood makes her fiction come alive with authentic detailing and highly memorable characters."
—*Booklist*

HOUNDS AND JACKALS

HOUNDS AND JACKALS

BARBARA WOOD

TURNER

Turner Publishing Company

200 4th Avenue North • Suite 950
Nashville, Tennessee 37219

445 Park Avenue • 9th Floor
New York, New York 10022

www.turnerpublishing.com

Hounds and Jackals

Cover design by Gina Binkley
Interior design by Mike Penticost

Library of Congress Cataloging-in-Publication Data

Wood, Barbara, 1947-
Hounds and jackals / Barbara Wood.
p. cm.
ISBN 978-1-59652-870-3
1. Sisters--Fiction. 2. Americans--Italy--Rome--Fiction. 3. Americans--Egypt-
-Cairo--Fiction. I. Title.
PS3573.O5877H68 2012
813'.54--dc23
2012006394

Printed in the United States of America
12 13 14 15 16 17 18—0 9 8 7 6 5 4 3 2 1

This book is nostalgically dedicated to my husband, George.

HOUNDS
AND
JACKALS

CHAPTER 1

"*Y*OU'VE GOT A PHONE CALL. JENNY'S SCRUBBING. SHE'LL RELIEVE you so you can take it."

Mrs. Cathcart waited patiently while I passed a haemostat to Dr. Kellerman. Not taking my eyes off the field I said, "I'd rather not leave right now. Who's calling? Can I call back?"

"I don't think so, Lydia. It's your sister, Adele, calling from Rome. She says it's urgent."

My head snapped round on a reflex. "Italy?" I said out loud, stupidly. "Are you sure?"

"That's what the operator says. Rome. Person to person. And urgent, too. Jenny's scrubbing for you."

At that point Dr. Kellerman's gruff voice suddenly blurted out, "Jesus! He's gone straight-line!"

My eyes shot to the cardioscope. There was no pulse. In an instant Mrs. Cathcart vanished into thin air and was at once replaced by a room full of teeming, shouting, bumping people. In the distance a cool voice announced over the speakers: "Code Blue, Surgery. Code Blue, Surgery. Code Blue, Surgery." Automatically, with all thoughts of Adele and Rome erased from my mind, I sprang to my present duty. Dr. Kellerman's hands were around the patient's heart. I was rapidly opening sterile syringes of epinephrine and sodium bicarb. From out of nowhere defibrillator paddles were handed up to me. The sound of drapes being torn. Someone unburied the patient's leg, baring an ankle for a cutdown catheter. Someone shouted, "Back from the table! Clear!" The body on the table jumped. The scope remained even. "Give it to him again. Everybody back. Two hundred volts this time. Clear!" Still straight-line. "Get another amp of sodium bicarb. Lydia, hold the paddles. Don't drop them. Is this guy type and crossmatched? Let's get some packed cells up. And not a word to the family yet. Lydia, the paddles. Okay, clear!"

We all gaped expectantly up at the scope. There was a bleep. There was a second bleep. The third was irregular. The line wavered and twittered. "Okay, one more time. Let's get him out of 'fib.' Clear!"

This time it took. The two hundred volts from the defibrillator paddles had shocked the heart back into action. Clinically the patient had been dead three and a half minutes. Biologically he hadn't been dead at all.

"Okay, let's get out of here." Dr. Kellerman's voice was steady, reassuring. "Get an ICU bed up here, this patient has to be watched. Lydia, peritoneal suture, please."

As I slapped the needle holder into his hand, Dr. Kellerman tossed me a fleeting smile with his eyes. He was saying, "That was a close one, girl, but we won."

Bit by bit the emergency team trickled away, leaving us once again as we were, operating quietly in Room Two. But this time the mood was different, for we were apprehensive, and gave no thought to anything other than the patient so trustingly in our hands until he was securely in that ICU bed and being wheeled down the hall.

I surveyed the mess about me: the heaps of bloody sponges, the scattering of instruments and empty syringes, the bewildered-looking heart cart. It never failed to impress me as being a battlefield that had just undergone heavy siege and was now deserted. While I was shaking my head in dismay at the horrendous cleanup job before me, Mrs. Cathcart looked in again.

"Lydia, go take a break. Jenny's offered to clean up for you. Go make you phone call."

My eyebrows flew up. Of course, Adele in Rome. An urgent call. I had forgotten all about it.

One hand, sweaty from the surgical glove, held the phone to my ear while the other plucked nervously at the mask dangling about my neck. I dragged hungrily on a cigarette. It seemed the operator had been gone for hours.

"Hello?" I said testily.

The operator's impersonal voice crackled over the wire. "Still trying. Overseas lines are busy. Can I call you back?"

"No. It's urgent. I'll hang on."

"Certainly. Still trying."

I switched ears. She sounded as if she was talking through cellophane.

In these ostensibly quiet moments—the lounge was deserted—I thought back over the events of the past furious hour, wondering what message lay for me at the other end of the phone. After all, I had not communicated with Adele in over four years, and my supervisor had said the call had come from Rome.

Looking back at the chaos that had filled the last hour, I could not discern what had jarred me most, the message that I had just received a transatlantic phone call from my sister Adele, or the cardiac arrest that had simultaneously occurred on the table.

"One moment please," came the Italian accent. I had successfully reached the number Adele had left—a Residence Palace Hotel in Rome—and was about to be connected with my long-silent sister. In all my scattered thoughts about the operation, the arrest, and the numerous strains of the nursing profession, I was also trying to determine what on earth would prompt Adele to call me, and—even more puzzling—what in Adele's opinion would we both consider urgent?

My sister and I had, long ago, been very close. But that was before the abrupt deaths of our parents and brother. That ironic twist of fate that normally draws families closer together—the death of loved ones—had oddly pushed Adele and me far apart. It had taken a couple of years for the grief to make polite strangers of us both until, at last, four years ago we spoke our mutual good-byes. I was twenty-two that day, Adele twenty-three. I was just learning surgery; Adele, how to charm men. She had spoken vaguely that day of traveling, and I had touched a little upon my serious commitments. Then we had parted with a limp handshake, as though a church tea had just adjourned. And in all that time, until this morning, I had not heard from my sister, Adele.

"Liddie? Liddie, is that you?"

Instantly the ghost of Adele stood before me. "Yes, is that really you, Adele? My God."

"Oh I'm so glad I got you. Oh Liddie, the most exciting thing! Just exciting! Can't wait to tell you!"

Her tiny, distant voice cried shrilly and prattled excitedly in an adolescent way. And as it rang familiarly over the wire, I stared incredulously at the wall opposite me. She called me Liddie! Adele called me Liddie as though we had parted only yesterday.

"Calm down," I said, feeling some of her excitement incense me. "What happened? Are you all right?"

"Of course I am! I'm just great. I'm in Rome, Liddie!"

"I know that."

"Oh, I'm not hurt or anything. But this is urgent all the same. Liddie, can you come to Rome?"

"Can I what?"

"Oh listen. I've sent you something that will explain it all. You should receive it any day now, because I gather you haven't yet. I sent it airmail. Maybe I should have registered it. Now I'm sorry I didn't. Oh Liddie, you must come, please!"

There was a strain, a note of panic in her voice that made me sit up. Adele was obviously extremely happy and excited about something, and yet at the same time an old instinct (she was, after all, still my sister) alerted me that all was not quite as it seemed. "What's wrong?"

"I can't tell you now. But it's just fantastic. I must tell you *in person*. Can you come to Rome?"

"Of course not. Don't be silly." This was Adele. Impetuous and capricious. "I can't leave work. Now tell me what's hap . . ."

"Oh hang your silly job. *You've got to come.* Listen, Liddie, I'm in a hurry . . ."

Her voice stopped abruptly. After a moment I said, "Go on, I'm listening." She did not reply.

"Honestly, Adele. Stop being so dramatic. I did not make this outrageously expensive phone call to play games. Whatever it is you want to tell me, then tell me. I'm not going to drag it out of you. Adele?"

The line went dead. Idiotically I took the receiver from my ear and looked at it. "Hello? Adele? Operator?" I tapped the receiver with my finger. The hospital switchboard answered. "My call was cut off," I explained. "Can you reconnect me?"

"Just a moment, please."

I waited. I listened. The receiver at my ear sounded like the ocean. I heard some clicks, some breathing. Eventually she came back on. "I'm sorry, your call was not disconnected. The other party hung up."

"What? That can't be."

"Would you like to put the call through again?"

"But Adele didn't hang up. Someone disconnected us. Maybe the overseas operator. Or someone at the hotel."

"I'm sorry, but they said your party hung up. Shall I send it through again?"

After a moment's pause, I debated only fleetingly whether or not to pursue Adele from here in the nurses' lounge or to try her again in the privacy of my flat. So I said, "No, I'll try later, thanks." I took a quick shower in the locker room, dressed in street clothes, and announced to the front desk that I was leaving half an hour early. Nobody minded.

Fog met me at Ocean Avenue like a white brick wall, and it felt refreshing after such a hectic day. I looked forward to a peaceful evening in my Malibu flat, reading a silly novel or engrossing myself in a piece of needlepoint. My hours after work were never terribly extraordinary. Tonight would be no exception. Other than, of course, the conversation I planned to have with my sister.

In exasperation I waited with the phone to my ear while the person at the other end went off to find someone who could speak English. Having gone through the overseas operator with a person-to-person call, and having been told that Adele Harris was not registered at the Residence Palace Hotel in Rome, I then directed the operator to give me anyone at the desk, because surely there was some mistake. With my own money, therefore, I bought the minutes in which to speak to a stranger on the other side of the world who seemed to be trying to tell me, in an incredible rush of foreign language, that he did not know my sister.

"I only speak English," I said slowly. "Please. You don't understand. My sister *is* there. Find someone who speaks English."

So the Italian gentleman politely put the phone down and went off in search of someone who could speak my language. Knowing that this might take half an hour, I sat with great resignation in my easy chair and chewed my lower lip. This was getting a bit ridiculous.

"Hallo?" The voice startled me. The man had been gone only a minute.

"Yes?" I sat up.

"You wish Miss Adele Harris? She is not here, madam. She has left the hotel."

"Are you sure? Then where has she gone?"

"I do not know, madam. She did not say."

"Yes, well, you see, I'm her sister. Calling from *America* and I was just talking to her this afternoon. There, at your hotel. She must have left a message for me. A number where she can be reached. *Surely.*"

"I am sorry, madam. No message."

"For Lydia Harris? You're sure?"

I could almost hear him shrug. "Miss Harris has left some time ago. Her room is empty, and she has paid her bill. She said nothing."

"I see." Of course, I did *not* see. "Well, thank you. Good-bye."

"Good-bye, madam."

My face was warm from the flames in the fireplace. My eyes stared glassily. That child, I told myself, was always a scatter-brain. Calls me in surgery, demands to speak to me, tells everyone it's urgent, then laughs when she gets me, then gives me no hint what it's all about, then hangs up on me. And leaves her hotel! Adele, you brat.

I was about to hurl the telephone into the fire when a knock at the door aroused me from my tantrum. It was Shelly, my neighbor, a cocktail waitress who worked nights and slept days. She had a battered parcel in her hands.

"Hi girl, can't come in. This came for you today."

"Oh?" I took the box wrapped in brown paper. It was dented and frayed. The address was in Adele's hand.

"Postman didn't want to leave it on your step, so I offered to take it for you. He made me sign. Do you mind?"

"Not at all. Thanks a lot. Come in for a drink."

"I'm in a hurry. Say, what do you think it is? Is that your sister?"

Adele's name was printed in the corner, just over the address of the Residence Palace on the Via Archimede in Rome. "That's her all right."

"Isn't she the one who never even sends a Christmas card? What is this, your birthday?"

"Hardly. Thanks, Shelly. I owe you."

I closed the door staring at the package in my hands. This must be the article Adele said she had sent airmail, and wished she had registered. Important enough to have it registered. More than a souvenir perhaps . . . Suddenly realizing that there must be a letter of explanation inside, I broke out of my reverie and tore savagely at the paper. It fell away with ease, revealing a plain white box. Stuffed inside was Italian newspaper and some table napkins from the hotel. At the core of this padding I felt something hard. As I was about to tear this last away I spotted the corner of a small piece of stationery and, withdrawing it from between the wadded paper, read the word *Careful* on it. That was all.

So I carefully peeled away the makeshift wrapping and eventually stood in the middle of my living room with the most incredible object in my hands.

CHAPTER 2

ABOUT EIGHT INCHES LONG AND MADE OF A CREAMY SMOOTH material which I guessed to be ivory, the object could best be described as something resembling a fat letter opener, which was tapered at one end and carved at the other. Rather like a miniature walking stick, the yellowed piece of ivory was fashioned at one end in the head of what appeared to be a most unusual dog.

I must have stared for some length at this "thing," for when I finally came out of the spell, I saw that my fire had died and that the room was growing chill. Walking languidly to my chair I cradled the ivory "dog," the box and its wrappings in my arms, and sank down in bewilderment. With great care I dissected all the pieces of paper and cardboard, but found, with dismay, no further communication than that small piece of stationery with the word *Careful* printed upon it. That was all. No letter. Nothing to tell me what this object was or why Adele had sent it.

And was it so precious that she would make a transatlantic call to inform me of its coming? That she wished belatedly she had registered the package? And then, of course, the greatest puzzle: why send it to *me?*

I turned the ivory over and over in my hands. It appeared to be very old, but I was no judge of this. And what sort of dog's head had been carved at the larger end was also a mystery to me. If, indeed, a dog. And such an odd shape it had altogether. Rather like a taper candle with the "dog" at the base. What sort of use was this, or had this item been put to?

My real dilemma concerned what I was expected to do next. Adele had wanted me to come to Rome, but why? And was I supposed to bring this trinket with me? Whatever it was. But then, why had she left her hotel with no message for me?

The next decision was no hard one to make. If anyone could give me a clue as to what this object was, it was Dr. Kellerman, for he was a collector of antiques and oddities. I gave him a quick call, then left my flat and drove the ten miles to Dr. Kellerman's house.

"I would like your opinion on something," I said after making myself comfortable in his study. Accepting a glass of wine, I turned to the roaring fire in the fireplace. Dr. Kellerman's study was a room I always liked, for it was warm and brown and replete with leather furniture, ancient maps, and busts of forgotten men. The plush carpeting subdued all sounds and the tiers of books that lined the walls loomed close to shut out the chill of a foggy night.

"Always glad to be of help, Lydia. But please don't make it such a brief stay. You always flit in and out like a jack rabbit. Let the fog keep you in a while." He sat next to me, the firelight reflected in his eyes. "Now then, what is it you want my opinion on?"

I told him about the afternoon's phone call with Adele, then brought him up-to-date with my latest bout on the phone and my discovery that Adele had left the hotel. Then I explained about the package, its contents, and the simple note. Lastly, I retrieved the "dog" from my handbag.

At first he said nothing. Turning the object over and over in his hands, Dr. Kellerman went into deep thought as he studied it closely. I saw in his eyes, beneath those heavy white brows, that I had caught his interest with this thing, and I began to realize that I might possibly have come into possession of something rare. Even valuable.

"From Rome, you say?"

I nodded.

"Very odd. I've seen this somewhere before, but I can't quite recall." His blue eyes seemed to be scanning unseen pages. "This looks like a dog, but it isn't."

"No?"

"The ears. See how long and pointed they are. And the snout. Queer looking animal. Wild, I would say, not domestic. And it's ivory all right. But what . . ." He tapped the pointed end in his palm. "Where have I seen it?"

Dr. Kellerman's gaze went around the room and over the thousands of titles lining his bookshelves. I, too, scanned the spines of those fabulous books and realized with a thrill that, surely, in all of this, we would find a photograph of this very object.

"I know!" he said suddenly. "It's not Italian at all. And I know just where I've seen it, too."

He stood and strode to the farthest wall, which was lined from floor to ceiling with shelves of books. Dr. Kellerman's hand reached directly for a volume at eye level. A book titled *Ancient Egypt Brought to Life*. He winked at me in the same manner he had done many times over the operating table and returned to his seat next to me on the couch.

"That's no dog, Lydia, it's a jackal. An Egyptian jackal. And it's a game piece."

"A what?"

"A game piece. Like a checker or a chessman. And I'll bet you," he flipped quickly through the leaves of the book, passing by hundreds of color photographs, "I'll bet you it's right in . . . Aha!" He slapped his hand broadly on one page. "Here he is! Our jackal."

My eyes grew wide in amazement. If not the actual piece we held in our hands, the one in the photograph was a close twin. I listened while Dr. Kellerman read the brief description of an ancient Egyptian game called Hounds and Jackals, an illustration of which accompanied the photograph of the ivory jackal. The game board, fashioned of ebony, was engraved with intricate designs and bored with symmetrical lines of holes. The pointed end of the game piece sat in the hole while a throw of knuckle bones decided the movement of the piece. Although it is not known today how the game was played, nor what were the exact rules, it seems there were several of each, hounds (looking more like ordinary dogs) and jackals, and that they might have been handled the same way as black and red checkers. I was thoroughly impressed.

"If this is genuine, Lydia, I would say it is quite valuable." Dr. Kellerman handed me the book. I gazed down at the mate of my jackal. "If your piece is genuinely ancient Egyptian, and I'll wager it is, then I'd say you've got quite a souvenir there."

"Yes, I guess so." I stared in wonder at the ivory jackal in my hand. But why send it to me? I'm certainly no Egyptologist. I'm not even interested in things like this."

"Is your sister?"

"Not that I ever knew of. But she always did have a flair for the mysterious, for the romantic. She always liked palm readers and believed in ancient curses. I suppose she came across this in Rome and thought she'd thrill me with it." But I frowned as I said this, for I did not believe it. Nothing of what I had said so far rang true. Indeed, I refused to believe the only explanation I could come up with for such a gesture. That Adele was trying to give me a message.

"You say she wants you to go to Rome? And she didn't say why? Well," he rubbed his chin. Unlike most surgeons of his age—he was in his fifties—Dr. Kellerman had a beard. "Then I think your sister is trying to tease you to Rome. For some reason, she wants you there. And for some reason, actually for *good* reason, she knew you wouldn't come, so she has used a ploy."

"That doesn't make sense, even for Adele. Not after four years. She'd write. Even a short letter. But not . . ." I fingered the bizarre jackal. "Not this . . ."

"Why not?" Dr. Kellerman stoked the fire and wrinkled his face against flying sparks. Of so many people, including doctors, he was one of the few whose opinion I valued. And yet, for the first time, I was hesitant to go along with him. "I don't know. I just don't know. Surely she'll call again."

"Possibly. Better yet, why not just go to Rome?"

"Go to Rome!" I laughed and touched his arm. "Silly. Then who would you throw your clamps at when things didn't go right?"

"There's always Jerry."

"Yes . . . there's always Jerry." A handsome young anaesthetist with four children. A man I had once had an affair with.

"You never go anywhere, Lydia. It would do you good to get out of the country."

"I go places," I protested loudly.

"Of course you do. Let's see, last year it was Columbus, Ohio for the Operating Room Nurses' convention. Before that it was Oakland for the California Nursing Association convention. The year before that . . ."

"Dr. Kellerman, I'm just not an international traveler."

"I'll say you're not. Columbus and Oakland, Jesus! You almost went to Hong Kong once, as I recall, but you chickened out."

"That's neither here nor there, Dr. Kellerman. As a matter of fact, I think I'll travel home. I'll take this book and my trusty dog and wait patiently for my wayward sister to call back. Which I'm sure she will." I rose and carefully laid the jackal back in my handbag. "Can't imagine why she hung up on me that way. And then check out before calling me back. Oh, Adele."

As I got ready to leave I noticed Dr. Kellerman staring up at the enormous clock over his fireplace. After a moment he said, "When did you get Adele's call?"

"When? Oh, let's see. It was during the heart stat. About one o'clock I'd say."

"And when did you return it?"

"About an hour later. Why?"

"So it was two o'clock in the afternoon here when you spoke to her."

"About that, Why?" I, too, began to gaze at the ornate old clock that ticked softly.

"If I recall correctly, Rome is about nine hours ahead of us. So that would mean it was somewhere around eleven o'clock where Adele was."

"Okay."

"And that would mean she probably checked out of her hotel close to midnight." Dr. Kellerman looked down at me. "I find that rather odd. Don't you?"

I stared back. "Yes, I do."

"Was the operator sure your sister hung up and was not disconnected? Then why on earth would she call you, hang up and suddenly leave her hotel in the middle of the night?"

I returned my gaze to the clock, imagining the sleeping city of Rome at midnight, Adele paying the drowsy clerk, looking for a taxi in the deserted street.

"But this is ridiculous!" As I was about to protest that my sister, no matter how flighty and unpredictable she might be, would never make an urgent call long distance and then hang up in the middle of her own sentence, I caught the vacant expression on Dr. Kellerman's face. He was staring distantly into the fire, and I suspected he was not thinking of either Adele or my jackal. A recent widower and a man inclined to reclusive living, Dr. Kellerman's sole interest in life was his patients. And I knew his mind was now drifting back to the near death we had had on the table today.

So I said with forced flippancy, "Well, ridiculous as it seems, I'm sure there's a logical explanation for it all. Adele will call me back and clear it all up. In the meantime I'll use this jackal as a letter opener or something."

Dr. Kellerman walked me to the car, our hair and shoulders beading with fog, and breath steaming from our mouths. He lived in a nice neighborhood, old and elegant, but a lonely one.

"I just wish at times you would stay longer, Lydia."

I returned his smile. In the three years I had been scrubbing for Dr. Kellerman we had become very good friends. "Good night," I said softly and drove off into the white night.

My initial reaction when I returned home was to stand rooted to the floor, my mouth hanging open. Then I flew into a rage on the spot and stood with my arms akimbo. "Good God!" I cried.

My flat had been broken into.

It was nothing that a casual observer or even a friend might have noticed, for the evidence was slight. Only the inhabitant of this immaculately kept flat would have caught the tiny signs of disturbance. It struck me at once as I entered the door, even—I guess—before my eyes caught anything, as though the very air of the room had been disturbed and was no longer the same. And then I saw the true signs: the lampshade ten degrees askew, the telephone an inch farther from the edge of the desk, a drawer not quite closed. My flat is as well maintained as the operating room I work in, even to extremes, yet this is the way I live. As a result I knew within the first ten seconds of walking through the door that my privacy had been breached.

I was not yet at the point of wondering who could possibly have done this, or even *why,* when I automatically went to the phone and dialed Dr. Kellerman's number. I was in a state of nerves and near tears with anger, for it enraged me terribly that a stranger had helped himself to my privacy. This I could not tolerate. It was not until Dr. Kellerman arrived a short while later and posed the most obvious question to me that I suddenly realized how indignant I had been about the entry, for he asked, "Was anything stolen?" and I had not, until that point, considered burglary. All I could think of was the insufferable crime of trespassing.

A brief but thorough search decided conclusively that nothing had been taken. Not the smallest thing: no jewelery, not the television, nor any money or other valuables. The place had simply been searched, not robbed.

I shook my head incredulously. "Nothing is missing, Dr. Kellerman. Absolutely nothing. And it was a neat search, too, not your average ransacker. Everything was put back close to how it was found so that I wouldn't notice the intrusion. But I did, anyway. I don't understand. Who'd want to search my flat? What were they looking for?"

I sank wearily on the couch next to him and stared into the cold fireplace. Dr. Kellerman likewise stared ahead, his sharp blue eyes full of thought and speculation.

After a while his voice asked softly, "May I see the box your jackal came in?"

I looked at him in surprise. "Heck of a time to change the subject, don't you think?"

"Just let me see it, Lydia."

I stood and started to walk to the desk, when I stopped and considered for a moment. Just where *had* I left that box and its unexpected contents? I looked about the room. No, not in the bedroom. I hadn't carried it in there. Then I looked down at Dr. Kellerman. He was smiling at me with his eyes, as though a mask covered his mouth. "It's gone," I said flatly. "Of course. Something was stolen after all."

Sinking once again on to the couch and cradling my chin in my hands I ruminated over this newest development. "So . . . someone broke in here and searched the place and then took my jackal box. He took the string, the wrapping, the cardboard box, the stuffing paper, and the note that said *Careful* on it. But why? Was he after the jackal?"

"It would seem so."

"But who'd want it? And why take the box and wrappings?"

"And don't forget, Lydia, that whoever it was knew the jackal arrived today. He also used the opportunity of your absence to break in here."

My eyes grew wide in disbelief. "Do you mean I was being watched?"

"How else would they have known when to come in? What they didn't count on was your taking the jackal with you, otherwise—I'll wager—that would be missing too."

I considered this theory for a moment, and it left a bad taste in my mouth. At that point I rose, strode to where I'd dropped my handbag, retrieved the object in question from it, and returned to my place on the couch where Dr. Kellerman and I sat for a good length of time staring at the jackal.

Finally he said, "Call the police, Lydia."

"No," I said before even thinking. "This isn't a case for them. They won't find any fingerprints or clues and you know it. What would they have to go by?"

"Your apartment was burgled all the same and something was stolen."

"Oh Dr. Kellerman, be reasonable. What could the police do for me? Find that battered old box and return it to me? Tell them that was all that was stolen and I want it back? No, not the police." I rolled the jackal between my fingertips. It was cool and smooth. The face of the animal was eerie, its mouth drawn back in a kind of leer, its eyes long and human-like. The ears were abnormally tall and pointed, giving the jackal a devilish look. It was truly a curious object. "Well, the jackal is solid," I said, "so that rules out international jewel thieves." This I said jokingly but I meant it seriously. If anyone was after it, I was groping for their motive. "I want to know why they are after it. I don't like this business, it's taken me so completely by surprise that I don't know which way to move. I am not a person used to mysteries or surprises. I live in an orderly world where answers come from scientific methods. From one o'clock this afternoon my life has taken a twist. A phone call from a sister whom I haven't spoken with in four years. A package in the mail containing a most phenomenal gift with no accompanying explanation. And now . . ." I spread my hands out to indicate the flat " . . . this. Whatever significance this jackal has, it is pretty damned important to someone. And I want to know why. I want to know because it is *my* jackal and it was *my* flat that was violated. I wonder . . ." My mind drifted again, being a confusion of annoyance, bewilderment, and impatience. "Can it have monetary value? You said it would be valuable if genuine."

"Yes, but not all that much. One piece of an entire game set," he shrugged. "A collector maybe. But not enough for someone to break into your apartment."

"And then steal the box and wrappings! That's the puzzling part. What is there about this thing?" I held it up to the light as though the ivory might be transparent and the answers could be seen clearly at its core. "There were others, you say."

"In ancient Egypt, yes, but today I don't . . ."

"If it were, Dr. Kellerman, if this jackal were the only one in existence, then would it have great value?"

He shrugged again. "Possibly. But then of course, we know for sure it's not the only one."

"Of course. The photograph in your book. There are others. Then why *this* one? Unless . . ." A thought was beginning to gel. "Unless someone were trying to collect an entire game set, and needed the last jackal to complete it. Would an entire set of these be valuable? The hounds and the jackals?"

"Priceless, I would imagine."

"All right. Suppose someone was very near to completing an entire set, gathered say over the years, and needed only one or two more pieces. My jackal would be valuable to that person. It might even force him to rob me of it."

"That's ludicrous, Lydia. Such a collector would simply approach you and offer you a price. You're thinking in terms of late-night movies, Lydia, and not being at all logical. Any collector of rare objects would try to secure your jackal on a business level, understanding that it would only be a trinket or souvenir in your possession, reduced perhaps to a paperweight. I think, Lydia, that you're overlooking the most important factor in the whole puzzle. It's not the breaking and entering, or the stolen box and wrappings, or even the possible value of the jackal."

"What then?"

"It's your sister Adele."

"Adele!" I clasped my hands together. "Of course! She started this whole thing. But wouldn't that just bring us right back to the nameless collector? Suppose he tried to buy it from Adele and she wouldn't sell. Suppose she refused his offer and mailed it off to me. That would explain a lot."

"Yes," he said slowly, but I could see by his expression that this idea did not settle easy with him. I know how he felt. The more we examined it, the more mysterious it all became. Nothing seemed to fit. Somehow, if the jackal had been hollow and had contained stolen diamonds, the entire thing would have seemed a lot simpler.

What I said next startled me more than it did Dr. Kellerman. "I have to go to Rome."

He said, "What?" as though I had just told him the moon was made of green cheese. I turned to face him and saw those soft blue eyes, so filled with kindness and concern, staring at me disbelievingly.

"You know I have to." Once I had said it, the idea seemed all right. There was only one way to get to the bottom of all this, and that was to talk to Adele. That she would have the answer I did not doubt. Besides, I knew for certain that my flat would be entered again, and the second time might not be such a lucky one for me. I might be in residence.

"Lydia, don't," said Dr. Kellerman quite simply. He gave me no doomsday warnings, voiced no wild fears, and expressed no deep anxiety. He merely said, "Don't" and all the warnings, fears and anxieties in the world were sounded.

"That's why she called, Dr. Kellerman. That was her real purpose. Not to tell me the jackal was coming but to summon me to be with her. She didn't get a chance to tell me why. And I think it's important. There was something in her voice . . ."

I shook my head decisively. "I must go. After all, she is all the family I have."

"But four years . . ."

"Is not so long when you consider that we are of the same flesh and we lost the same mother and father. A bond as close as that is just not weakened by years or miles. If I ever called Adele on the other side of the world and said simply, 'Come here, I need you,' she would. And you know that."

Poor Dr. Kellerman shook his head. "Lydia, it's not safe. Oh, this age of liberated females. I was born too late."

Now I patted his hand as though my own father sat next to me, and said, "Don't worry. I'll go the Residence Palace Hotel and find Adele and give her back her impulsive gift and cry a little while about the good old days. Then I'll come back and be your lacky again. It won't be such a long time, really."

"I don't like it, Lydia." There was something else, too, but he said it with his eyes. Unfortunately I did not read this second plea, for I heard only what his voice said. That other message, the silent one spoken with a gaze of longing, did not penetrate my exterior of self-sufficiency. Indeed, it was not until it was too late that I finally realized what Dr. Kellerman had tried for so long to tell me, but never could.

But that was to come later. For now he was trying to be gently persuasive and it was not working. He knew me to be an independent, autonomous female of the liberated variety, and once I had made up my mind, he knew there was no changing it.

"I thought you would be pleased to see me go off to Europe."

"But not this way, Lydia. Something's wrong about all this. And the man or men who ransacked your flat will be back. Or maybe they will follow you. You're not safe, not while you have the jackal."

"Then I'm going to return it personally from whence it came. I still have a passport from that Hong Kong trip I never made. My smallpox vaccination is still good, and I have money in the bank. Will I need a visa?"

"Not for Italy. Lydia . . ."

"In the meantime I'll move in with Jenny. I'll tell her the apartment house is being fumigated. Then I'll send a cable to Adele at that hotel. Tomorrow I'll tell Cathcart I have to leave for a family emergency and then catch the earliest plane possible. In fact, I'll make my reservation right now." I started to move towards the phone.

"This isn't like you, Lydia."

His words struck me with an unexpected impact. I averted my head and stared for a moment at the one glowing ember in the fireplace. How strangely true were the words he had just spoken. Since graduating from nursing school I had lived alone, and I had never, in all that time, committed a rash, regrettable act. Now, all of a sudden, one phone call, one parcel in the mail and I was as irrational and flighty as my sister, Adele. In one afternoon I had suddenly become all the things I had once condemned her for.

Yet it could not be helped. In that moment, on that unreal and distraught evening, the actions I planned seemed to be the only reasonable answer to the problem.

If only I had listened to Dr. Kellerman.

CHAPTER 3

*H*E SAW ME OFF AT THE AIRPORT, AND FOR THE FIRST TIME IN three years, Dr. Kellerman kissed me. I hugged him in a daughterly fashion and assured him once again that everything was going to be all right.

Los Angeles International Airport was busy and hectic at this hour of the morning, and yet Dr. Kellerman spoke quietly to me as though we were alone in his study. His hands were firmly on my shoulders as he said for the sixth time that morning, "This is folly, Lydia. You should have called the police and let them handle it. The burglars never came back. For all you know, it wasn't the jackal after all. Maybe they stole something and you don't even realize it. I think you're imagining it all. Your sister is a scatter-brained, selfish woman. She is luring you to Rome with a ruse. The burglary was only a coincidence. It could have happened any night."

But I was confident. "No, Dr. Kellerman. You're wrong. My sister is mixed up in some funny business, and I think she wanted me to help her out of it. The more I think back on our conversation, the more I am convinced of that. She was afraid of something. Maybe that's why she left the hotel so soon, and why she couldn't leave a message. Maybe there's something more to this jackal," I patted my handbag where it lay, "than meets the eye. After all, Dr. Kellerman, you're only a surgeon. What do you know?"

He kissed me for the second time in three years, and it was on the lips. "Cathcart isn't happy. She knows no one else can scrub for an old crocodile like me. You've never seen me throw a Balfour retractor across the room."

"I'll be back before you know it."

"And who else hands me my sutures in such nice tangles as you do? Oh, Lydia . . ."

Dr. Kellerman shook his head in resignation.

At his suggestion I exchanged some money for lire, purchased a crossword magazine, and boarded the plane early. Our good-bye was, to my surprise, somewhat strained. As soon as I was on board the TWA 747 and setting up house in my window seat, I ordered a glass of bourbon. As we taxied away from the airport, I found, with relief, that the seat next to me was empty and would remain so until New York. I desperately needed the next few hours to think.

Once again, as we said good-bye, I had not read in Dr. Kellerman's eyes what other, more sensitive women might have seen. Looking back, of course, I see it now. As a consequence I departed from Los Angeles with the erroneous notion that, should any unforeseen mishap befall me in Rome, no one would mourn the loss.

And then, for some reason, my thoughts drifted from Dr. Kellerman to Jerry Wilder, the intriguing anaesthetist who was the portrait of familiness and faithfulness and who had everyone fooled. Strange that after two years of giving no thought to our brief, bitter affair, I should think of it now. As the jet lifted off the ground and I felt the gentle pressure on my body, I listlessly recalled my last night in Jerry's arms.

He had said to me half-jokingly, half-seriously, "The trouble with you,

Lydia, is you're all nurse and no woman. With you, medicine comes first, and I really don't think you have any other interest in life."

I had laughed into his neck, hiding the hurt of hearing truth in his words.

"Oh don't get me wrong, Lydia, you're a darned good surgical nurse. Probably the best one in our whole department. You're an efficient little machine in the operating room and turn out good work. But the problem is, you don't change after hours."

"You're just saying that because I only date doctors."

But now he grew very serious. "Not at all. Most nurses date only doctors—married or single. But in your case it's different. I don't know . . . you're different."

I suppose that had been Jerry's way of saying the love affair was over, and yet that hadn't bothered me, since for me the love affair had never really begun. In the short three months we had gone out, not once had I ever thought in terms of loving Jerry, nor had I ever given myself totally to him. Physically yes, spiritually no.

The 747 reduced itself to a soft roar, the pressure eased, and my ears popped. I was on my second bourbon, listening to classical music through the headphones, when I finally confronted my situation head-on.

Here I was, for the first time in my life, on a 747 jet to a foreign country to look for a sister who might not be at the other end. Furthermore, and what truly nonplussed me now, was the undeniable fact that I had, for the first time in my superbly organized life, given only scant thought to my career and had abandoned everything for one ridiculous folly.

And yet, even in recognition of my foolishness, I continued to go forward with determination, not really knowing what I expected to find in the end.

I had a seat partner on the transatlantic leg of our journey, but fortunately she was a quiet little Catholic nun, who spent most of her time sleeping or studying a book. The flight from New York to Rome was estimated at seven hours, and we had three more to go; Rome was fast becoming less of a theory and more of a reality.

I tried to make myself comfortable for a nap, for I had not slept well the previous two days. Adele's call had had an uncanny effect upon me, having done no less than trigger off an avalanche of memories which I had, for several years, been able to avoid and was only too content to forget. But her voice had opened a door in my brain, and once opened, it could not be closed again upon the past, which consequently began to rush at me. Our childhood, our adolescence, the death of our family, our eventual drifting apart, and our final good-bye four years ago. It all came rushing back to me as if Adele and I had parted only yesterday.

On the phone she had called me Liddie.

I screwed up my eyes tightly, but everyone knows that burying your head in sand doesn't shut out painful memories. Her face was before me, shining in all its *Vogue* make-up and framed by the very latest hair fashion. Her enchantress smile was laughing at me, teasing me for my serious outlook on life and trying to seduce me into becoming a vagabond. That gipsy sister of mine! She was so unlike me with her style and personality that always got her invited to parties. I used to say of my sister Adele, "She could charm the warts off a frog," and I believe she could.

Without realizing that I was truly a collector of "final good-byes," I relived my last meeting with Adele, and I remembered every word and gesture.

"Honestly, Liddie, it's time I was going. I know you don't seriously want me for a roommate—you always did value your privacy—so I'll just move on. And besides, I don't think America is big enough for me. I want to go places. There's so much to do before I'm thirty."

"For God's sake, Adele, you're only twenty-three."

"Seven years isn't much time. Oh, you have your life all nicely planned, Liddie, with everything falling neatly into place. A niche for everything. And I'm sure it will all go as you plan. But me . . ." She had sighed dramatically. "I never know what tomorrow will bring. I have a lot of living to do before I'm thirty."

"What's so special about thirty?"

"Oh, Liddie, thirty is old, and I don't want to be old."

"Adele." I had shaken my head at her in resignation, thinking of how rootless she had become since the loss of our parents, thinking of how drastically she had changed. "It's really time you thought of a career."

"I have one!"

"I hardly call marrying a rich man . . ."

"Oh Liddie!" There was scolding in her high laugh. "I'll bet you never marry. You're just too . . . too *liberated* for that. Good God, you'll be a Mizz all your life!"

I spread the airline blanket over myself up to my chin and pressed my face against the window in hope of glimpsing the world below. But it was still dark—we would arrive at Leonardo da Vinci Airport at 8:30 a.m.—and the cabin was dim with sleeping bodies. All I saw in the glass was my own reflection, just a poor imitation of Adele's beautiful face, with none of the electricity and allure. It was a good face, mine, but not an exciting one. I had the eyes required in an operating room; those that could communicate almost any thought over a surgical mask. Still, we greatly resembled one another, Adele and I, and people had sometimes taken us for twins.

A movement at my arm brought me back from my reverie to the 747 where I found the Catholic sister rising from her seat. "Excuse me, but I have friends further forward. I asked the stewardess, and she said it's all right for me to sit with them. Do you mind if I leave? You'll sleep better if you're alone, I'm sure." And she retrieved a plain bag from under the seat and trundled away up the aisle.

As I stared after her, seeing her small body disappear into the sleeping shadows ahead, I was startled by the arrival of a stranger. He was grinning down at me in a familiar way and had a holdall in one hand. "Mind if I sit here?" he asked.

I shook my head.

In an instant he was sitting, his bag under the seat, and the safety belt fastened in place. "You're sure you don't mind if I sit here? Our Catholic friend has gone to join someone of her own cloth, and by all outward appearances, she isn't coming back. Ah, crossword puzzles. Are you a buff?"

I must have been staring at him with blank eyes, for he repeated, "Are you a crossword buff? The magazine in the seat pocket. Hm?"

I looked dumbly down. "Oh yes. I mean, no. Just when I fly."

"You fly a lot?"

I thought of Columbus and Oakland and wrinkled my forehead "Not really. The puzzles pass the time. I never finish one though. Care to try?" I carelessly handed it to him, and to my surprise he eagerly took it. "Thanks. Is the logic problem still virgin?" He flipped the pages. "Aha! Here it is. Wow, looks like a toughie. Thanks a lot. These last two hours are going to be the longest."

I continued to stare at my new companion while he plunged wholeheartedly into the puzzle spread ritualistically on his tray. There was something almost religious about the way he approached the logic problem, smoothing down the page, shifting in his seat, squaring his shoulders, and touching the pencil tip to his tongue in schoolboy fashion. He was, I would guess, thirtyish, dressed well, with stylish hair and sideburns, and with a rather distinctive profile. Although it had been my desire for the past nine hours to gather as much seclusion as possible, and although it was I who hadn't said much, it was nonetheless I, in the end, who sat staring with mild interest at the person next to me.

When he suddenly looked up at me, I jumped, realizing how intently I had been staring. "Hope you don't mind my sitting here. Best seats these, two across. I was back there," he waved a hand over his head, "by the johns, and after five hours they begin to give off quite a fragrance. On my left was an old snorer, and on my right squirmed the brat you now hear screaming at psychologically-placed intervals. I sort of kept an eye on this side hoping for an opening. After a few hours on these big jets, people invariably get restless and musical chairs results. I'll bet if you made a serious study of it, you'd find that on the average transatlantic flight, no more than ten per cent of the passengers arrive in the same seats in which they departed. It was charitable of the nun to move before I either stuffed a sock in the snorer's mouth or wrung the brat's neck, or both!"

I continued to stare at him, trying at the same time to visualize a serious study of musical chairs.

He studied my face for a minute and then, having not been able to inspire a dialogue with me, turned away saying, "Yes . . . well. Anyway, this is definitely one of the tougher logics . . ."

I smiled weakly as he picked up the crossword magazine and turned my attention to the genesis of a dawn in the distance. It reminded me at once of another dawn I had sat up to watch. I was eighteen years old and sitting in the bay window of our living room that looked out over a dew-covered lawn. My sister, Adele, a year older than me, was not at home. She had gone out that evening on a date and was not back yet. My parents and younger brother, having spent the weekend in San Diego, were supposed to have been home some hours ago. So I had sat by the bay window looking out at the beginning of a dawn and wondering where in the world everyone was.

Then there had come the sudden knock on the front door by two uniformed policemen.

"Ever done one?"

I snapped my head up.

"Logic problem. Ever done one?"

"Uh, no. Don't have the patience."

"I know what you mean. Some can be real corkers. Like this one." He laughed and shook his head. Ramming the puzzle magazine in the seat pocket in front of him as a gesture of frustration, he cried softly, "I give up."

For the first time since leaving Los Angeles I felt like smiling. Whoever my new, talkative companion was, he had an easy manner about him. I surveyed him again, taking in the attractive grey eyes and athletic tan. He wore a business suit, one as yet unwrinkled by the ravages of transatlantic travel, and indeed his entire portrait was refreshing and undogged, as though he had just boarded the plane. Such a contrast to myself, I realized a little dismayed, with my uncombed hair, neglected make-up, and crumpled dress bearing a few embarrassing dinner spills.

"John Treadwell," he said next, extending his hand.

Offering my own, I said diffidently, "Lydia Harris." The handshake was strong.

"Is that Miss or Mrs.?"

"It's Ms."

"I assumed that. But is it *Miss* Ms. or *Mrs.* Ms?"

I laughed and shook my head in surrender. John Treadwell, it seemed, had the ability to draw even an oyster out of its shell. "It is *Miss* Ms. And just plain Miss will do. I'm not terribly definite about the latter."

"That's good. Totally emancipated females frighten me, but a little liberation never hurt any woman. May I call you Lydia and ask what you do in this life?" "Yes and yes. I'm a nurse."

"Is this a vacation?"

"Not really. I'm going to Rome to take care of some . . . personal business." I thought of the jackal lying in the bag between my feet. "Family affair, you might say. And what do you do in this life, Mr. Treadwell?"

"Stockbroker."

"Are you going to Rome on vacation?"

"It's business for me, but no doubt I'll sneak in a little pleasure with it. I've been there before, so I won't waste time in getting lost like I did the first time. I'll be at the Exelcior. Where are you staying?"

Hesitating only slightly, I said, "The Residence Palace Hotel."

"Ah yes, on the Parioli Hill. Very nice district. Residential neighborhood. Did your travel agent recommend it?"

"Well, no. My sister is staying there and . . ." My voice gradually dimmed.

"Excuse me, I'm not trying to be nosey. Say, if you do have a free afternoon, please look me up and I'll be glad to show you around the city. For fifty lire we can take the bus all over town."

I made a sound of agreement and fell to staring ahead. Then I thought of Adele and the jackal and my uncertain tomorrow. And I wondered when I was going to wake up.

CHAPTER 4

I FELT THE PLANE BEGIN ITS GRADUAL DESCENT AND I SAW BY my watch, with great relief, that we would soon be in Leonardo da Vinci Airport. John Treadwell resumed some small-talk with me, saying something about Spanish Steps and leather gloves, but I was not listening. While my expression was polite, my mind was racing in many directions at once. I couldn't tell which moved faster—my thoughts or my heart.

On Italian soil, after the plane had come to a definite halt and the stewardesses had thanked us in four languages, I gripped my handbag and my coat with a theatrical determination and followed John Treadwell to the terminal. Going through customs together, he offered me the share of his taxi, a proposal that relieved me somewhat, for the thought of going blindly into the city frightened me a little.

During the twenty-odd mile ride from the airport, John Treadwell and I hardly spoke. We both sat looking out through the window, watching the beautiful countryside speed by us. Our driver was a chatty little man, who sped past other cars and through traffic lights and told us about his sister's cooking. But we ignored him.

John explained that my hotel was not inside the city walls, which had no significance to me, but that it was in a good district all the same. Instructing our driver to drop me first, he explained, "There's a good bus service around this neighborhood because it's wealthy. And if you want to walk, it won't take you long to get to the walls."

"What's inside the walls?"

"Rome, of course. Ah, here we are."

After many twisting and narrow roads through what appeared to be an enchanting residential neighborhood, the cab turned into the Via Archimede and eventually pulled up in front of the Residence Palace Hotel. Its exterior was not imposing. Rather plain, blending in with the blocks of flats around it, the hotel's one distinct feature was the small theatre adjoining it that claimed to show American films.

When I saw on the meter that we owed the driver nearly 6,000 lire—and I hastily calculated that to mean around ten dollars—I tried to force my share upon John Treadwell. He would not take it.

"I'll let you pay me back by accompanying me about the city today or tomorrow. You and your sister. Is that a deal?"

"I think that would be nice, Mr. Treadwell."

"Call me John." He was leaning out of the taxi window with a grin. "We Americans have to stick together. Deal?"

"Deal. And thank you."

I watched as the cab rattled off down the road and disappeared around a bend. Then I turned to face the hotel.

Its façade was peaceful. No one went in and out of the double glass doors, no phrenetic doorman struggled with impatient tourists, no stream of taxis bottle-necked at the curb. Unlike the usual bustling metropolitan hotel that is like a circus by day and a Christmas tree by night, the Residence Palace Hotel was the quiet sort of refuge I might seek for myself. It certainly was not Adele's taste.

Adele. My heart raced. She would have received my cable and would be inside waiting for me. After four years would we be sisters or strangers?

Would there be minutes of awkward silence, or would we fall into a rush of words? How bizarre to be reunited with her again like this, under these circumstances.

I went inside. The lobby was dark and austere, not at all pretentious. The rug was a bit threadbare and the plants dusty, but it bespoke an air of elegance that told of better days. On an easel-type bulletin board was tacked a notice in oriental characters, listing, I supposed, the events planned for a touring group. At the top of the notice in English was printed "Takahashi Tours, Kyoto."

There were a few people milling about the desk, all of them Japanese. With white sailor hats and heavy cameras they prattled delightedly over a selection of postcards. But Adele was not there. I wound my way past them and approached the receptionist.

"Excuse me. Do you speak English?"

"Yes, madam." He gave me a charming smile.

"Oh thank goodness. I wonder if you could help me. I'm looking for my sister, Adele Harris, who was staying here four days ago. She might still be registered here, and there might be a message for me, Lydia Harris. Would you check please?"

"American?" he asked.

I nodded vigorously.

"We have no Americans today, madam. In Rome we have few tourists. Very bad year. They go inside walls. They stay near Foro Romano. Here we have groups.

"Last week we have Air France, today we have Japan. On Thursday Yugoslavia is coming. But no Americans."

"She isn't with a group. She's alone. But I think she might have checked out two days ago. Will you check please?"

"Certainly." He turned away for a minute and consulted a large book. Presently he said, "I am sorry, Miss Harris is not registered."

"Oh dear," I said sadly. "I was afraid of that. Then she really did check out. Are you sure she left no forwarding address? I really must reach her."

The man looked totally confused. "But the name is not familiar to me. When did you say she was here?"

"Two days ago. She placed a person-to-person call to America from this very hotel. So I know she was here. I also sent her a cablegram. She must have got it. Now if you would please look up her record and see if she left any message for me, Lydia Harris. I'm her sister."

"I do not recall the name, madam, but I will check for you. Excuse me please."

Something was not right. The man's manner, or possibly that nebulous state we call intuition, sent off a little warning signal in the back of my mind. For some reason, I don't know why, I did not expect the man to come back with any good news of Adele. I was right.

"I am sorry, madam, but we have never had a Miss Adele Harris registered in our hotel. Possibly another hotel in Rome."

"It was the Residence Palace," I said evenly. "She spoke to me very possibly from this lobby. Now, I know she was here. She sent me a package with this return address. I would like you to check again, please, a little more carefully."

The man was unperturbed by my manner. "Certainly, madam, excuse me." He disappeared this time, and as he did so I leaned an elbow on the desk and once again scanned the lobby. The Japanese group, I saw, was growing—getting ready no doubt for an excursion. Coming from the dining room not far away I heard the clatter of dishes and the excited talk of late breakfasters. In the large sitting room that adjoined the lobby and was furnished with overstuffed chairs and couches, a few tourists wrote letters. On the walls hung large ornate mirrors and antique engravings of Roman archaeological sites. There was occasional statuary and heavy curtains.

Then my eyes rested on him. I don't know what it was, but something about him caught my attention. Slightly taller than myself and well dressed, he was swarthier than most Italians and wore huge sunglasses that hid most of his face. He leaned idly against the wall reading an Italian newspaper. I could not discern why this particular man should attract my attention so, but when I tried to look away and ignore him, my head turned involuntarily in his direction again.

"I am sorry, madam," said the Italian receptionist with great regret in his eyes. "I have looked and looked. I have even gone back two months, but there never was an Adele Harris in our hotel."

I gaped at the man incredulously. What he was saying to me didn't make the slightest sense. "But that's impossible!" I cried. "I know she was here!"

He spread out his hands, palms up, helplessly.

"Now look. I called this very hotel two nights ago. It was after midnight, and I spoke to someone at this very desk. And that person told me Adele had paid her bill and checked out."

He shrugged and shook his head at the same time.

"Maybe she was here under a different name. Maybe . . ."

"Madam, please. No Americans in this hotel. Not for long time. They go to Hilton or Holiday Inn. Business is bad in Rome now. In three months we have few single tourists, just groups. I know, I see them. I see all guests."

Exasperated beyond belief, I sighed and took a step back. Obviously I was going nowhere fast. "Then why was I told on the phone she had paid her bill? Who is on at night?"

"Luigi Baroni."

"Fine, can I speak to him?"

"He comes in tonight, madam."

"Great." I looked around the lobby. The Japanese had left, but the stranger with the paper was still there. I had an odd feeling about him that I could not shake off. "Then I guess I'll have to take a room. You do have one, don't you, with a private bath?"

"Certainly, madam."

As I registered and paid, I let my anger subside and decided that there was a simple explanation for all of this. I was just going to take a nap, shower, eat in the dining room, and then threaten Luigi Baroni with his life if he didn't tell me where Adele was.

The receptionist tapped a bell and a porter in a red and white striped apron picked up my one suitcase. *"Prego,"* he said, pointing for me to go first. As I swept past him I gave one quick glance over my shoulder.

The man with the newspaper had gone.

After a perilous ride in a lift the size of a telephone kiosk, and a quick inspection of my enormous suite, I lay back on the bed to test its comfort and fell instantly asleep.

Six hours and three bizarre dreams later I awoke, at first not knowing where I was and cursing the backache I had from sleeping in one position. I had been exhausted, but now I was refreshed and a little better equipped to face my new world. My room, I quickly found, was not a room at all but a flat elaborately furnished with antiques, old rugs, and the same fascinating engravings that could be seen throughout the hotel. My accommodations surprised me. This was not what I had expected. There was an entrance hall, a sitting room, something like a small dining room, a large bedroom, a dressing room with a gigantic wardrobe, and a bathroom so large that my voice echoed. Above all, it was a spacious suite with white plaster walls and polished hardwood floors that held an air of refinement despite the age of the place. Going off the sitting room was a wide balcony and louvred doors which opened on to a splendid panorama of the flats next door.

With a smile I stood out over the garden below and realized that if my room were just one over and around the corner, I would see the city of Rome. As it was, my view fascinated me anyway, for it was full of the sort of thing I would later find to be the common characteristics of Rome: reddish brown buildings, a balcony at every window, and potted plants on every available space. Down below, in crowded little yards grew jungle-wild shrubbery and concealing trees. From each balcony hung green and brown plants of every variety. This first impression was quite an eye-opener, but I was soon to become used to this "garden city" of red-brown and overgrown trees.

Taking a bath in the bathroom that reminded me of an operating room, I wondered vaguely what I was going to do if the night receptionist denied having spoken to me, and if any chance of finding my sister here became hopeless. Then what? Back to America?

As I dried myself on a towel—characteristically large and plush—I thought of the trip home, of explaining to Dr. Kellerman, of using the jackal as a paperweight, of waiting for my flat to be searched again.

I stopped suddenly and straightened. It is strange how mental processes work, particularly memory, for very often if one cannot recall something and one works hard at trying to remember, nothing materializes. Yet when it is put out of the mind and one thinks of something else, that lost memory returns. It happened to me just then. Thinking of Dr. Kellerman and an assortment of unrelated things, it suddenly occurred to me why I had been attracted to the man with the newspaper.

I had seen him before.

Of course, it was definitely him, no mistake about it. John Treadwell and I had just gone through customs and were looking for a taxi. Searching the area, I had spotted a dark man with wide sunglasses reading a newspaper, and for some reason I had given him fleeting consideration. Possibly it was his not quite Italian looks. Or the way he seemed to be reading and *not* reading the paper. Whatever, I had seen him briefly at the airport before getting into the cab.

Now he was at the Residence Palace Hotel.

I dressed in great haste. Before leaving the room I retrieved the jackal from my handbag, looked at it for a moment, then wrapped it tightly in a handkerchief and buried it at the bottom of my bag. With the handbag tucked securely under my arm, I flitted down the stairs.

This old style of Italian hotel was a challenge to the most organized of minds, for although ostensibly I stayed on the third floor in room 307, I had to go down six flights of stairs to reach the ground. This phenomenon I guessed was due to the fact that the building was on the slope of a hill and therefore tiered. As I galloped down, my hand sliding along the polished marble banister, I heard my footsteps echo and I had the momentary impression of being in a church. Once again those white plaster walls, the occasional antique piece of furniture, the wrought iron fixtures, and that incredible silence all about me. As I passed quiet doorways and dusty ferns, I told myself that this was the quaintest and most charming place I had ever seen.

The dining room was large and, again, old, with the characteristic statuary, framed engravings, and faded tapestries on the walls. As I wolfed down a plate of spaghetti which was, I was certain, better than any I had eaten in the United States, I imagined that in the days before air-conditioning the singular design of this hotel afforded the coolest possible atmosphere. I wondered at the same time, however, what the Residence Palace might be like in the dead of winter.

Two glasses of wine put me in an excellent mood, after which I retired to the grand lounging area of the lobby, sat at an antique writing desk, and started a letter to Dr. Kellerman.

"Yes?" I swung round on hearing my name.

A stout Italian with a shiny head stood behind me. "I am Luigi Baroni. You wish to speak to me?"

"Oh yes!" Hastily I gathered my stuff together and crammed it in my handbag. As I did so, I felt the hardness of the jackal against my fingers and made a mental note to find better, safer quarters for it. "I'm Lydia Harris. I believe I spoke to you the other night."

"Oh?" His face was blank.

"Come now. Surely you don't forget a call from America. It was after midnight and I was looking for my sister. You said she had just checked out."

"I'm sorry, madam, I received no . . ."

"Then someone else answered the phone. Look, I spoke to someone at this hotel!" Losing patience, my voice began to grow shrill. "Who else works that desk at night?"

"No one, madam. I have been alone these past weeks. Since the slow tourist business we have had to let people go . . ."

"Now wait a minute." I tried to speak slowly, knowing my voice was carrying everywhere. "I rang this hotel two days ago, I spoke to a receptionist who sounded strangely like you. He said Miss Adele Harris had paid her bill and checked out. Now I want to see the receipt for that bill."

"But, madam . . ."

"I am trying to keep my patience. I want to look at the records."

"But they are private, madam. I cannot allow . . ."

As I was about to point a rude finger at the man, a third voice intervened and said, "Perhaps I can be of help." My heart gave a leap when I saw who it was. With enormous sunglasses hiding his eyes and the newspaper rolled under his arm, it was the same swarthy gentleman I had seen at the airport and then in the lobby that morning.

"I could not help overhearing your conversation, and I wondered if, as a fellow tourist, I might be of some assistance."

I gaped at the man, who spoke excellent English in a soft and nasal voice. He had short curly hair, copper skin, and was of average build. His suit was the Ralph Nader variety, black with a white shirt and narrow tie. I don't know why, but I took an instant dislike to him.

"It's all right, thank you, but I can handle this."

"You say you are looking for your sister."

"She was staying here, yet this gentleman claims there's no record of her. Now I definitely spoke to someone . . ."

The stranger said something in Italian to the receptionist. The other man merely shrugged.

"Then it is simple," he said. "We will look at the records for ourselves."

When the receptionist started to protest, the stranger held up a hand and said most pleasantly, "We are only trying to save time and trouble. Tomorrow the young lady will go first to the American Embassy and then to the police. At which time we will all look at the records."

The Italian, unmoved by the threat, said, "You must understand my position. Our files are private. I cannot let anyone see them without special order. If you must go to the police, then you must, but we have the privacy of our guests to consider."

"Certainly," said the other man. "This young woman has come all the way from America to find her sister only to discover she must go to the police for help."

"I would like to help, *signore*."

"Then may we speak to the manager?"

"But of course!" The receptionist turned away and I suspected he was glad to be relieved of the responsibility. As he hurried away from the desk I looked again at the man who forced his aid upon me, and wondered what he looked like behind those glasses.

"You really don't have to bother, Mr. . . ."

"Forgive me. My name is Ahmed Rasheed."

My eyebrows must have raised. Why I should be so surprised to meet an Arab in Rome, I don't know, except that from the very first—at Leonardo da Vinci Airport—I had had an odd feeling about him. Now my feeling was downright uneasy.

"I'm Lydia Harris. I really can handle this myself."

"It is no trouble at all. The Italian people are superiorly hospitable and accommodating. And this is a very fine hotel. We shall find your sister in no time."

We? I wondered.

The receptionist returned with another man, who was introduced as Mr. Mangifrani, the assistant manager of the hotel. He had been briefed on the situation. With a wonderful smile and very gracious gestures he invited us into his office where, after an offer of tea, we were allowed to go through the past guest lists.

"I am terribly sorry for the inconvenience, Miss Harris. I truly wish we could help you further. But as you see, your sister was never registered here."

He was polite and generous, and afterwards I felt a little guilty at my outrageous behavior. It was not like me to shout in a public place—it was not like me to lose my cool at all. Mr. Mangifrani, so characteristic of the Residence Palace Hotel, had been more than helpful and anxious to serve. Yet he could not produce my sister.

"Perhaps," began Mr. Rasheed, who for some reason continued to remain with me, "your sister was only visiting someone here and that person is the one who checked out. When you called, the receptionist simply was in error as to who exactly checked out."

I could not deny the logic of this, with two exceptions. Why had Mr. Baroni insisted he had received no transatlantic call, and where was the cable I had sent?

"Well, that's that, I guess. Thank you for your help, Mr. Rasheed."

"May I buy you coffee?"

"No," I said too quickly. "I think I'll just go up to my room and relax a while. Adele will turn up, I'm sure. Good evening."

I turned pertly on my heel and walked away as fast as I could. A little wary of the lift, I decided to take the stairs back to my room, only to remember after the third flight that I had three more to go. Then, also remembering that there was no television in my room and nothing to read, I turned and went back down to the lobby.

As I reached the desk, the Japanese group was pouring through the doors. They chatted in high, singing voices and grinned pleasantly at me as they passed. A few of them did not enter the hotel, but continued instead down the street. On an instinct I followed them, walking past the American cinema and up the slight incline of the Via Archimede. My intuition was rewarded. We all walked into a small store not far from the hotel called The Daily American.

As the air rang with Italian and Japanese, I perused the cigarettes, candy bars, and literature the seller had to offer. Very few books and magazines were in English. It was a difficult choice between Agatha Christie and Alfred Hitchcock, and as I flipped through each book to decide which to buy, I casually raised my head and glanced through the large window.

Mr. Rasheed was standing on the other side of the street watching me.

"Oh . . ." I began, suddenly fumbling with the books. "How much, please?"

"Cinquecento lire, per favore."

"Okay." My palms were moist and clammy. They shook slightly. "I'll take both."

After I handed the man my lire and he returned my change, I summoned the courage to look out of the window again. He was not there.

Stepping uncertainly into the night, I felt a premonition. In the soft glow of Via Archimede's street lights and in the gentle air of a true Roman evening, I knew beyond a doubt that Adele was in trouble.

Perhaps this was not all intuition and guess work. As I strolled along the pavement towards the welcome glare of the hotel, I reassessed the situation. It was possible that this was all a misunderstanding. It was possible Adele was with a friend. The friend had checked out. Over the transatlantic line the misunderstanding arose. Very simple. Adele was somewhere else in Rome.

Unfortunately, no matter how tidy this little explanation was, it still left unanswered my two most pressing mysteries. Where was the cable I had sent, and why had Mr. Baroni insisted he had never received a phone call from America?

As I braved the lift and rattled upward to my floor, I decided that it would have been very nice to talk this over with Dr. Kellerman. I also realized, as the lift jerked to an uncertain halt and the doors squeaked open, that I found myself missing Dr. Kellerman and wishing he were nearby.

I was stretched out comfortably on my bed when the phone buzzed, startling me. Then I stared at it as if waiting for it to rectify its error and redial the proper party. But as it continued to buzz with determination I realized the call might actually be for me and, in a rush of excitement, that it might be Adele.

"Hello?" I said in a hurry.

"Hi. John Treadwell here."

"Oh." My voice fell. "Hi."

"Hey, I'm sorry."

"Oh no, I didn't mean it. I thought it was Adele calling."

"Want me to hang up? She might be trying to get you now."

"No, John, I doubt that she is. She might not even be near a phone."

"Don't you know where she is? I thought she was meeting you at the hotel."

"Well, unfortunately there's been a mix-up of some sort. It seems she isn't here. Wrong hotel, I guess."

"What're you doing now?"

"Reading *Stories to Stand Your Hair on End*."

"Care to go out on the town?"

"Oh . . . no thank you, Mr. Treadwell. I mean, John. I'm tired really."

"Tomorrow morning then. I'll be at your hotel at what hour? Eight? Nine?"

In my current mood I was not terribly interested in getting involved with John Treadwell, but as I was about to refuse his offer, a nagging little voice reminded me of something I had temporarily forgotten—that it seemed Ahmed Rasheed was following me. "Eight would be just fine. I'll meet you in the lobby."

"Great. And we can look for your sister, okay?"

"Fine, thanks. Good night."

As I hung up I began to think that befriending John Treadwell might actually be a very wise idea, considering the situation with Adele, the strange Mr. Rasheed and being new to Rome.

As I turned out my light and settled back in that strange bed, thinking of the foreign city that lay just beyond my windows, I found myself thinking again of Dr. Kellerman. I suppose that, just as his presence had always been a comfort to me, that he had always "been there," so it was now, during a moment of frustration and doubt, that even his presence in my mind had a consoling effect.

Dr. Kellerman had eyes so ice blue and wintry that one look from them could make you shiver under the hot operating room lights. And yet, afraid of him though a nurse or intern might be, dislike him though you might, you could still sense his strength and the security that he brought to the surgical team. No matter how desperate a moment might be on the operating table, how panicky his assistants might feel, Dr. Kellerman had an aura of complete control and command about him.

I often likened him to the captain of a ship who, during a violent storm at sea, would stand to fight at the helm and thus inspire the crew. I had felt like that in Dr. Kellerman's presence during emergencies, when I would look at the blood and hear the rapid electrocardiogram monitor and think, "Oh God, we'll never make it!" But then Dr. Kellerman's voice would be calm, his hands steady. And I would think, "He knows we'll do it. Look at him, he knows we can do it." And somehow we would. So it was with these thoughts that I drifted off into an uneasy sleep.

CHAPTER 5

W HEN I HAD ARRIVED THE DAY BEFORE, I MUST HAVE BEEN very tired, for when I stepped into the sharp morning with John Treadwell it was as though I was seeing my surroundings for the first time. The Parioli district consisted mostly of blocks of flats and quiet hotels, interspersed with small shops and an occasional private house. The streets were narrow and winding beneath the towering buildings of reddish brown masonry, and looming over these little streets were hundreds of balconies all overgrown with green and brown plants. The pedestrians who passed us, some Italian and some foreign, were friendly and greeted us generally in English. An occasional car rattled by now and then, a few bicycles, and one tourist bus. The pavements were cracked and tree-lined, and overrun by cats. Even before the doors of the hotel I saw a coven of cats prowling as if waiting for some likely tourists.

I liked what I saw. It all struck me as so foreign and charming.

"Shall we walk?"

"Is it far?"

"Couple of miles to the walls. Downhill all the way. And we pass through some delightful scenery. The Villa Borghese, for example. Or, if you're anxious, we can grab the number 52 bus. It takes us into the heart of the city for only fifty lire."

Anxious wasn't the word. I had to find Adele before all else, and it was not going to be easy. She was why I had come to Rome, and until I found her I would not rest. Besides, I had awakened that morning with the memory of Mr. Rasheed and, trying to assure myself that the times I had seen him were merely coincidental, I had asked for his room number. But Ahmed Rasheed, it appeared, was not a guest at the Residence Palace Hotel, which would make it terribly coincidental seeing him first at the airport, then in the lobby, and then outside the magazine shop.

"Can we ride? I'd prefer it."

"Sure. Come on."

We walked down to the corner and stood under a sign that said *Fermata*. While we were waiting, John briefed me on some of the sights I would be seeing and I stooped to stroke the cats that ran up to greet us.

"Rome is a cat city," said John as he checked his watch. "I've been here three times before, and each time I'm just as impressed by them."

"There are rather a lot."

"Just wait."

A big green bus pulled up and we climbed in the rear door. Since it was no longer the "free" hour, we dropped fifty lire coins into the slots and took the white tickets. I sat by a window while John gave me a running commentary on everything we saw.

Looking back, it is difficult to say which amazed me more—the traffic or the trees, both of which came in great numbers in Rome. As I was soon to learn, Romans loved gardens and greenery as much as they loved driving their cars. When I was not gaping open-mouthed at the fantastic road congestion, I was exclaiming over the abundance of trees, shrubs, and flowers that grew everywhere.

Although the predominant color was a sort of pinkish rust, many flashy new hotels and stylish glass office buildings sped by. Next to old Renaissance façades stood the concrete and chrome of Madison Avenue.

Having come from a city of few contrasts, I was quite fascinated by the variety of Rome.

Of course, that was outside the walls. Once we passed through one of the ancient gates of the Aurelian walls I was struck by an entirely different beauty. The private residences were surrounded by high walls and lush green gardens, while official buildings were elegant and timeless with their straight lines and classical ornamentation. And everything was the same brownish color.

"It's amazing," I said, "I've never seen a city like this!"

"The Romans are very particular about how their city looks and as a consequence have strict rules about construction within the walls. All new buildings must look like the old ones."

"So that's it. I thought it was my imagination. How incredible!"

"There is one exception which I'll show you later. We're almost at the end of the line. Where do you want to go first?"

I did not know the answer to that. How did Romans go about finding missing Romans? With Adele the only lead had been the Residence Palace Hotel, and that had led me nowhere. "I don't know, John."

"Hungry?"

"I could have some coffee."

"Great."

We left the bus and stood on a busy street. I could not stop being awed by the general scheme of the city and therefore had a difficult time concentrating on Adele. John led me down a side street and into a little shop that stood next to a florist. Looking exactly like a turn-of-the-century pharmacy, the snack bar had a counter to stand at and one table in the window. We chose the latter, drawing looks from the local people who, apparently, were not used to tourists in their midst. Americans in Rome usually eat at Harry's American Bar or Wimpy's.

"So tell me," said John as he poured a copious amount of cream into his strong coffee, "what's the problem with your sister?"

I looked at him. "I'm sorry. I didn't tell you?" Briefly I recounted the circumstances that brought me to Rome and watched as his handsome face turned into a frown.

"That's some story!" he said after a moment.

"You think so?" All of a sudden I was anxious for his opinion, since it would be fresh and objective and might therefore let me know whether I was being a little hysterical. "Am I worrying for nothing?"

"No, I wouldn't say so. If I got an urgent call from a long-lost relative on the other side of the world, received some weird thing through the post, had my place searched, then found that my long-lost relative was still lost, I'd be really worried."

"I was afraid you'd say that. Adele must really have got herself mixed up in something this time."

"May I see this jackal?"

"I don't have it with me. But don't worry, it's in a safe place."

"I see. That valuable, huh?"

"It must be. At least that's what all the mystery points to." Then I thought of Ahmed Rasheed, who I had not mentioned to John, and wondered how he figured into it, if at all. "I appreciate your concern, John, but I know you're busy here in Rome."

"Nonsense! I always enjoy a mystery. Especially when it involves a pretty girl. But as you say, we have to find your sister. The American Embassy might be able to help. She could have left a message for you there."

"Of course! I hadn't thought of that."

"And besides, maybe when we get back to your hotel there'll be a message waiting for you. She knows you'd be staying there."

I smiled with relief at John Treadwell. He had done a great deal to ease my anxiety.

"But first the Forum. I insist. Just in case the news isn't hot at the Embassy, which would spoil your entire day, we should leave it for last. Besides, I want to see you smile like that more often, so I'm going to show you the delights Rome has to offer."

Although reluctant, I could not decline John's offer to have a cheerful morning. With his charm and his good looks, and his hand exerting a little gentle pressure on mine, John Treadwell was a very persuasive man. And besides, Adele couldn't be far, and after four years another hour or two wouldn't hurt.

I don't think I closed my mouth once during our walking tour, and all I could think of over and over again was why didn't someone tell me it was like this. As if the Renaissance and Baroque styles and beautiful gardens weren't enough, the classical antiquities were positively breathtaking. Although I had never had a great love for ancient history, I could easily imagine cultivating one after I visited the vestiges of the Roman Empire.

In one small area we saw the Forum, the Colosseum, the Palatine Hill, and the Capitoline Museum. Of the Victor Emmanuel Monument John said, "This was the one exception I told you about. Romans call it the 'wedding cake' because it's a big white monstrosity in the heart of their rose-colored city."

I laughed. "Fascinating. It should have a bride and groom on the very top." I stared at the unending traffic that passed through the Piazza Venezia and fought for parking spaces in the middle. It was all so strange, so foreign.

And as I stood and stared, I began to get some idea of what my sister Adele must have found here.

Then John said, "It's nearly one o'clock. Want lunch?"

I looked at him in surprise. "That late already? Let's go to the Embassy."

But he shook his head. "Siesta time. It'll be closed. We'll have to go after five when they reopen. What you're observing is the second of four rush hours in Italy."

"Then let's walk around some more."

From the heart of Imperial Rome we walked northwards to visit the Trevi Fountain and the Spanish Steps. These two points of interest, among the most popular of tourist attractions, were strangely deserted.

"And it's not because of siesta," said John. "Tourists don't take an afternoon nap, they continue to tour about. But no one is here. It's the same all over Europe. High prices, no tourists."

"I like it better this way."

We waited until four o'clock, when the Trevi Fountain was turned on, and then began a slow trek to the American Embassy.

John was the ideal companion as we strolled the smaller, less crowded streets, for he kept the conversation light and, sensing my apprehension, told occasional jokes that kept me laughing. In the afternoon sunlight his hair turned a golden brown and became tousled by the wind in small-boy fashion. The more we walked and talked, the more thankful I was that the nun had moved.

The American Embassy was an enormous imposing structure on the Via Veneto and just waking up as we got there. I must have known that this was my biggest hope to find Adele, for as we stepped from the sunlight into the dark interior I felt my heart race.

The news was bad. There was no message from Adele and they had not heard from her.

"I'm sorry about dinner," I said, in the rattly old green bus as we started our ascent up the Parioli Hill. "But you must understand. If I'm to find Adele at all it will be by staying at the hotel. You do understand?"

John nodded. Although he had wanted to treat me to one of the stylish restaurants on the Via Veneto, I could see he sympathized with me. The police had been little help since we had no evidence, no clues, not even a photograph to give them, and I did not blame them. The Embassy had been an even bigger disappointment, for, if Adele had wanted to get in touch with me, she could easily have done it through them, and she had had four days to do it in!

"Then let me buy you dinner at the hotel," said John.

I looked into his smiling eyes and felt myself less willing to argue. What I really wanted to do was go to my room, soak in a hot bath, and wait for my sister to decide to show up. But John Treadwell was a difficult man to say no to. He reminded me of a neurosurgeon I had once known, who had had the remarkable ability to make everyone in the operating room laugh during the most trying of cases, who always had a grin, a pun or a good word on his lips, and who had one night committed suicide in the doctors' locker room. He had been able to dispel other people's gloom, like John Treadwell, but apparently had no idea of how to cope with his own.

"Well?" said my companion. "Dinner at the hotel?"

God, but the Embassy had been a disappointment. Right now I really did need the company of this man.

"Dinner at the hotel," I conceded.

John agreed to wait for me in the lobby while I quickly ran up to my room. I murmured any number of excuses to him for this, but the reason I kept quietly to myself. Or rather, two reasons. One, I harbored a small hope that Adele might have come to my room and slipped a note under the door, and two, to check on the jackal. What's the saying? Once searched, twice shy? Whatever, after the affront of having my flat rifled I was wary of any further break-ins. Not that I really expected it, but it was in the back of my mind . . .

The jackal was just where I had left it and the room had not been disturbed. There was also no note from Adele. Dragging a comb through my hair and rubbing some lipstick on my mouth, I hurried back to join John.

We had a veal scaleopini dinner and good rich Italian coffee, and afterwards I was persuaded to take a stroll around the Parioli district. Passing brightly-lit pavement cafes, flower sellers on every corner, and entire families out to enjoy the evening, I was able to relax on John's arm and enjoy, if only briefly, the beauty this city had to offer.

"What does SPQR mean? It seems to be on everything," I asked.

"Literally it is Latin, *Senatus Populusque Romanus,* which means the Senate and People of Rome. In the days of the Republic before the Caesars it meant something and was then later carried over into Imperial times, but had little more than figurative significance. Today Italy has a president and is a democracy once again, so I imagine they've borrowed this noble bit of heritage and are carrying on a tradition. I kind of like it."

"It's even on the plastic rubbish bags!"

"So it is. You'll see SPQR on ancient monuments and on traffic signal boxes."

"You know a lot about Rome."

"It's a fascinating place."

"How long will you be here on this visit? What does that mean, a shrug? Because of me you haven't had a chance to get down to the business you came here for."

"Well, actually my job is traveling, going back and forth between our home office in New York and our international offices in London and Rome. I'm on an expense account, and if I take a day or two extra, no one will mind."

"Well, thanks. I really don't know what I would have done without you. I'm not a seasoned international traveler, even though I'm a big girl. And I never was good at coping with mysteries or surprises. Mine is a very orderly, predictable life."

"Is that what an operating room is like?"

"Mostly. Except for an occasional emergency that disrupts things." I thought of the cardiac arrest that had happened at the same time as Adele's call.

"Like your sister?"

I laughed. "Yes, like my sister." We stopped on a crest from where we were able to see the lighted city below us. A temperate breeze rustled my hair and stirred the autumn leaves all about us. "John, who ever said big cities were all alike?"

"Someone who's never seen them."

"God," I whispered. A black ribbon divided the glittering city as the Tiber River ran its ancient course separating east from west. I shivered a little and John Treadwell gently put an arm about my shoulders. It was at this moment that a truism struck me with such a force that I held my breath for an instant. As I gazed at this city that was something out of a dream, it occurred to me that I might be falling in love with it. And as I realized I could fall in love with Rome, I wondered at the same time why I had never come here before. Then I had my answer.

Although until now I had thought that my life was a rewarding one, the truth was that this was not so, and that my life was sadly unfulfilled.

"John, I'm getting cold. Can we go back?"

"Of course." He led me away and back to the warm streets and friendly crowds. The hotel was bright and glary and, right now, very inviting. I stopped in the lobby and thanked John for a wonderful day and for having tried his hardest to find my sister. Taking a moment to look at me, John then said, "When am I going to see this mysterious jackal of yours?"

"Come by tomorrow and I'll introduce you, okay?"

"Deal." He hesitated, and I guessed what he was thinking. So I said, "I'm exhausted, really I am. I'm going to soak in a hot bath and fall asleep instantly."

"I can't talk you into a nightcap? A glass of Benedictine or Grand Marnier?"

I shook my head weakly. "Please, this has been a tiring day. I wouldn't be much company."

"Oh, I don't know." Yet he did not persist. Instead of pressing it, as I feared he might, John only put his hands on my shoulders, lightly kissed my forehead and whispered, "I'll call you in the morning. Good night, Lydia."

"Thank you, John. Good night." As I watched him go, hailing a taxi out front, I thanked Providence for having brought the two of us together. His presence and his help had made my first big step very easy. From now on I was certain I could make it on my own.

At least those were my thoughts as I crossed the large hall towards the stairs until I ran into Mr. Rasheed. Or rather, he planted himself in my path.

His intrusion startled me.

"Excuse me, Miss Harris. I was wondering, have you found your sister yet?"

"Uh . . . no, I haven't." He still wore the huge sunglasses and carried the same newspaper. Both objects to hide behind. And since he was not a registered guest at the Residence Palace I wondered what on earth he was doing there again.

"I was waiting for you," he said, as if reading my thoughts.

"I beg your pardon?"

"In case you had not found your sister, I thought perhaps I could help since I speak Italian and know this city quite well . . ."

"Thank you," I said uneasily, "but I have help, and I've done everything

I can. The police and the Embassy were unable to furnish me with any help. But I'm not worried. She can't be far. Maybe she went on a junket to Naples or something."

"Have you enquired at the Egyptian Museum in Vatican City?"

My eyebrows shot up and I fell back a step. "What?"

Ahmed Rasheed's face remained impassive. I could not see where his eyes were or what he really looked like. "It was only a thought. Good night then, Miss Harris. I wish you luck."

I stared after him stupidly with my mouth hanging open, and did not move until the Japanese tour group suddenly filled the hall. Then I spun round and dashed up the six flights of stairs two steps at a time until I got to my room, where I double locked the doors, including the louvred doors that led to the balcony. Then I slumped on to the edge of my bed, feeling my heart pound against my chest, and tried to absorb the startling implication of the Arab's words.

Ahmed Rasheed must have known about the jackal!

I was already awake when the phone buzzed and I nearly broke my neck answering it. "Adele?" I said breathlessly.

"Sorry, it's only me," came John's voice. "Did I wake you?"

"No." I squinted at the sunlight pouring through my windows. "I've been up a while. Couldn't sleep very well. I'm just waiting and waiting."

"How long do you intend to keep that up?"

I shrugged over the phone.

"Now I thought it would be a good idea if we got out for a while. I'm not interested in going to the office today and I haven't yet let them know I'm in town, so what do you say we play hooky?"

"I don't know, John."

"Just for a couple of hours. My God, you're letting the neatest city in the world pass you by! What do you want to say when you get back to LA? That you sat in a hotel room the whole time? Come on, I have a very special place to take you."

Again I looked at the inviting sunshine and felt my determination begin to wane. John Treadwell was too much to resist. And besides, after tossing and turning all night over Ahmed Rasheed's cryptic words, intimating that he knew of my jackal, I had decided to tell John about him. But I wanted to do it in person.

"All right," I said. "For a while anyway. If Adele shows up . . . well, *she'll* just have to wait for *me*."

"That's the spirit! Now listen, I have an errand to run, so why don't you just meet me? Go to the Colosseum, you remember the way. Once you're there, cross the street and go up the Oppian Hill. You can't miss it. I'll meet you in front of the Domus Aurea. That's what I want to show you. Nero's Golden House."

"Sounds great. What if I get lost?"

"You won't. You can't miss the hill, it's all green and looks like a park. Ask anyone around. Just say 'Domus Aurea' and they'll point you in the right direction. Look, it's nine now. How about meeting at ten? I'll be out front with the tickets."

"That's fine. I'll see you at ten."

I debated a moment about taking the jackal with me to show to John, thought better of it and decided, at the last minute, to change its hiding place. The ivory devil should be secure until the evening, when I would show it to John.

My spirits lifted greatly once I was out in the dazzling daylight. No mysterious men followed me. Nothing unexpected occurred. Just sunshine and people and blue sky. The number 52 bus dropped me off at the Piazza San Silvestro. From there I struck out on my own, keeping the Tiber to my right as a guide, and enjoyed a positively enchanting walk to the Forum and Colosseum. In those few minutes of window gazing and flower sniffing, I was able to forget my real reason for being in Rome and to just lose myself in its allure.

At the Colosseum, I saw the familiar "cat ladies" and feline tribes that are so peculiar to this city. Old Italian women with tattered black shawls and paper shopping bags went from ruin to ruin treating the cats to pasta delicacies. At such times I wished I had packed a camera.

John was right. I had no trouble in locating the Domus Aurea. After a pleasant walk among sculpted hedges and under trees I came to an iron gate that stood open, disclosing on the other side a handful of restless tourists and a small carnival-like ticket booth. Surmising this to be the entrance John spoke of, I wandered in and took a seat on a marble bench. My watch said five past ten, but John was not yet there.

The man in the ticket booth was smoking a cigarette and reading a newspaper. The five tourists, pacing like caged animals, looked occasionally at their watches, too, and then glanced towards another pair of iron gates set most strangely into the hillside. Beyond these iron bars there yawned a blackness so formidable that I had the fleeting impression of Christian martyrs about to face lions. I saw no evidence of the Golden House or any of the grandeur I had seen on the Palatine Hill. There the greatest people in Roman history had lived: Augustus, Tiberius, Livia, Caligula, Claudius, Messalina . . .

I looked again at the cavern beyond the bars. Yet *this* was Nero's abode, the most formidable tyrant in Roman history and one of the most shocking figures in all world history. I had at one time read *Twelve Caesars* by Seutonius. I had read of the madman, the butcher, the decadent Emperor of Rome who had supposedly killed Saints Peter and Paul. This was his house.

My reveries were interrupted by an opulent lady whose thighs made a rustling sound as she walked. "English?" she said.

"American." I squinted up at her silhouette haloed by the sun.

"Wonderful! So am I." She sat next to me and placed a pudgy hand on my arm. "Isn't it exciting? Isn't it positively thrilling?"

"The Domus Aurea?"

"Rome, my dear! Are you with a group?"

"Alone."

"Us, too. The groups have been suffering this year because of inflation. But my mother and I have been saving for this trip for years and nothing could change our minds. Have you been in there yet? No? This is my second time. You just won't believe it when you get inside, especially after you've seen the beautiful palaces on the Palatine Hill. You have? Well, this is nothing like that. It's terribly dark and mysterious. Like the Black Hole of Calcutta. You can just imagine ghosts living in there. Why, it's positively spine tingling!"

I looked again at the blackness beyond the iron bars, a blackness that stretched deep into the hillside but left little trace on the hilltop as to what lay concealed beneath. I had the brief impression of a burial vault.

"Of course the Golden House once stood in the sunlight, but the centuries have buried it. Inside is the most fantastic labyrinth you'll ever see. There are a few murals left, some mosaic floors, but it's all so deathly and formidable. It's my favorite spot in all of Rome!"

I smiled politely at the woman with the bright red lips and taste for the supernatural. She was excited and animated, and I felt a little of it inspire me. Whatever lay beyond that twentieth-century iron gate belonged to another realm, a mysterious one, hidden from the daily vagaries of our modern era.

"Nero still dwells within those walls," she chatted on. "His ghost has actually been seen!"

"That's pretty exciting." I looked around for John. It was almost twenty past ten.

"Listen." She put a fat hand to her ear. "The last group is returning."

Following the subdued sounds of feet and voices, I strained to see movement beyond the bars. Then a spark appeared. It grew, and as it grew I saw it was a flashlight held by a guide who led a few tourists back to daylight. The gates squeaked open and one by one the tourists tipped and thanked the Italian in different languages. As they walked solemnly past me I searched their faces for a reaction, just as in a cinema queue one looks at the people coming out to glimpse what they thought of it.

But these faces were strangely blank. No one spoke. It was impossible to read their thoughts. Then I had a fantastic curiosity to see just what indeed remained of the monstrous Nero.

My American friend was saying, "Shall we go in?"

"Well, I . . ." Looking around, I saw the others take their places with the rotund little guide. "When is the next tour?"

"In an hour."

As I stood I took one last look around. John was not in sight. "Yes, let's go in." I ran to the booth and impulsively bought a hundred lire ticket. When I joined the small group the guide was just counting heads. Then he shouted, *"Sei!"* to the man in the booth, who then scribbled the number six on a piece of paper. When the guide addressed us he said, "You alla speak English. Is good. Giovanni speak English best. One language. Some-a day I have German, Francese, mama mia, even-a Greek! Today she's easy for Giovanni. We go, eh? Stay close to papa."

He pulled the gate open and the six of us stepped intrepidly into the cold tunnel. "She's easy to get lost. In a Nero's house she's easy to get lost. Stay with papa. No walk away."

We all clung to one another as we tripped over the uneven floor and followed Giovanni's weak flashlight deeper into the earth. The farther we went, the darker the blackness became, until my eyes ached from straining to see. For the first time in my life I had an idea of what it must be like to be blind, and the thought frightened me. Giovanni's light was like a beckoning finger. We had to follow.

When we bumped to our first halt, we all gaped at the room around us and the many doorways leading from it. While Giovanni spoke, extolling the crimes and atrocities of "Neroni Imperatori," I realized with a chill the need to count heads before entering and to stick close to the man with the flashlight. Totally black and labyrinthine, the insanely laid-out palace of Nero was an easy trap for the innocent strayer.

We shuffled from room to room, listening raptly to the Italian's oration of the legends surrounding this most mysterious of Rome's monuments, and I wished belatedly that I had waited for John.

The six of us had been trundled through narrow halls and chilly rooms for about ten minutes when it happened. Giovanni had just imparted a few ghost stories about Nero's hauntings and was leading the others from the room, while I held back to take a last look at the mural before me.

In the next instant there was a blow on my skull, a searing pain, and then a blackness even greater than that in Nero's Golden House.

CHAPTER 6

I AWOKE WITH A RINGING IN MY EARS AND AN ACRID TASTE IN my mouth. At first, when my eyes fluttered open, I perceived a prism of colors in a variety of shapes—none of which made any sense. But as consciousness gradually returned, my surroundings formed a picture.

The sound, I discovered, was a young woman talking in a high-pitched voice. The colors and smells eventually presented themselves in the form of a room of sorts, which I could not immediately identify. The ghastly taste was a medicinal one. I must have made a face over this last, because it prompted words from a man close to my side.

"She's awake now. Lydia? Lydia, can you hear me?"

I gaped at John Treadwell in amazement. What on earth had he to do with this absurd setting? "Of course I can hear you."

"Atta girl. You sound well enough anyway."

Again there was that high, melodious speech as the young woman fussed over me. I had no idea Italian could sound so sing-songy.

"I'm all right," I moaned. But I didn't mean it. There was a pain at the back of my head and, after a brief exploration with my fingers, I found an enormous lump. My entire body felt weak and drained, my stomach frightfully nauseous. The symptoms of shock were easily recognizable. I do not normally say words like "Jesus Christ," but I did then and followed it with the usual, "What happened?"

"You had a nasty fall, Lydia. You slipped in Nero's Golden House and whacked your head hard."

"Oh wow." I felt truly wretched. My skull throbbed, and that general post-car accident rottenness had come over me. I wished at that moment I could have gone unconscious again. "My head is killing me."

"Poor Lydia. You've got a grandaddy lump. If only I'd arrived on time."

I waved a limp hand at him. "Not your fault. I was too impatient to meet the ghost of Nero. And it appears I met him. Oh wow." I struggled to sit up, but John had the upper hand. With two hands on my shoulders he gently persuaded me back down where my head lay pounding on the pillow. "Am *I* sick!"

"The doctor's seen you once, and he's coming back. Just rest, Lydia."

"Doctor?" Now I finally took a better look at my surroundings and found myself to be lying on a cot in what appeared to be an emergency examining room, where I was being kept company by John Treadwell and an Italian nurse with a moustache. The walls were yellow and cracked, the furniture wormy. Along a counter by the sink stood the usual paraphernalia of a doctor's office. On one wall hung a faded picture of some indeterminable Roman ruin congested with cats and in the air was that heavy "hospital" fragrance.

It was not exactly Santa Monica Emergency, but it would do. When the doctor returned I was relieved to find he spoke excellent English and had some idea of what to look for in skull injuries. He discussed my condition with me on a professional level—after I had disclosed to him my occupation—then he gave me a thorough neurological examination. So far no brain damage. Even though it felt as though the back of my head would explode all over the room any minute, I was pretty safe from concussion or subdural haematoma.

For this I was very thankful.

Although he wanted further tests and to send me to the radiology department, I protested, explaining that I knew the danger signs to watch for and that I would contact him in the event of any change in my condition. Little mollified by this reassurance, the doctor requested that I sign certain legal forms absolving the Italian government of any further responsibility, since I was, in effect, "checking" myself out.

This I did gladly, for—sick though I was—I was very anxious to be out of the hospital and back at the Residence Palace Hotel. John was reluctant to take custody of me and sided with the good doctor's suggestion that I remain in the hospital. But my own strong will won. Although I felt wretched, I still had a good hold on my mental faculties, and indeed these sharpened by the minute. As the forms were placed before me for signature, my mind was already rapidly forming a new and startling idea.

In the Domus Aurea, *someone had slugged me.*

Resolutely I slid into my shoes and leaned heavily on John's arm. My professional training told me that the throb in my skull should be heeded and that a few hours of medical observation would be the wise choice. However, a mixture of fear and anger rendered me irrational enough to make me anxious to return to the hotel and get to work on figuring out this latest turn of events.

After all, my "accident" was no accident. It had been done on purpose by someone who had knocked me out cold for some very specific reason. It was my intention to find out just who had done this and—more important—why.

As we rattled over the ancient bridge and away from Tiberina Island where the hospital stood, I aired these thoughts to John. He was predictably reserved.

"I don't want to accuse you of romanticizing, Lydia, but I just can't accept your theory. I mean, the Domus Aurea *is* a weird place and it fires any imagination. Walking through those dark rooms and listening of tales of Nero's hauntings, it would . . ."

"Oh, John Treadwell," I whispered, as if that said it all.

He watched me pout for a few minutes, then said, "You know it gave me an awful scare. I saw the ambulance drive away just as I got to the Oppian

Hill, and I couldn't believe it when they said you'd been hurt. First I went to the Salvator Mundi on Mura Gianicolensi, because that's where foreigners are usually taken. I had a heck of a time trying to find you when I saw you weren't there."

"John," I interrupted. "You'll just have to believe me, that's all. One minute I was standing with the group as conscious and sound minded as ever, and the next I was lying on the floor with a lump on my head where someone had struck me."

He held my eyes with his. "All right, if you insist on that, then who was it and why? *Why,* Lydia?"

"I don't know." I was thinking of Ahmed Rasheed. I decided not to tell John about him. Not just yet anyway. "Somehow my sister has managed to involve me in some sort of trouble and I don't like it. I won't run, John, I won't ignore it. I have always faced problems head-on, even if they seemed insurmountable, and I will always challenge them. Maybe I'm talking through my hat, but that was no accident in the Domus Aurea."

I pressed my cheek against the window and gazed out as rose-colored Rome sped past. Through the ringing in my ears I heard the gentle voice of Dr. Kellerman saying, "And who else hands me my sutures in such nice tangles as you do?" I could have used his advise and company just then. Even just his presence would have made everything seem all right. But Dr. Kellerman was 10,000 miles away and in another world. He was in Santa Monica, working quietly in a cool operating room, while I was rattling around Rome with a throbbing head.

"Lydia?"

I looked at John. He had been talking and I hadn't heard a word. "I'm sorry."

"Promise me you'll stay in your room this afternoon. Lie down and take care of yourself. Head injuries are tricky things."

"I know. I'm a nurse, remember? If I develop any symptoms I'll go back to the hospital. But until then I have more pressing things to do."

"Just don't be irrational, Lydia."

Now I laughed. "You don't know me very well, John Treadwell. I haven't committed an irrational act in my life."

"I don't know about that. From what you tell me, in the past few days you haven't committed a rational one."

I stared at him in amazement. He was right.

At the Residence Palace Hotel I made the customary check at the desk for Adele, receiving nothing, and then said good-bye to John in the lobby.

"I hate to leave you alone, Lydia."

"I'll be all right." My head was pounding so loudly I was certain everyone could hear it. "I know how to take care of myself. First I'm going to write a letter to a friend back home . . ." My voice drifted as I pictured Dr. Kellerman again. "Maybe I'll just telephone him. Then I'm going to sleep for a while."

"I'll come back around eight o'clock for dinner. Okay?"

"Please come back, but I don't know about eating." When I turned to go he put a hand on my arm and said quietly, "You think you know what's going on with Adele and the jackal, but you don't trust me enough to tell me about it."

His words surprised me. "First of all, John, I have no idea what's going on with Adele and the jackal, not even the scantest of theories. Second, I *do* trust you or else I wouldn't have told you as much as I did. And third, any idea I have on this mystery I'm keeping to myself only because I don't want to involve you in this absurd melodrama which you so witlessly wandered into. I want to be fair to you, John."

"If you want to be fair to me, Lydia, let me help you as much as I can. You think someone is out to harm you. You might be right. If that's the case, then you'll need protection."

"I'm safe as long as I'm in this hotel. Thank you for your concern. I do appreciate it. But right now I want to be alone for a while. Let me take some aspirin and sleep this off. Later, when my thoughts make more sense, I'll tell you exactly what I think. Right now . . ." I sighed heavily, "right now I feel wretched."

With a reluctant shrug he put his hands on my shoulders and looked deep into my eyes. For the briefest instant I wished Dr. Kellerman was standing before me, then I smiled gratefully at John and let him kiss me on the lips.

"I'll be back later, Lydia. If you need me, call. Okay?"

"Thanks, John, I will. And I'll see you at eight."

I approached my suite with great apprehension. It was not fear of another physical attack, but rather a wariness of what I would find on the other side of my door; an intuitive expectation that, if true, could turn this adventure into a nightmare.

Unfortunately I was right. What I had been wary of had indeed come to pass, and the evidence of it was so distressing that I wanted to cry.

My room had been searched.

The job was not as neat as the one on my Malibu flat and was obvious instantly. Drawers not fully closed. A cupboard standing open. My suitcase lying flat rather that on its side. Even the bed had been hastily checked.

I stood dumbly in the doorway with my head throbbing, and I suddenly felt very helpless. At the Domus Aurea one of those five tourists had knocked me unconscious in order to give himself or an associate time to search my things for the jackal. Along with this realization came another: they would probably stop at nothing to get it.

Casually I strolled to the curtains that hid the balcony and rested my hands at their junction as if to part them. As I did so, I slowly lifted my foot and tapped a toe against the hem of the curtain. A reassuring hardness told me the jackal was still safe and that its place of concealment in the curtain seam had been a wise choice. I was glad now I had changed its hiding place. At least for a while the jackal was still mine.

However, that also meant I was still in danger.

Drawing the curtains apart I stared through the glass door to the flats opposite. So that was it, my Big Choice. Either I could give up the jackal and go back home unscathed to my quiet life and Dr. Kellerman, or hang tenaciously on to it until Adele and myself were killed for its possession.

An easy choice to make.

"How do you feel, Miss Harris?"

I gasped and swung round. Ahmed Rasheed stood in the open doorway, poised on the threshold of my room.

"Why do you ask that?" I placed a hand at my chest as if it would calm my racing heart.

"I overheard the telephone call made to this hotel from the hospital on Tiberina Island. I enquired after your condition and was told of the accident you suffered. The Domus Aurea is a chancy place for the unaware visitor. Uneven floors and low ceilings."

"Yes, it was stupid of me."

As we watched one another across the room I saw that for the first time his face was exposed to me, for he had removed the sunglasses to reveal large eyes with thick black lashes. Ahmed Rasheed had a way of looking through people, as though able to penetrate them with his eastern eyes.

I ran a hand across my forehead and noticed that I was perspiring. The back of my head felt as though it was about to fall off, and the painful throbbing was causing an ever-increasing nausea. Yet I held my ground and stared right back at the Arab.

"Have you found your sister?"

I felt like saying, "You know I haven't," but answered merely, "No."

"That is unfortunate. I fear your stay in Rome has been visited with unfortunate circumstances. I wish I could be of help."

"You can, by leaving," I said rudely. "I don't feel well at all." Quite boldly I strode across the room and placed a clammy hand on the door. Knowing I was suffering a delayed form of shock and that I was about to be very ill, I was anxious to be rid of this man at any cost.

"You do not look well," I heard his voice say above the hammering in my head. "You are very white, Miss Harris. Miss Harris?" I saw a dark brown hand extend towards me and I suppose he took hold of my arm. "Can you hear me?"

"I'll be all right in just a min . . ." Then my knees gave out under me. When I expected to feel the floor slap my face, instead two strong arms were about my waist, and by some magic I was propelled away from the door. As the room swam around me, I felt myself being laid upon the couch, my feet raised, and a blanket fluttered over my body.

In the next instant my fainting spell passed and I was looking up into the fantastic eyes of Ahmed Rasheed. "I'm sorry," I said, reluctantly thankful that he had been there to help me.

"I know what happened at the Domus Aurea, Miss Harris, and I think you would be better off in the hospital. As a nurse you should realize this."

I tried to lift my head but could not. The nausea had passed yet the throbbing remained. "What do you mean, you know what happened? And how did you know I was a nurse?"

He offered an apologetic shrug. "I know a lot about you, Miss Harris, just as I know about your sister and why you are looking for her."

"What?"

"You see, I know about the jackal."

After he had secured me on the couch, Ahmed Rasheed called the desk for assistance, so that in the next moment a maid was at my door with a tray of tea and rolls, and an extra blanket. In what sounded like excellent Italian, Mr. Rasheed instructed the woman to check on me every hour, that I would be asleep, and that the management was to be kept informed of my condition. More than accommodating, the woman reassured me in rapid Italian that I would be given special consideration.

"They are a hospitable people," said Mr. Rasheed after she had gone. He was sitting in a chair by the bed and watching me closely.

"You're very generous yourself, Mr. Rasheed, but this is really an awful lot of fuss."

"Do you think so?"

I did not reply. I drank the tea, which was delicious, and four aspirins set to work on my head. But I had to know one thing.

"Who are you, Mr. Rasheed?"

For the first time he smiled, and it was an engaging gesture. "I am simply Ahmed Rasheed."

"It's not all that simple. Do you know where my sister is?"

"Unfortunately, no."

"Did you say something about a jackal?"

Again he smiled and the simple expression erased all the mystery from his face. Reluctant though I was to admit it, I conceded to myself that this stranger was very intriguing to look at. "You are wise in your precaution, Miss Harris. I refer to the ivory jackal your sister posted to you and which I believe you have brought with you to Rome."

I attacked my lower lip with my teeth. "I don't know what you're talking about."

"Of course not." He stood up at this point and assumed an air of flippancy. "It was not I who struck you in the Domus Aurea, and it was not I who searched your room. Yet I do not expect you to believe this or to trust me. If you did, I would think you a fool, which you are not."

"Where is my sister, Mr. Rasheed?"

"I truly, truly wish I knew. Rest now, Miss Harris, and perhaps we can talk later."

"I don't think we have anything to talk about. Besides, I have a friend with me in Rome and he will be all the help I'll need."

"Of course. I trust you will feel better. *Inshallah.* Good-bye."

I waited for his footsteps to echo down the marble hallway, then I carefully tiptoed to the door and locked it. The excitement of the day was taking a heavy toll, and it was all I could do to drag myself back to the couch and collapse on it. My thoughts were jumbled, my emotions raw. The peace and security of my Malibu home and few friends seemed as far away as Mars, and about as accessible. Adele had involved herself in some dangerous intrigue and had unwittingly dragged me into it, too. Now all of a sudden I had in my possession an object, the value of which I could not determine, that someone—possibly several people—was after. And because of it my life was now in danger.

With my mind thus occupied I fell fast asleep on the couch and slept soundly for several hours until a rapping at my door roused me. Stumbling over long afternoon shadows cast across the floor, I pressed my cheek against the door and said, "Who is it?"

The maid's voice replied, *"Scusi, Signorina. Una lettera."*

"Just slide it under the door, please."

"Non capisco, Signorina."

"Never mind." I fumbled with the lock and opened the door a crack. As she handed me an envelope she asked, *"Come sta?"*

"Fine, just fine. Thank you."

I locked the door and leaned against it with a sigh, staring foggily at the letter. Not yet awake, and feeling the beginnings of a headache, I was in no condition to question this unexpected mail. Some colorful stamps sat crookedly upon a flimsy airmail envelope, and a familiar hand had written my name and the hotel's address. Still not awake, I casually tore open the envelope and unfolded the single piece of thin paper with a letterhead inscribed in both Arabic and English—The Shepherd's Hotel.

The same familiar handwriting had scratched a brief, hasty note to me. It said simply,

Liddy,

You must join me at once in Cairo. I'll be at this hotel. Will explain everything when you get here. Hurry.

Adele

CHAPTER 7

I FLEW BY ALITALIA JET JUST HOURS AFTER RECEIVING ADELE'S
letter and with great apprehension and misgivings. At least, I
was able to console myself, now I knew where my sister was and
I should soon be getting answers from her. It was for this reason that I did
not call Dr. Kellerman in Rome but had put it off until I saw Adele, so that
I could at least tell him when I should be returning. Yet there was a nagging
fear at the back of my poor lumpy head that Adele might elude me once
again, and the prospect of being alone in Egypt was far more formidable
than my brief sojourn in Rome.

As I worked my way to the bottom of a third bourbon and water, I took
a mental account of the situation. A tiny consolation was that Ahmed Rasheed did not know of my departure—of that I was certain—and it appeased
me somewhat to be out of the reach of that enigmatic man, whose mere
presence put me on edge. An even larger consolation was that, upon reading Adele's note, John Treadwell had insisted on coming with me. Once his
mind was made up there was no dissuading him, for he was of the firm

belief that he was now as deeply involved in this mystery as I, and that his emotional involvement with me precluded any other plans he might have had. This last, John's ardent protesting of great fondness for me, did not pass without effect. It had been a long time since any man had displayed such emotion for me and I was moved by it. To say that I loved John Treadwell at this point would be premature, for the circumstances did not truly allow me to think of much other than Adele and her blasted jackal. Yet I knew that if we had met in saner conditions and at a more conducive time I most likely would have fallen in love with John Treadwell quite easily.

As it was, his presence next to me as we cruised above the Mediterranean had a pacifying effect. I was able to sort my thoughts more easily, reassess my financial situation, and even try to think of possible alternative plans if I couldn't find Adele.

"She might just have you following her around the world," said John.

I nodded and saw my reflection in the black sky beyond my window. We would be landing in Egypt at 3:00 a.m. "It isn't fair to you, John, abandoning your work this way."

He took my hand and said reassuringly, "We've gone over all this before. I'll stay with you till you find your sister. I have never been to Egypt before, but I can imagine it's no place for a young woman traveling alone. One imagines such sinister people in Cairo."

I nodded again, thinking of Ahmed Rasheed. Once more I had decided not to tell John about him. He was back in Rome and I had escaped his unnerving presence. Why make matters more confusing?

Cairo International Airport, set in the desert fifteen kilometers from the city, had to be awakened for our arrival, John and I being the only two passengers to disembark from the plane. A number of uniformed Arabs, all pleasant and friendly, were required to process us as we passed through customs, by the visa desk, by the Bank of Egypt, through health control, etc. As we exchanged our currency for Egyptian pounds and obtained temporary visas, John and I found ourselves being greeted by friendly, laughing people. Free at last to pass into the airport itself, after numerous well wishes and welcomes in Arabic and broken English, we trod carefully over the floors that were being washed and had no difficulty in obtaining a taxi.

A grinning Arab took our cases and ushered us into his little car, which was interior decorated with flowers, paper birds, and colorful beads. John said, "Shepherd's Hotel, please," and we were on our way.

Although the roads were deserted at this dark hour, our drive was as harrowing as if we had sped a hundred miles an hour on the Harbour Freeway. The driver was maniacal, and I had a sinking feeling that they all might be in this city. Remembering the hair-raising traffic in Rome I guessed that I would have to be many times more watchful in Cairo.

As it was darkest night I saw little of Cairo from the taxi, but was vaguely aware of passing from flat desert into sprawling suburbs, then narrow streets and finally into a "downtown" section. We drove around a large square that was sparsely lit with orange street lights, and as we sped past a large towering building our driver pointed and said, "Hilton," as if we should be impressed. Two blocks later we pulled up in front of the Shepherd's Hotel.

Tired though I was, I jumped out of the cab and hurried up the steps, pushed open the heavy glass doors, and went directly to the registration desk where a sleepy receptionist was startled by my arrival. First he said something in Arabic, then said, "Welcome in Cairo," and gave me his best grin.

I, too, curved my mouth into a hopeful smile and said a little breathlessly, "Can you tell me the room number of Adele Harris? She's an American. Adele . . . Harris . . ."

"Certainly, madam." He opened a large book, fell upon the last page, and ran his finger down the lines. "How is that name again, please?"

"Harris. H-A-R-R-I-S. Adele Harris."

I watched that brown index finger go down the line, come up and go down the line again. Then I saw the Arab's eyebrows begin to come together on his forehead and his smile disappeared. His next words stabbed me. "I am sorry, madam, we have no one of that name in our hotel."

"Well . . ." I knew I was dreaming and that I would wake up any minute. "Of course she's here. She wrote and told me she was. Look . . ." I whipped her letter out of my bag and thrust it at him almost accusingly. "See? Your own stationery."

"Yes." He closely examined the envelope. "But where she has written her name there is no room number." He was pointing at the return address. "She has not told you her room number."

"Can she have checked out already?"

"I will look for you, madam."

I stood for what seemed to be several years, leaning on that spacious desk with its postcards of pyramids and sphinxes. Somewhere behind me a clock ticked and footsteps whispered over the polished floor. At what point John joined me I do not know, but as I stood anxiously on that spot with my eyes bulging towards the registration book, I felt his hand reassuringly on mine. When the receptionist said sadly, "We never had a Miss Harris in our hotel," I thought I was going to cry.

"But you must, don't you see?"

"Lydia," said John quietly, "let's just get a room and figure this out in the morning."

"Can there be another Shepherd's Hotel?"

"No madam," said the clerk. "This is our paper." He handed me back Adele's letter, and I could see he was truly sorry. "Why would she say she is here if she is not?" He shrugged, "I cannot tell."

"Lydia," said John again. "Come on."

"Where *is* she!" I cried. The lobby was beginning to carousel about me and my head was throbbing again. The pain was unbearable.

The receptionist was saying something about having only one room left because of Henry Kissinger and a pick up in tourist trade, but I did not care in the least. Adele had again led me to a dead end, and in a city so foreign that I might have been frightened had I not been so angry.

A chatty bell-hop led us to my room on the eighth floor, trying his high-school English on us and beaming when we understood him, and then went on to offer any number of services to alleviate my distress. All I wanted was to be left alone. Only twelve short hours before I had been brutally attacked in the Domus Aurea, and I had not had a chance to recuperate. And it did not appear I was going to get any rest in Cairo. Not yet at least.

John could not have expressed more concern. He held me gently against him, cradling me in his arms, and took all my weight as we walked down the hall to the room. The bell-hop was hastily discharged and John took care to see that I laid down upon one of the twin beds, that my shoes were off my feet, and that I was generously covered with wool blankets. I could not protest. The darkness of the room was a great relief and I was too exhausted to argue.

After a moment of moving softly about the room, latching the door, opening the window a crack, and setting our suitcases in the wardrobe, John came back to me and sat on the edge of the bed. I couldn't see him clearly, only an obscure silhouette against the darkness, but I sensed in his patient silence the smile that must be on his face. When his hand gently touched my forehead and my cheeks, I imagined the concern that shone in his eyes. When his lips were upon mine, I pictured the kind face of John Treadwell and saw him as clearly as if the sun shone.

I kissed him back. My arms curled up around his neck until I held him as tightly as I could. I was clinging to him, clutching him in my fear and my anger. Then I murmured his name and felt his body mould to mine. His arms collected me to him as our kisses grew hungry. In that moment I could give no thought to Adele or the jackal or Egypt. Here was John—real and palpable and filling me with his strength.

In the next moment he released me, resting me back on the pillow. He whispered, "Not now, Lydia. I want you to sleep first. Tomorrow everything will be all right."

He kissed my closed eyes and I felt his weight rise from the bed. The ardor remained, covering me with warmth and a glow, but I was indeed exhausted by now and, after only a second, quietly succumbed to sleep.

At first I did not know where I was. My eyes stared absently at the ceiling as my thoughts gradually came together in some vague coherency. I was lying fully dressed in bed. My head ached. I felt ravenously hungry. Thin cracks of light showed between the curtains, and next to me was a vacant but slept-in bed.

"Good morning."

I lifted my head. John was standing over me, grinning.

"Good morning," I said thickly.

"Feel better?"

I rubbed my eyes. "Ask me in a few days. What time is it?"

"Damn near noon." He sat on the edge of his bed and studied me. "I've been out all morning, Lydia. I'm sorry—no news of Adele."

I was not surprised. Slowly and clumsily I pulled myself out of bed and went into the bathroom. Cold water on my face was remarkably therapeutic so that, as I washed myself and dragged a brush through my hair, I felt my body begin to stir with life. I also remembered the goodnight kisses.

"I went to the American Consulate and then to the American Express office," I heard John say from the other room. "I checked all the major hotels and finally put in a word with the police. They were all more than anxious to help, but couldn't."

"Far out . . ." I murmured, and then looked around for the bottle of aspirins.

"I did learn one thing, however—that your sister definitely came to Egypt."

I stuck my head round the door. "What?"

"You remember all that red tape we had to go through at the airport last night? Every arriving visitor to Egypt has to go through the same thing and fill out the same forms. Well, so did your sister. The police have her regis-tered as a tourist who arrived here four days ago. In fact, Visa Control says the date of her arrival was two days *after* she left the Residence Palace Hotel, if what you had been told on the phone was true."

"So Adele left Rome in the middle of the night and showed up here two days later. Where was she in the meantime?"

"You got me."

"Could they tell you if she is still here?"

"As far as they know, she has not left yet. But wait a minute, Lydia, the police are checking the airlines for us. We'll soon find out if she's flown the coop again."

"But then she is probably still in Egypt!"

"And it's a big country, Lydia, and Cairo is the largest city in Africa. This is one easy city to get lost in. She could be anywhere."

"But she *is* here and knows I will be at this hotel. All I have to do is wait for her to come to me."

"Yes . . ." said John hesitatingly.

"What's the matter?"

"Oh, I was only thinking." He tried to appear casual. "Maybe that isn't the wisest thing to do, sit around here."

"Why not?"

"Well . . ." He rose from the bed and took hold of my arms, saying seriously, "You were in grave danger in Rome, Lydia, and you are probably in even more here. I don't think you should stay."

"And go home? Not on your life." After all, I had shaken off Ahmed Rasheed. "I'm perfectly safe."

"That's what you said in Rome. You're not safe while you have the jackal. I think you should get rid of it, Lydia."

"Never! I've gone through a lot for that little rascal, I'm not giving it up now."

"But what I mean is, you can let them have the jackal—whoever 'they' are—and then look for Adele."

I shook my head violently. "No. The road to Adele is through that piece of ivory. As long as I have it there's always a link between me and my sister. After all, she sent it to me for a reason. If I gave it up I might also give up the chance of ever finding her again."

"Then at least let me take care of it for you. I can hide it . . ."

I continued to shake my head firmly. "That jackal and I have come half way around the world together and he is as safe as ever. I'm capable of taking care of it, John, as well as myself."

"Oh, Lydia. All right, you win." Impulsively he threw his arms about me and kissed me. "There's obviously no talking reason to you." Then he said, "I suppose I'm just as committed to this thing as you are, whatever the heck is going on!"

I kissed him for saying that. It was hard to imagine what I would have done without John all that time, and even though I would have managed somehow, it would not have been as smooth. I had a lot to thank him for.

"Hey, you know what? I've never even seen this jackal that I'm risking life and limb for. I don't even know what it looks like."

"Then it's about time you two were introduced." But as I moved away from him to dig the jackal out of its special hiding place, there was a sharp rap at the door. Muttering something about "making up the room," John flung the door open to reveal Ahmed Rasheed standing on the other side.

"Good afternoon, Miss Harris," he said nasally. His manner was smooth, deceptive.

Taken off guard, I still managed to say hello. Then I went to John's side and put my hand on his arm.

"I trust your accommodations are not lacking?"

"Not at all, thank you." His eyes were hidden again by those sunglasses, and I was thankful for that.

John gave me a quizzical look, then studied the Arab before us. "Is this a friend of yours, Lydia?"

"No he isn't. Just someone I met in Rome." I could not look at him. I was too shaken.

Then Mr. Rasheed said, "I was hoping we could talk alone, Miss Harris."

"That's not possible. And I really can't imagine what we might have to talk about."

"You can't?" He smiled secretively. "Perhaps I have come at the wrong time."

"Any time is the wrong time, Mr. Rasheed. I don't care to talk to you," and I began to close the door.

"But it is you who are mistaken, Miss Harris . . ."

"Listen mister," said John now. "Miss Harris doesn't want to see you. I think she's made that clear. Now kindly pull your foot out of the doorway or I will put my fist in your face."

"There is no need for violence, Mr. Treadwell. I am leaving. However, Miss Harris, should you change your mind about talking to me, I will leave the telephone number of my office at the front desk."

At this point John slammed the door in Ahmed Rasheed's smiling face and swore under his breath. "Who is he, Lydia, and what does he want? How did he know my name?"

"This whole thing is just dreadful, John. And my head feels monstrous. Can we please go somewhere for coffee?"

I changed my clothes and freshened up before we went up to the dining room on the roof. Served by very amiable Egyptians, and treated to a view of the city through the yawning windows, I felt worlds better and was able to give John the entire story of Ahmed Rasheed without coloring it with my small fears and suspicions.

"I wish you had told me about him sooner," said John, frowning. "He seems to know a lot about you. I wonder how he knows me and how he ties in with this jackal business."

My hands were working at the strap of my handbag, twisting and knotting. Inside, secure on my lap and swaddled in a scarf, was the jackal. I knew it was my imagination, but the bag seemed to be getting heavier each day.

"At least he wasn't the one who hit me yesterday. Of that I'm certain. The guide at the Domus Aurea counts everyone going in, and no one can enter without being part of the group. And Mr. Rasheed was not part of the group."

"But he still could have been the one who searched your room."

"I don't know, John, somehow I don't think so. There's something funny about him."

"I'll say there is!"

"That's not what I mean. What I mean is, if he's after the jackal, he could have got it by now, by one sinister means or another. There's more to it than that. Almost as if he was waiting for me to lead him to Adele."

John carelessly buttered a croissant. "What is that supposed to mean?"

"I don't know. Only that something more important than the jackal is afoot here. As though Adele has stumbled upon something very important and that certain parties are anxious to find her as well as me."

"If it's not the jackal they want, then why has your room been searched?"

"For the jackal, John, but only to use it as a clue to Adele's whereabouts. Somehow I think 'they' believe the jackal will lead them to her."

"Sounds awfully far-fetched, Lydia." He sipped his coffee and gazed at a point above my shoulder.

"I know, but then so is this whole odyssey. Somehow . . . I get the idea that everyone is waiting for me to find Adele. I don't know . . ."

I picked up another slab of tasteless goat's milk butter and spread it on a roll as I looked around the huge dining room. Only half full at this time of day, it had an air of intimacy and solitude. The waiters stood ready to attend to our slightest wish, and the other tourists—mostly French—murmured quietly.

Then I saw the fat man. Standing almost hidden behind a potted palm tree, he appeared to be watching us very carefully. But more than that, for I had come to accept being spied upon, the little fat man was in some way familiar to me. Those extraordinary glasses that looked like the bottoms of Coke bottles.

Our eyes met across the room.

"John . . ."

"Yes?"

I nodded in the direction behind him, trying not to be obvious. "Have you ever seen that man before?"

He shifted in his chair. "What man?"

I pointed at the plant, but the spy had gone.

"Where, Lydia?"

I squinted. "No one now. I guess I imagined it. I thought I saw someone familiar to me . . ."

"Oh? What did he look like?"

"Never mind. I was only imagining it."

While the lump on my head was starting to go down, its effects still continued to plague me so that I was anxious to be in my room again and lying down.

"You'll want to see Cairo," said John as we walked to the lifts.

"Certainly I will. But not now. I have to nurse my brain for a while."

He conceded and escorted me back to my room. "You take it easy, Lydia, and don't worry about that Rasheed character. I won't let him get near you. Now get some sleep while I go to see what the police have found."

I didn't bother undressing, but lay at once upon the bed while John drew the curtains, kissed me good night, and hung a Do Not Disturb sign on the door. Sleep, however, was not to be had. Although aspirins were again taking care of my throbbing headache, my wildly flying thoughts would not let me rest. Why had Ahmed Rasheed followed me to Cairo, and what did he think we would want to talk about? And who was that fat man, obviously watching me and so elusively familiar?

After half an hour I impatiently gave up and decided to go downstairs. If Adele was to be found, if answers were to be got, they would not come to me lying in a dark room.

Fully aware of what curiosity had done to the cat, and totally aware of the possible folly I was about to commit, I decided to make a telephone call to Ahmed Rasheed.

Going down in the lift I found it quite easy to rationalize the telephone call. First of all, I did not think there was going to be any avoiding Mr. Rasheed in Cairo anyway. And secondly, I was certain he had information about Adele, and I was determined to learn why he was after her.

Anyway, these were my thoughts as I stepped out of the lift and into the lobby. Those were my thoughts when my eyes fell upon John Treadwell standing by the desk, deeply involved in an animated talk with the fat man who had spied on me. However, those were not my thoughts as I withdrew into a recess where I could stand unseen, for it occurred to me just then why the fat man had been so familiar.

He had been one of my group in the Domus Aurea.

After a moment they walked off together, getting into a lift and laughing quietly. I must have stood frozen for some time with my mouth hanging open, for I could not imagine what John and the fat man would have to say to one another. But even more disconcerting had been their manner, as though they were not strangers at all but friends.

Because of this I forgot my phone call to Ahmed Rasheed, and decided to join John and his fat friend. As calmly as I could I watched the old-fashioned dial above the lift glide past each number until it stopped at the top. Then I stepped into the next lift and pushed number eight. It seemed to take forever going up, and I felt my palms getting moist and clammy. Something called feminine intuition was beginning to take over from reason and it was putting insane thoughts into my head. If the fat man was in the Domus Aurea with me, then what was he doing here in Cairo and talking familiarly with John? Although the answer would have been obvious to anyone else, I refused to let it enter my mind and, instead, invented some half-baked theory that possibly John had approached the fat man to ask why he had been spying on us.

A myriad of thoughts deluged my brain at that moment, none of which were at all rational. Events were happening too fast, and shock was beginning to take over. Jet lag, exhaustion and abnormal stress were all making me behave irrationally.

The eighth floor was still and quiet, with not a sound coming from anywhere. The maids had come and gone, and the guests were all out enjoying the city. So I trod softly along the red carpet, not anxious to announce my arrival, and looked this way and that.

All the doors were closed except one at the end, which was an inch or two ajar. I pushed it cautiously open. Strangely, I was not terribly surprised to find John lying face down on the floor. This whole affair was so ridiculous and fiendish. It was a nightmare peopled by boyish stockbrokers and mysterious Arabs and fat men with thick glasses. Now John Treadwell was lying unconscious on the floor and it seemed only proper that I, too, should faint. I said, "Oh John," saw the room go very black, and joined him on the floor.

CHAPTER 8

I AWOKE IN TOTAL CONFUSION. MY FIRST SENSATION WAS ONE of pain in the back of my head. But it was a familiar pain and did not alarm me. Struggling to a sitting position, I muttered the traditional expletives, groaned a little, and finally, when full consciousness returned to me, took a studious look at my surroundings.

The room was totally foreign to me. Although only barely lit, the illumination was sufficient to tell me that it was not a hotel room, nor did it belong to any public official such as the police or a doctor. In fact, only the scantest of inspection told me I was in a private house.

It was a bedroom. An unpretentious room with not much furniture but a lot of clutter. The walls were laced with all sorts of photos, randomly placed, some framed, some not. The mirror of the dresser was also framed with photographs, smaller ones, many faded and old. The dresser top displayed all the usual paraphernalia of a man's personal life: hair brush and comb, crumpled tie, opened mail, matchbooks, an old book with an Arabic title, toiletries, etc. Other furniture, such as the bed upon which I was sprawled and two small chairs, were unmatched and stood upon a threadbare oriental rug. Beyond the door I heard no noise, although through the bottom crack came white light.

And then it struck me.

In alarm my eyes flew back to the dresser top. The tie, the bottle of after-shave lotion, the absence of any lace, could all mean only one thing. I was in a man's bedroom. And it took little in the way of brain to discern that the man was an Arab.

Boldly now I stepped off the bed in my stockinged feet and tiptoed to the door. No sound. Not the remotest tinkle or click. Whoever was out there (for surely I had not been left alone!) was being darned quiet. I pushed it open a crack and set my eye against it. All I could see was bright light. Not really knowing what to expect on the other side, I gingerly pushed the door all the way open and entered a warm, well-lit room. Somewhere in the background a radio was softly playing Arabic music, and an unfamiliar though pleasant scent pervaded the air. All about me I saw a setting of total foreignness: white walls that were adorned with paintings of Egyptian antiquities, shelves cluttered with ancient statuary, a floor dressed richly in a handsome oriental rug. On top of a very old television set stood a vase of dried flowers and a portrait of President Anwar Sadat. There was an overstuffed couch cluttered with books and a desk nearby equally bedecked with books, papers, and envelopes. The windows were all shuttered so I had no idea of the time.

When Ahmed Rasheed appeared from the next room wiping his hands on a towel, I must have ogled incredulously at him, for he laughed and had to repeat himself several times.

"Why are you so surprised, Miss Harris? You knew you were coming here."

I stepped back from him, then screwed my face into the biggest frown and tried desperately to remember. However, my most recent recollection was finding John Treadwell on the floor. After that there was nothing.

"You walked out of the hotel with me and we rode in a taxi together. You do not remember this?"

"No . . ." I stood rooted to the spot. If I had legs, they were not mine to command.

"My poor Miss Harris! I was afraid you would not remember. Please sit down and I will explain."

"Yes, of course . . ."

He hurriedly cleared a space for me on the couch, sat me down, then left the room for an instant. He returned with a tray of tea and biscuits. Handing me a cup, he sat beside me and went on, "I was on my way to visit you when I found you on the floor in Mr. Treadwell's room. I was able to rouse you and escort you from the hotel. I am well known to the manager and explained to him that you are a friend of mine and were not feeling well. So I brought you here to my home in a taxi. Now do you remember?"

I stared into my tea for some minutes before shaking my head. The throbbing was subsiding and I began to think what a terrible mess I must look. A myriad of impressions went through my mind but few made any sense. A vague memory of bright lights. Flashing lights. And people. Many people. None of it cohered. I shook my head again.

"Perhaps it is just as well," he said quietly. "Please drink the tea, it will do you good."

I sipped the tea, wishing it were bourbon, and watched the man over the rim of my cup. I must have looked like a cat, poised to run, because he said, "Please be assured that you are safe here."

I wanted to say, "From what?" but instead I asked, "How is John doing? Is he all right?"

Mr. Rasheed averted his eyes. "It all happened very quickly. Passing by the open door, seeing you lying there . . . very awkward you understand. If I hadn't been known at the Shepherd's Hotel . . ."

"What's going on?" I asked at last, mildly surprised at my boldness.

He blinked his bovine eyes. "I beg your pardon?"

I rattled my cup into its saucer as if to announce the return of my strength. "I'd like a few explanations, Mr. Rasheed, if you don't mind. Like, for instance, just who you are and why you have been following me."

The air hung heavy with silence. From all four walls echoed the pounding of my heart. I did not care for the position I was suddenly in. This man's prisoner. Where no one knew I was.

"You deserve an explanation, Miss Harris, and I wish to apologize for any discomfort I may have caused you. But you see, it was not really yourself I was following, but Mr. Treadwell."

I blinked stupidly. "John?"

"I was waiting for him when he arrived at Leonardo da Vinci Airport, and followed you both to the Residence Palace Hotel."

"You were following John Treadwell?"

Mr. Rasheed momentarily examined his fingernails. I knew he was deliberating on what to tell me and what to hold back.

"And besides," I blabbed on, "just who are you to follow people around, and what sort of thing is John involved in that requires him to be followed?" My God, I thought, first Adele, now John.

"I will come to all of that, Miss Harris, but you must please allow me the opportunity of explaining. You see, ah, I was indeed following Mr. Treadwell in Rome and had been expecting him to return that day. However, I had not expected him to return with company, that is yourself, and therefore decided to watch you for a while to determine what connection you had with John Treadwell."

I gaped. "What do you mean you expected him to *return*?"

"Mr. Treadwell had been in Rome, in the Residence Palace, just a few days before."

"What?" The room took a small spin. Possibly I was still hallucinating from the bang on my head. "You mean John had been in Rome days before he arrived with me?"

Mr. Rasheed nodded slowly.

"Wait a minute. I don't believe you. Who are you anyway?"

"That you are entitled to know. I work for the Egyptian government. I am an investigator, as you would say."

"Egyptian government!"

He grinned. "I can show you my credentials, but they are in Arabic."

My eyes narrowed. "What sort of investigator?"

"I cannot tell you exactly, Miss Harris, just as an agent of your own government cannot divulge all of his information. Let us say that I am a policeman of sorts, and Mr. Treadwell is my assignment."

"Oh wow." I ran a hand over my forehead in a symbolic gesture of being overwhelmed and tried to take all this in. I also took a minute to sit back and look at Ahmed Rasheed and was surprised to find that possibly he was not so sinister as I had previously imagined. What I saw before me was a swarthy man in his early thirties. He wore slacks and a white shirt with the sleeves rolled to the elbows. His hair was thick and black and his face forcefully Semitic. When he spoke it was with careful speech and a curiously intriguing accent.

Yet I still did not trust him.

He drank some more tea before continuing. "When I learned from your conversation that you were a friend of Mr. Treadwell, I thought that your own movements might give me a clue as to those of Mr. Treadwell."

I was both uppity and indignant at having the invasion of my privacy so lightly spoken of, so I refused to drink any more of his tea—policeman or not. Yet as the information he gave me began to trickle down into that small part of my rambling brain that controls reason, the significance of what he had said suddenly hit me between the eyes.

"He was at the Residence Palace days before I got there?"

"I saw him there myself."

"But he never mentioned . . ." My voice went the way of all good intentions. I looked again at Ahmed Rasheed and found him staring at me. "Go on, say it," I whispered, although I did not want to hear it.

"I am certain you have guessed it now, Miss Harris. John Treadwell knew your sister, Adele."

I screwed my eyes tightly, and when I opened them again the room was still there. The dingy walls, the oriental carpet, the perfume of the tea, the faint Arabic music in the background, it was all still there. And so was Ahmed Rasheed, secret policeman, with enigmatic eyes.

"You know I don't believe that."

He shrugged. "I did not say he knew her well. I saw them have lunch one day at the Residence Palace."

"He was a registered guest there?"

"Yes he was, but under another name. He was registered in the name of Mr. Arnold Rossiter and shared a suite with two men." Mr. Rasheed watched me closely for a reaction. That I had never heard of Arnold Rossiter must have been pretty obvious.

"Was one of them a fat little creep with thick glasses?"

His eyebrows raised. "Why yes!"

So that explained the mystery. John and the fat man *did* know one another. "He's in Egypt. I saw him today with John, just before we all decided to take a nap on the floor."

"So his friends are here with him. I am not surprised."

I shifted uncomfortably on the couch. Somehow this was all too bizarre. Here I sat in the flat of an Arab, who claimed to be a secret policeman, trailing my friend John Treadwell who it turned out had lied to me and had known my sister Adele in Rome. I felt my stomach sink by degrees.

"John Treadwell knew my sister, did he? So that means he flew to New York in order to accidentally sit next to me on the plane in order to come back to Rome and pretend not to know Adele. I'm sorry, Mr. Rasheed, but it makes little sense to me."

"And to me as well, Miss Harris."

"If John knew I was coming to Rome then Adele must have told him she was going to call me to come. So why the secrecy?" Of course I already knew the answer. "He or his friend must have been the one who searched my Malibu apartment."

"Was it searched?" He seemed surprised.

I closed my eyes with a nod. Then my stomach sank further. "So John also knew who socked me on the head at Nero's Golden House. In fact, he was in on it."

"I'm afraid that is all true, Miss Harris." Ahmed Rasheed sat expectantly hovering before me, waiting for me to say something more. Just one more thing.

I hated to concede, but I had no choice. "Then you know I still have the jackal, don't you?"

He said, "Yes."

We continued to sip tea as if we were at a garden party, after which he brought out a bowl of oranges and spoke for some length on the qualities of Egyptian fruit. I was not listening, of course, I was trying to make some organized sense of this whole mess. I was also suddenly very sad. I did not want to believe what Ahmed Rasheed said, yet it all seemed to fall into place. And to discover that John Treadwell had been deceitful was a terrible blow. I did not know what to think.

So what had *I* to do with all this? And why should I believe it anyway? The words of a mysterious stranger who made me a prisoner in his flat. Why should I believe what he said of John Treadwell? A man I was falling in love with.

A second cup of tea was delivered into my hands and I stared at it. "Would you possibly have something more medicinal?"

"I beg your pardon?"

"Bourbon, scotch, vodka, even cheap wine?"

"I am sorry. I have no alcohol."

"Oh . . ."

"As a Moslem I do not drink it. Perhaps you would prefer coffee to the tea, or juice maybe?"

"No." This was absurd. "Not at all. This is fine." I sipped the tea. It really was delicious. "Now will you answer me another question, Mr. Rasheed?"

"Certainly."

"What is Mr. Treadwell involved in?"

His smile turned pearly. "I am sorry, Miss Harris, but this is confidential and I cannot . . ."

"Let me rephrase that." I put my cup on the coffee table and squared my shoulders. "What is John Treadwell involved in that my sister Adele has become involved in that *I am now involved in*?"

"Miss Harris, I can truly understand your feelings, but I am not at liberty to tell. Yes, you are now involved in this just as you believe your sister is, although she may be innocent."

"*Of what?*"

"I cannot say." His voice remained calm and steady. "Please believe me, it is better this way. The less you know of the entire matter the safer it is for you."

"Now listen, Mr. Rasheed. I don't care if you're the head of the Egyptian CIA, I don't have to put up with this. We have an Embassy in this country . . ."

"A consulate."

". . . that I can go to at once. They won't cotton to an American citizen being held against her will by the Egyptian police . . ."

"Miss Harris."

". . . and not even told why."

"Miss Harris, please. I do understand your feelings. Now let me explain. Please? First of all, the Egyptian police, as you put it, are not holding you against your will. I am not the Egyptian police and you are not being 'held.' I brought you here for your own safety."

"Why? Because John and his fat friend had a fist fight? Maybe they had an argument about who should pay the hotel bill. I don't know. But I was safe in the hotel, of that I'm sure. The Domus Aurea was different. I appreciate your picking me up off the floor and brushing me down, but I didn't need to be spirited away to some Ali Baba's hideaway."

Ahmed Rasheed tried to hide his amusement and I realized how fanciful I had become. It was unlike me.

"And besides," I continued in a more dignified, collected manner. "I would like to know the significance of that damned jackal and why everyone is so anxious to get hold of it."

"Unfortunately, Miss Harris . . ."

"Yes, yes I know. You are not at liberty to tell me. Are you at least at liberty to return me to the hotel now?"

His manner altered suddenly. As his face clouded I said, "So I *am* being held against my will."

"No, that is not it. You see, what you said a moment ago about not needing protection, that you were safe in the hotel . . ."

"Yes?"

"There is more to it than that. You are *not* safe in the hotel now, Miss Harris. And you cannot go back."

"But why?"

Finally his eyes lifted to meet mine and they held me so tightly it was as if his hands were on my wrists. I could not move. "What happened? Tell me?" I whispered.

"John Treadwell was not unconscious. He was dead."

The room grew faint and distant, and Ahmed Rasheed seemed to disappear altogether. I felt my body turn to jelly and my stomach turn over. Visions paraded before me, and vague recollections. Had I really seen them or had I dreamt them? On the way out of the Shepherd's Hotel, my fist pressed against my forehead, Mr. Rasheed's arm about my waist, confusion at the door, badges flashing, someone saying, *"Aywa! Aywa!,"* bright lights and police uniforms.

"Now I remember," I whispered. "The police at the hotel."

"A chambermaid had found you both on the floor in John's room. When she reported it at the desk I overheard and took it upon myself to go up and see. You were trying to get up, so I helped. It took us a few minutes to reach the lobby and by then the police were there. Much confusion, however, aided our departure. My papers allowed us to pass."

I stared stupidly at Mr. Rasheed, my head resting on the back of the couch.

He went on, "The maid gave a poor description of you. All she could say was 'American woman, American woman.' We have many Americans in this city."

"But my passport . . ." Considering all I had been through, my brain was still functioning. "My passport is at the desk."

"I took it for you, along with your suitcase and handbag. Fortunately you had not unpacked in your room. I told my friend at the desk you were leaving. Apparently Mr. Treadwell had registered you in his name, so that you were not responsible for the room. At any rate, for the moment no one knows to look for you. They have no name, no description . . ." He tried his best to smile.

My mouth felt wooden and my tongue had difficulty in moving. "What do you mean 'for the moment'?"

"The Egyptian police are very thorough, particularly when it comes to an embarrassing and scandalous murder. The authorities will expect them to solve it. Before too long the police will examine their records for all passports that were registered with them in the last few days. Yours will be among them, and it will not be long before a process of elimination will have them out looking for you."

"Along with the description they got off the passport."

"That is not as important as the fact that you cannot go to another hotel in Cairo. The police will be watching for an American woman with your passport number."

"I see." I sat up straight and folded my hands in my lap. I could still see John Treadwell lying on the floor, his hair tousled in that familiar little boy way. Tears flooded my eyes. Before I started to cry I managed to say, "Thank you, Mr. Rasheed, for getting me out of there. If you hadn't come when you did . . ." I shook my head. "In Rome I thought you were my enemy."

"But you see? We are on the same side."

"And which side is that?" My voice was sharp and bitter.

"To find your sister."

Suddenly, those words held no importance any more. As I settled back into the couch and drove my fingernails into the skin of an orange, all I could think of was John, dear sweet John who had been so kind and helpful. Now he was dead and I didn't even know why. For all I knew, this Arab had murdered him.

When I felt his hand on my cheeks I realized I was crying, for he was wiping my tears away. He said as he did so, "Do you know that Allah intended for us to be happy always, that is why he gave us laughter. But he also gave us tears to make the laughter that much sweeter. I suppose you loved John Treadwell. I am terribly sorry that it is I who give you such bad news."

"I'm crying for the man I thought was John Treadwell, not the man he really was. He had lied to me from the start, if what you tell me is true, and continued to deceive me to the last moment. And if I am to believe you about his friendship with the fat man, which I admit I witnessed myself, then it would seem John had a hand in the Domus Aurea incident. I couldn't love a man like that, and I don't. I am crying for the loss of someone I never even knew except in my imagination."

Yet as I sat there, a half-peeled orange in my hands and salty tears on my cheeks, I felt sorrow gradually change into anger and frustration. It would be a waste of time to mourn a man who had played me for a fool. This whole nightmare was getting out of hand. It had become damned serious business. A man was murdered. I nearly was. And all because of the jackal.

I looked again at Mr. Rasheed. "So you are hiding me from the police. Isn't that illegal?"

He shrugged, but it was not flippantly. "You did not murder John Treadwell and you would not be able to tell them who did. Therefore you would be of no help to the police and little would be accomplished with your arrest. It is foolish to let them take you. It would be a waste of time for everyone and would delay finding your sister. Yes, I am hiding you from the police and, yes, that is illegal. But it will not be for long. Tomorrow my office will make full explanations and clear you with the police."

I bit into the orange and it sprayed all over the room. Mr. Rasheed was right, it was delicious. He watched me as I ate, those unsettling eyes staring sharply and revealing nothing. He knew more, much more than he was letting on, and I had to know.

"Mr. Rasheed, I have become involved in some nasty business. Apparently you, the Egyptian government, are looking for my sister as well as I. Apparently John was also involved in the same thing as my sister. I might soon be hunted by the Cairo police for the murder of a man. You must understand that I have questions. It is only fair to answer them. I have a right to know what I've unwittingly fallen into and what John Treadwell was mixed up in that got him murdered. I also have a right to know why you are looking for my sister, and what the significance is of that jackal."

"Yes, you do have those rights." He smiled patiently and reached for an orange. Peeling it he said, "However, believe me, Miss Harris, it is only for your safety that I do not tell you all these things. You are better off not knowing. There are other people involved, people who would stop at nothing to get information regarding your sister. And if you were to fall into their hands . . ." He paused for dramatic effect.

"Like that Arnold Rossiter you mentioned."

"Precisely."

"So you are hiding me from him too?"

"As a matter of fact. I am."

"Why so concerned with my safety, Mr. Rasheed?"

"Because if you were to be murdered I might never find your sister."

"I see."

We sat in silence for some time, listening to music. It seemed to be coming from a flat nearby, a monotonous clamor of Egyptian music. It all sounded the same to me, but it was also intriguing in its foreignness. I realized that my foot was tapping on the carpet.

"Can I offer you anything else, Miss Harris?"

"Just answers if you please."

"I had been following Mr. Treadwell for some time in order to learn the nature of, shall we say, a certain *matter*. In Rome I saw him make the acquaintance of Adele Harris, they were friendly for a while, then he left for the United States. I knew your sister had mailed the jackal to you, and I knew she had asked you to come to Rome. What surprised me was to find you arriving with John Treadwell. I could not tell if you were part of his group, or rather, Arnold Rossiter's group, or if you, shall we say, worked with your sister. Or if you were just totally innocent of it all, which I believe you are now. We all left Rome together after you received the letter from your sister. I had not anticipated John's murder and I cannot imagine why they did it."

"Arnold Rossiter's men?"

"Yes. Or so it would seem." Ahmed Rasheed frowned. "This has made a great complication of everything."

"So then, what you were doing was using me to find Adele. In fact, that's what you're doing now, using me as bait."

"It is the only way, I am afraid. Your sister is either hiding or she is being held captive somewhere. Whichever is the case, she will try to contact you."

I ruminated over this. Hiding or captive. Very intriguing. "So even though John Treadwell was the man you were after, the investigation still goes on after his death. But now it has shifted to my sister."

"She always was suspect. But now she is our prime suspect."

"In what, Mr. Rasheed?"

"I cannot tell you."

"Then tell me this. Did John Treadwell give her the jackal?"

"I do not know."

"So she might have had it before she met him, and possibly they were both involved in this *matter* before they even met one another in Rome?"

"Yes."

"In other words, John sought her out to make friends with because of the jackal. When she got rid of it he came after me."

"It would appear that way."

"Then what I don't understand is, why didn't John just take the jackal? He certainly had lots of opportunities."

"It is because you were more valuable to him. You were going to lead him to Adele. Why should he ruin his good relationship with you by stealing the jackal when what he already had, in effect, was you *and* the jackal."

I nodded thoughtfully. "He had both of us all right. Eating out of his palm."

"I beg your pardon?"

"So, then, Adele is the key to this whole mystery."

"Yes, she is. However, it might not be as serious as you suspect. Your sister might be as innocent of the affair as you are, and she may have been brought into it unwittingly, just as you are now. I cannot say. On the other hand, she might also be guilty of serious crimes. We do not know, and that is what I am trying to find out."

I slipped another slice of orange into my mouth and thought for a while. "Do you know how my sister left Rome? Did you know that it was in the middle of the night?"

"No, I did not know this. She was there one day, and the next she was not. I had carelessly lost her."

"So you don't know if she left on her own or if she was kidnapped."

"As you say, I do not know. I had thought you might. But my few questions in Rome told me how little you know."

"I wonder where she is . . ."

I fell to staring blankly ahead. Somehow I felt very detached from the whole business, as though I was standing back and watching it as I would a play. Lydia Harris had got herself into some stupid trouble, and it was going to be interesting to see how she got herself out of it. If she could at all.

"Are the police the only ones you are protecting me from?"

His hesitation was my answer.

"So whoever killed John might also be after me. Then why didn't they just kill me in Rome and steal the jackal then?"

"I do not know, Miss Harris."

Suddenly my eyes flew open and I searched the room for my suitcase. Reading my thoughts, Mr. Rasheed said, "Do not fear, I have not touched your things. The jackal is still in your possession."

"You really are a cop."

He laughed at this and handed me an already peeled orange. "Not exactly, but that will do for now."

"And you work for the government which would mean Adele is involved in a federal crime, one of the big ones. Oh, what a mess." I was extremely tired and felt like crying again. In less than twenty-four hours I had been nearly killed in a Roman dungeon, hopped on a jet to the mysterious Middle East, lost my sister a second time, got myself on the wanted list of the Cairo police, and gone into hiding in the home of some mysterious Arab who couldn't tell me who he was.

From some point far away I heard my tired voice say, "What am I to do now?" I did not appreciate having to make the appeal, to appear so helpless. I was used to standing on my own two feet, and in an orderly world that had no room for surprises. But that world was thousands of miles away.

"I am afraid you cannot go to a hotel—the police will find you. In my position with the government I will be able to clear you, but that will take time. And then, of course, whoever killed John will be watching the hotels for you. I would prefer that you remain here, where you will be safe."

I narrowed my eyes at this. For all I knew Ahmed Rasheed was John's murderer. I still did not trust him.

"You are safe as long as you are here."

What choice had I but to trust this man and hope he was telling me the truth? It would certainly do me no good to get arrested just now, or to be found by the man who killed John Treadwell.

"My home is your home," he said.

I suppose I stared at him a little incredulously at that moment, when his words finally struck home. Stay here, I thought wildly. Without trying to hide it, I let my eyes wander about the room, taking in the haphazard scatter of books and papers, the chaotic design of the rug, the shuttered windows and the threadbare couch we sat on. Stay here? And where, exactly, was here? In the flat of a man who, for all I knew, had killed John Treadwell and wanted to kill Adele. A man who made many claims but backed up none. A man who was dark and spoke with an alien accent and who had unsettling eyes.

"You do not trust me," he said flatly.

"No, I don't."

"What choice have you, Miss Harris? I think the word is gamble. Will you take the chance that I am not a friend and return to the hotel? And gamble your life?"

I met his eyes as boldly as I could, but that nauseating headache was returning, the thumping lump on my skull, and it clouded my judgement. Suddenly, all I wanted to do was lie down and be alone.

"It is evening now in Cairo," he said quietly, like a man talking cautiously to a wild animal. "The streets are dark and crowded. Even if you do not trust me, your chances are better alone against me than against the men who killed Mr. Treadwell."

I heard my small voice say, "How do I know you didn't kill him?"

Mr. Rasheed did not reply. Instead he continued to hold me with a steady, arcane stare, and there was no way I could penetrate the mask.

"I'm tired," I said finally, "and a little fed up. And I'm in no mood for heavy decisions. All right, maybe you did and maybe you didn't kill John, but I'm in no frame of mind to take the gamble. You could have killed me at the Shepherd's I guess, or maybe you're waiting for me to find Adele, and then do us both in."

I put my hands on my hot cheeks and found they were flushed. "My God, this can't really be happening."

"Then you will stay here?"

"I really have no choice, have I?"

Mr. Rasheed smiled. Then he stood and cleared away the teacups and orange peel. While he was gone for the moment I tried to evaluate my situation. Suppose he didn't kill John? That still didn't mean I was safe with him. What if he was keeping me from Adele instead of waiting for me to find her?

The possibilities were many. At this point I could only trust my intuition that he was what he said he was and let it go at that. After all, he had saved me from the city police and all *that* entailed. He had not taken my jackal and run. And . . . I looked about his flat—this strange man's flat—it did *seem* safe.

When Mr. Rasheed returned I slid gracefully to my feet and discovered how truly tired I was. This seemed to be my regular state of being lately, and I wondered what it must be like to feel normal.

"I have another room, a small sitting room where I will sleep," he said.

I glanced about me again. This bachelor flat was in desperate need of tidying. Even more than that it lacked organization, although this impression was helped by the fact that it was the home of a Middle Easterner and that the furnishings and effects were quite alien to my eye. I thought of my own flat; the red, white and blue decor with polished chrome and glass. Although not ultramodern it was at least fashionable and very neat.

This place was cluttered and personal.

It seemed so absurd to say, "I hate to put you out," and yet I did. Fatigue overcame me and my head began to ache even more. I wanted to be alone and to sleep, even in this stranger's bed, because my body could go no further.

He opened the door of the bedroom. "No one will know you are here, Miss Harris. You will be entirely safe."

I appraised the voice and manner of this strange man and wondered why I was so willing to trust him for the moment. John Treadwell was murdered and the police were looking for me. Somehow I was going to have to get out of this mess, with or without Adele, and back to the world of sanity. So I took a long look at the Arab before me and half-wondered if I would soon wake up from this nightmare. I stood in the middle of a strange flat with its pictures of Anwar Sadat and random ancient Egyptian statuary. My sole companion was an alien looking man who spoke oddly and who had me completely at his mercy. Suddenly all semblance of civilization and normality were gone. Nothing of the world I knew, the real and sane world, remained. I was on the other side of the planet from the life and friends I knew, and the feeling it left me with was cold and hollow.

"Please," he said, his fingers touching my elbow. "It is late."

"Yes, of course." I moved as if in a dream, because I believed I was in a dream. As I stepped into the bedroom I saw that my suitcase and handbag stood in the corner.

"You are all right now?" he asked behind me.

"Well, yes, thank you. But . . ."

"Good night, then, Miss Harris."

"Wait a minute." I turned.

"Yes?"

I looked around the bedroom and flapped my hands helplessly. "Thank you anyway," I said feebly.

He nodded. "You are safe. No one knows where you are. And I will watch the Shepherd's Hotel for your sister. It is very simple, really."

"I know, but . . . well, I mean . . ." I could not recall when I had ever before been at such a total loss for words. "What about tomorrow?"

"Tomorrow is in the hands of Allah. Whatever comes will come. Tonight we will sleep and pray. Tomorrow there will be another sunrise."

I shivered in the warm room. The hard, nacreous eyes of Ahmed Rasheed were piercing me. I do not know which caused me greater dread, John's death or my position in line to join him. In my experience as a surgical nurse I had seen death in many forms, and as a teenager I had felt death strike me personally as it took my parents and brother. Therefore, we were no strangers, death and I.

However, this was different.

"Were you in love with him?" I heard a voice ask.

I stared blankly at Ahmed Rasheed. In all my preplanned, well-managed and very organized life I had never been "in love" with any man. This was something I had never before questioned, even though all my friends had experienced countless love affairs and everyone had expected me long

ago to have found "the right man" and eventually marry. Yet this never happened and I always supposed it was because of my preference for reclusive
living.

Now, all of a sudden, standing in a dim room with faded wallpaper, with
Arabic music in the background, staring into the eyes of a total stranger, I
was questioning my entire past.

"No, I was not in love with him. But I'm sorry he's dead."

"He is with Allah."

"I suppose . . ."

"Good night, Miss Harris."

"Yes," I whispered. "And thank you."

"In Egypt we say *shokran*."

"*Shokran.*"

"*Affuan,* and good night."

CHAPTER 9

*I*T WAS THE CALL TO PRAYER THAT WOKE ME. MY EYES OPENED with a start, and I lay unmoving until I remembered where I was. Some light pierced the slats of the shuttered window, fresh early-morning light that also carried street sounds and voices from somewhere below. I lay listening to the distant wail of the muezzin while rearranging my jumbled thoughts.

The first thing to enter my mind was that this bed I occupied was extremely comfortable and I felt incredibly well rested. My next thought was of John Treadwell, first sadness and then anger. My anger turned to bitterness as I thought of what a fool he must have thought me, and how easily I had played into his hands. A little bit of charm, a handsome face and I had been ready to trust him with my life. Just which ired me more—his underhandedness or my stupidity—I was not certain, yet I knew one thing. Lydia Harris was not going to play the fool a second time, no matter how enchanting the man.

Then I thought of Dr. Kellerman. He would be terribly worried by now and angry with himself for having let me come. When I wondered who was scrubbing for him in my absence, I smiled, for I knew that whoever it was they were anxious for my return. He was a gruff old bear in surgery, but being the best surgeon on the staff gave him that right. Adele or not, I decided to telephone Dr. Kellerman today.

Lastly, my thoughts came around to the focus of all this insanity, my sister Adele. I wondered where she was at that moment and what she was doing. I wondered whether she was trying to contact me and if she was nearby. But most of all I wondered what the big mystery was that she had got tangled in.

I must have lain in bed for an hour before I reluctantly decided to get up. My lumpy head still ached and was screaming for aspirins, while my stomach was full of hungry lions. After I dressed, still hearing no sound beyond my door, I took a minute to look at the jackal. After Ahmed had left me the night before, and after I had listened to him walk away and turn out a few lights, I had gone at once to my bag and had found, to my mild surprise, the jackal exactly as I had left it. It had taken me a few minutes to think of a hiding place for it, and eventually I stuffed it into the pillow I was to sleep on. If anyone decided to sneak into my room during the night, he was at least going to have to fight for the jackal.

I took it out of the pillow now and, since I was fully dressed, slid it under my blouse and into the waistband of my slacks. Not terribly comfortable, it was at least in my possession and I wouldn't have to worry constantly about its safety.

I stopped to look at myself in the mirror. The blouse was loose and no bulge showed. In the last few days the value of this piece of ivory had multiplied many times over, so that now I almost felt as if I were carrying the British crown jewels in my hip pocket. Somehow the ivory held the secret to Adele's whereabouts, and it was my ticket to finding her.

Ahmed Rasheed was not home. This surprised and relieved me and, in a way, bewildered me. Still uncertain as to whether or not I was his prisoner or just a guest, I had emerged from the bedroom warily and ready for a fight. But he was not there, I was not being guarded, and the front door opened under my hand. Trying to figure this out, I took a quick look down the stairs that led from the flat, closed the door, locked it, crossed the room and flung open the shutters.

Noise and light and bustle and odors all met me at once in a kaleido-scope of life. I was four stories up and overlooking one of the busiest streets I had ever seen. When I saw the great amount of pedestrian traffic under-neath me, I quickly stepped back and closed the shutters again. In that in-stant I knew what Mr. Rasheed had meant when he said the streets were crowded and that my chances were better alone against him than out there. My God, there were hundreds of people jammed in that street below, and any one of them could have been the one who killed John.

I pressed my face against the shutter and tried to peer through a space in the slats. Directly across the way were flats, very old and grey, some with balconies, some with intricate harem windows, and many with closed curtains and shutters. There seemed to be no threat from that quarter. But below, in the press of humanity that clogged this street, how could I see who was down there? Especially without him seeing me.

I thought of the fat man with the Coke-bottle glasses, and inadvertently I shivered. Suppose he was out there? How certain was Ahmed Rasheed that no one saw us leave the hotel and that no one knew where I was?

I rubbed my fists into my eyes in an effort to think more clearly. The bump on my head still hurt and I needed aspirins for it. Although I was rested and temporarily safe, I was still none the less frustrated and bitter.

The more I thought of John Treadwell, the more incensed I became, not so much because of what he did, but because of how blind and naïve I had been. Was I really so pliant, so ready to be used? Apparently John Treadwell had found me so.

I spun away from the shutters and marched across the room to the couch and, slumping on to it, chastised myself for having been so ignorant. If Ahmed Rasheed had any plans for using me, if he intended to sway me with a bit of charm and words of comfort, it was not going to work. As of that moment, the only man in the world I trusted was Dr. Kellerman, and I would have given anything to have him with me. But he was miles away and in another world.

I leaned back and felt the jackal poke my side. The jackal. A game piece. An ivory toy that looked so harmless and yet was deadly enough to have caused a murder. So, it had still been in my bag last night. And what had that proved. That Ahmed Rasheed did not want it? Possibly that's what he wanted me to think. Maybe his leaving it alone had been a ruse, just a ploy to trick me into his confidence. All things were possible in this game, I had learned, and treachery from Ahmed Rasheed was no exception. I was resolved not to walk so easily into a second trap, not after John Treadwell.

A sound at the door made me jump. I got to my feet just as Mr. Rasheed entered with a newspaper tucked under his arm. Seeing my surprised expression he said, "I am sorry. I did not mean to startle you. I had not thought you would be awake yet. It is early."

"Yes, I know. Good morning."

He smiled and said, "*Sabah el-kheir.* I will make you some tea."

I watched him as he left me to go into another room, and I felt my body tense. Sounds came from beyond the door—dishes clattering, water running, a spoon or fork falling to the floor. A moment later he reemerged, smiling casually and removing his jacket. "I am making tea," he said.

I stood still, watching him move about the room, uncertain of my next words. Mr. Rasheed supplied me with a solution by asking, "Did you sleep well?"

"Yes, as a matter of fact, I did."

"Good, I'm glad. You needed it. Please sit down."

I sat on the couch and he sat on an easy chair opposite me. He continued to smile as he spoke. "I have been to the police this morning. I wished to waste no time."

"And?"

"The inspector who is handling the John Treadwell murder is a friend of mine. We had a private talk. I explained to him that you are probably the American woman they were looking for, and that you had nothing to do with the murder, for you are working with me. He has removed your description and passport number from the hotel bulletins and has stopped the search for you."

"Oh, thank God!" I breathed.

"Now you need not worry about that."

"That means I can check into a hotel. The police aren't after me."

"Yes, that is true." His smile faded and he frowned a little. "However, there is still the fact of Mr. Treadwell's murderer. He might still be watching for you."

"The fat man."

"Or Arnold Rossiter. And they know you have left the Shepherd's and have gone somewhere. Now they will watch the hotels."

"Mr. Rasheed, I do wish you'd tell me what this is all about. Why would anyone want to kill me?"

"It might not be as simple as killing you, Miss Harris. They will probably want to hold you as their prisoner in order to find your sister. That is my theory."

"And why," I said tiredly, "are 'they' looking for my sister?"

"Excuse me." He stood. "I think the tea is ready."

After he left the room, I went to the window again and, parting the shutters a little, tried to look down on the crowded street. Very few cars passed, for the pedestrian traffic was thick. They were predominantly Middle Easterners—half of them in western dress, some in the long night shirts, or *galabias,* some in turbans and *khaffiyehs,* some women with veils, others dressed very much like myself—all hurrying to their destinations, dodging the donkey carts, or walking arm in arm.

There was not one person who seemed concerned about this flat.

"I can assure you they do not know where you are."

I turned to look at Ahmed Rasheed. He carried a tray laden with teapot, teacups, and a mountain of thick pastries. Placing this on the low table before the couch he said, "When I took you out of the Shepherd's Hotel last night, I looked very carefully around the lobby. None of the men I know to be working for Rossiter were there. And besides, after having just committed a murder, they would be foolish to stay around."

I heaved a sigh and returned to the couch. "Still . . ."

He put a cup in my hands and pushed the plate of pastries towards me. "There is no one watching this flat, Miss Harris. I made sure of that myself before leaving you alone."

I could not resist taking one of the cakes and found it to be uncommonly sweet, like the tea, which had a half-inch layer of sugar at the bottom of the cup. The pastries were thick with custard and frosting and jelly.

"You must eat," he said, and forced me to have a second one.

Biting into it I wondered why all Egyptians weren't fat.

"I have a friend who works at the Shepherd's Hotel, and I have told him I am looking for your sister. He will watch for her and let me know if she comes to the hotel. Also, the customs officials at the airport have said that your sister has not left the country."

As I started to speak, he held up his hand, saying, "However, this does not mean she is in this country. I still await communications from Alexandria and Luxor. It is not difficult to go into the Sudan."

"Sudan! Why would she want to go there?"

He spread out his hands. "In that, Miss Harris, my knowledge is as limited as yours."

"And just when are you going to tell me the rest?"

"Soon, I assure you."

It seemed those were his favorite words and yet he did not assure me at all. When he pushed the plate closer to me, I said, "No thank you," and sat with my cup in my lap.

We fell silent at this point, and I did my best to avoid his eyes. It was not a rude stare at all, but rather a look of curiosity, of open interest. It was almost as if he found me novel.

This was ironic, considering what an oddity he was. Although his appearance was strange to me—with his dark cocoa skin, thickly-lashed eyes, and large nose—it was actually his manner of speaking that intrigued me. His voice had a soft nasal quality to it with occasional glottal stops. He could not say the letter P at all—it came out as B—and he had a rough way of saying the letter R, so that words like "first" came out in two syllables, "fir-rist." He spoke carefully and slowly, as if to be certain I understood him, and in excellent English. My mistrust of him was not because he was foreign, but because he was a stranger.

"I will go out now," he said suddenly, as if remembering himself, "and will return this afternoon. Please make my home your home, and all that is in it is yours."

"Thank you."

"*Shokran.*"

As he donned his jacket and headed towards the door, a thought occurred to me. "Do you mind if I use your phone? I'll reverse the charges."

"I have no telephone, Miss Harris. Few people in Cairo do, for it is an expensive luxury. There is a telephone exchange not far from here. Is it urgent?"

"Well, sort of."

"I would not want you to go out yet. Let us wait and I will take you. This way you will be safe. Good-bye."

I locked the door after him, listened to his footsteps fade away down the stairs and then went again to the shutters. Through a small opening I saw Ahmed Rasheed appear below and join the rest of the pedestrians in the busy street. When he was out of sight I took a little time to carefully study the crowd below, the windows opposite, and the rooftops. There was no one, not a single person who could possibly be watching this place.

I closed the shutters and returned to the couch. Not to be able to call Dr. Kellerman was a disappointment, but I was determined to press for the opportunity that evening.

I poured myself a second cup of sweet tea, and lay back to give some time to my thoughts. I suppose it was a form of escape, like a defense mechanism, to put the present out of my mind and to drift back to the past for a while. I did not want to think of John Treadwell, Adele, the jackal, Ahmed Rasheed, or the men who were out to kill me. I wanted to comfort myself with something familiar, something warm and pleasant. So I thought of Dr. Kellerman.

Two hours passed before I got up from the couch and went again to the window. The day outside was brighter and warmer, and more people were out in the street. After looking carefully about again, I began to believe what Mr. Rasheed had said, that no one knew where I was hiding. I felt a little better.

The tea was cold and the pastries were beginning to look too tempting, so I took the tray into the kitchen and did my best to clean things up and put them away. There was an ancient gas stove in this old and small kitchen, a chipped enamel sink, and no refrigerator. More photographs were hung on the walls, some small drawings of animals, little tapestries of Arabic design, and an old calendar. I washed the pot and cups, put them away, and set the plate of cakes on the table with a cloth over them.

Then I returned to the living room and, with a smile, thought again of Dr. Kellerman. You accused me of being too fussy, my mind said to the vision I had of him. You always said I was too orderly and too organized. Well, look at me now. Living out of a suitcase in jeans and a shirt, hiding out in a strange man's flat somewhere in Cairo, with the jackal sticking in my side like a hidden weapon.

God, I couldn't wait to call him.

Then, for some reason, another memory came back to me. Something buried, that I hadn't thought of for a long time. It had been a year after I had first started scrubbing for Dr. Kellerman. We had worked late one night trying to reconstruct an artery in someone's arm and Dr. Kellerman had taken me out to dinner afterward. We had some wine, ate rich food, and sat in a dim corner with a candle between us. After a little casual talk, he had gazed at me with misty blue eyes and said, "I've never told you how my wife died, have I?"

Surprised, I shook my head.

"Believe it or not, it was at our hospital. Just three years ago." He paused to take a sip of wine. "She started complaining one day of migraine headaches. No amount of aspirins would give her relief. So I told her to have her eyes checked."

Dr. Kellerman's voice was soft and steady. "But her eyes checked out normal. So . . . cautious man that I am, I had her go see Mike Roth, just in case . . ."

He took some more wine and I waited patiently. I knew Dr. Michael Roth. He was a neurosurgeon.

"Turned out she had a cerebral aneurysm. Blood in her spinal fluid. Angiograms confirmed it. In a matter of days her speech began to deteriorate, so Mike operated." Dr. Kellerman looked long and deep into his wine, the candlelight reflected in his eyes. "She died on the operating table."

I lost track of time in my reverie of Dr. Kellerman and things past. It was the muezzin and his enigmatic song that brought me back. For the millionth time I rose and went to the shutters, peered out, looked for anyone suspicious and came away feeling a little more secure. If anyone was watching this flat, they were being damned clever about it.

So I paced a while. The headache was subsiding and hence the constant reminder of danger to my life. Perhaps this was all a bit too melodramatic, I began to think. Surely there was a simple answer.

Then another thought struck me. One that surprisingly had not occurred to me before, but which should have. I stopped short in the middle of the room, arms akimbo with, I am certain, a look of revelation on my face.

How did I know for sure that John was really dead?

This question had fallen quite by accident into my random thoughts as the other collections of doubts and queries assailed me. Where was Adele? What did the jackal mean? Who was Ahmed Rasheed? Why should I trust him? Why should I believe that he hadn't killed John?

And then . . . why should I believe him that John was even dead?

This new development caused me to slump down on the couch and stare at my hands in dismay. Good God, it was possible that John was really alive and looking for me, and still my friend and not at all what Ahmed Rasheed had said he was.

But then what about his meeting with the fat man and why was he lying unconscious on the floor?

Sure enough, my head began to hurt again. So little was certain in this mucky business! About all I could be sure of was my own identity. I didn't even know what day of the week it was.

A new anger boiled up inside me—frustration over my helplessness. I wanted to be in command of this situation, but all I really was was a helpless pawn.

Was John still alive?

I took to pacing the floor again. Obviously proof was going to be hard to find. And I certainly couldn't go out looking for him, not back to the Shepherd's. The risk was too great.

Then I stopped because of something that caught my eye. I don't really know why, but as I walked past the dining table set against a wall, my eye fell upon the folded newspaper that Ahmed Rasheed had brought home that morning and had carelessly tossed down. I looked at it now with an uneasy apprehension. It was almost as if, without even opening it, I knew what it held.

I spread out the front page, saw the twisted Arabic lettering of the headline, saw the photograph of a covered body and a circle of legs and feet around it, and imagined that the wormy alphabet of the caption told that a murder had taken place at one of Cairo's finest hotels. It was a front-page story.

Tears welled up in my eyes. I felt a fresh sorrow for John's death, and this time I remembered him as I had seen him last.

I suppose my fantastic notion that John was not, after all, really dead had been a feeble effort on the part of my overworked mind to grasp at even the smallest hope. It had not worked. Nice though it was to imagine for a brief moment that John was really alive and that everything Ahmed Rasheed had told me was a lie, the fact remained that nothing had changed at all and that I was still where I was before, with the same puzzles taxing my brain.

Footsteps on the stairs brought me out of my reflection. I turned and listened. They started far away, slow and steady, but gradually grew louder until I realized they were coming close to the door. Suddenly they stopped and were followed by a light tapping.

Someone was knocking on the door.

I dashed at once into the bedroom and flung the door closed. With one hand on the jackal under my shirt, I inched the bedroom door open just slightly so that I stood pressed against it, one eye peering through the crack, and held my breath. The sound of a key made my heart skip a beat. Slowly the front door opened, the door that I had locked earlier.

Now my heart started to pound. I scarcely breathed. My face was pressed against the door as I stared wildly out with one eye. In the next instant someone entered the room, removing a key from the lock, and then quietly closed the door behind.

She was a young woman I had never seen before, approximately my own age, with black hair down to her waist, dark olive skin, and large searching eyes. She looked around the flat, keys still in one hand and a handbag in the other. She seemed to be listening.

I continued to hold my breath and wondered if she could hear the pounding of my heart.

Then she called out, "Mees Harees!" and I jumped.

She listened, looked around again, and called out once more, "Mees Harees!"

In one fleeting second I decided to join her. It wouldn't take her long to find me anyway, and hiding frightened in the bedroom was not an impression I wanted to make. So I decided to approach her directly with the most self-assured and fearless posture I could manage.

I flung the door open. "Yes?"

"Oh, Mees Harees." Her face broadened in a bright grin. "How do you do?" She extended a hand. Nonplussed, I took hold of it. In a ridiculously thick accent, she said, "I am pleased to meet you, thank you."

"Yes, well . . ."

Next she said something in Arabic. Seeing my blank face, she laughed, shook her head and pointed to herself. "Asmahan," she said. "I am Asmahan."

I raised my eyebrows. "How do you do. You already know who I am."

"Aywa." Then she rushed on in Arabic and I thought I caught the name Ahmed.

"Ahmed?"

"Aywa." She nodded vigorously.

Bewildered though I was, it occurred to me that I was in no danger from this girl. She had an openly pleasant face and a warm manner about her. She also laughed freely and didn't appear pretentious. None the less, I kept up my guard.

Asmahan prattled on a little longer in Arabic, quite as casually as if I understood every word she said, and then quite impulsively turned away from me and disappeared into the kitchen. For a moment I remained rooted to the floor, holding my elbow against the shaft of ivory in my waistband. After a second I heard sounds of dishes and then running water, and so I decided to join her.

Asmahan was making tea.

"Good morning, good afternoon, and good evening," she said in a high voice. "I speak English, how are you?" With a toss of her long black hair, she cast a twinkling glance over her shoulder at me and seemed to be waiting for me to react. All I could do was smile.

So she continued with the ritual of boiling the water, measuring the tea leaves and inspecting the cleanness of the cups. All the while she gave the impression of being completely at home and in familiar company.

When the tea was ready and we returned to the living room, my visitor made another attempt to communicate with me.

"I speak English," she said as we sat on the couch in front of the tray of tea and cakes. "Like this," and she held up her thumb and index finger about an inch apart. "Little," she said.

"I gathered that. And I'm afraid I don't speak Arabic."

Asmahan gave a shrug. "*Maʿalesh*. Tea, please, Mees Harees."

I took the cup from her, sniffed at the sweet mint aroma, and then drank gratefully. I hadn't realized until now that I was hungry. Or that it must be late afternoon.

Then she pushed the cakes towards me. "Mees Harees, Ahmed speak to me. You understand?"

"And he told you to come here?"

She frowned.

So I said it more slowly and she understood this time. "*Aywa*. Ahmed say Mees Harees is here. We are friends. You understand?"

"I guess so."

My caution was waning. In the presence of this loquacious and smiling girl it was difficult to keep a distance. Moreover, she had a key to the flat, knew my name and had been looking for me, and now claimed that Ahmed had sent her. I was sure that Asmahan was Ahmed's girlfriend or fiancée and had been sent either to keep me company or keep an eye on me, or both. Very clever.

"It's very nice of you to bother like this," I said, wondering just how much English she did understand. "And the tea is very good."

"*Aywa.*"As she drank, her hair fell forward over her shoulders, framing her lovely face and enhancing her large dark eyes. I could easily see what Ahmed saw in her.

Then we fell silent. Not awkwardly so, but silent all the same, so that we finished the tea and the cakes without speaking a word. Once in a while she would look at me and grin, and I would smile weakly back. But that was all. And I found myself anxious to have Ahmed return.

We washed the cups and pot together, again in silence; but we were at ease with one another. Asmahan had a way of extending friendship with her eyes and smile. I could not help, during the two strangely silent hours we spent together that afternoon, but find myself starting to like her.

Shadows were growing long on the street below when Ahmed finally came home. I was not surprised to feel a mingling of relief and pleasure to see him, because I looked upon him as my only link with the outside world and, hopefully, Adele. I still did not trust him but he was, after all, all I had.

His initial reaction at seeing the two of us was surprise, which was quickly transformed into a frown. Asmahan jumped up and ran to him, kissed his cheek, and then chatted in high-pitched Arabic to the accompaniment of wild gestures. He nodded and replied in single words, looking at me once or twice as I remained dumbly upon the couch. Finally, when Asmahan seemed to have run dry, Ahmed stepped around her and approached me. He said, "I am so sorry, Miss Harris, to have had this happen to you. What a shock it must have been."

I gave a puzzled look at Asmahan.

"I asked her to come here, Miss Harris, to be in your company, for it is lonely for you. But I had told her to come tonight after I was here. I explained that you were a visitor to our country who is in need of help.

But Asmahan was anxious to help you and to be your friend, and in her hospitality, came too early. I would have told you first. What a shock for you to have her come in so suddenly!"

"It was."

"Then forgive me, for the error was mine."

Very smooth, this man. "It's all right. She managed to give the impression that she was a friend. But at first, I'll admit, I didn't know what to do."

Ahmed Rasheed smiled—that engaging, disarming gesture. "Very well then, now we shall have some tea."

Oh God! I flew to my feet. Apparently the Arabs' answer to everything was to make tea. "Mr. Rasheed, please, tell me what you found today. Anything at all?"

"I must tell you I am sorry again, for we have found nothing."

I felt like saying, "Did you look?" but held my tongue.

"And now we will eat. You must be hungry."

"As a matter of fact, I am."

He and Asmahan had a brief exchange in Arabic, after which she turned and hurried off to the kitchen. Smiling at me, my "host" said, "Asmahan is anxious to prepare something special for you. I have told her not to, but it is her way of welcoming you in Egypt."

As soon as he said it, she reappeared with her purse and a paper shopping bag under her arm. A few words in Arabic and she was gone.

"Miss Harris, please sit down."

"Nothing at all? The Shepherd's Hotel? Visa Control? Can't you tell me anything?"

"I can understand your feelings, Miss Harris, and wish very much that I could bring you good news. But there is nothing. Not yet."

Another disappointment, but it didn't hit as hard. Maybe I was getting used to them.

"How did you and Asmahan converse?" he asked. Mr. Rasheed was sitting next to me on the couch. He leaned close once and I caught the faint scent of aftershave lotion. His eyes again seemed to be studying me.

"I really don't know. She didn't speak much English and I know absolutely no Arabic."

"But this is not true! You can say *shokran* and *sabah el-kheir*. And if you do not understand, you say *mahf hemtish*."

"Asmahan said one word a lot. *Ma'alesh*. What does it mean?"

To my mild surprise, he laughed. "It is the most important word in Arabic! It means, never mind."

"Oh." I felt myself grinning back at him.

"For Arabs, if you do not understand or are not understood, it does not matter. There is something more important than words. There is friendship. You and Asmahan are friends now, and yet you share no words in common. You see? If she speaks to you and you do not understand, she says *ma'alesh*, because it is not important. What matters is friendship. That is all."

How pleasantly simple that was, and how simple for him. No complicated relationships, no analysis of one's feelings, no pondering the nature of another's relevance. Just plain and simple friendship. I wondered if he really believed it.

"Some other words you will hear much are *ahlan wa sahlan* and *mehalabeyah*. This means simply welcome. You will hear many people in Cairo say to you *ahlan wa sahlan*, and they are saying welcome and peace to you. *Mehalabeyah* means this." He tapped his temple with an index finger. "It means someone is crazy. *Mehalabeyah* is a pudding we make out of rice and it is very popular. If we think someone is crazy, we say he has pudding for a head."

I laughed a little. "It's the same everywhere."

"Do you speak another language, Miss Harris?"

"Not at all. Unless you count the Spanish you naturally pick up living in Los Angeles."

"How is this?" He gazed at me earnestly, as if genuinely interested in what I had to say.

"Well, in Los Angeles there's a large population of Spanish-speaking people. It's because of our proximity to Mexico. You'll see Spanish written in a lot of places, particularly downtown, and you'll hear it spoken absolutely everywhere. Even the name Los Angeles is Spanish. It means The Angels."

"How interesting."

"Yes," I shifted about on the couch, "I suppose it is."

Now we, too, fell silent and it was an awkward moment. He had the good manners to stop staring at me, but I had the impression that a hundred questions stood on his lips.

"You will please forgive me, Miss Harris, but I have met so few Americans."

I turned in surprise.

"You are curious to me. Well . . . perhaps that is not the correct word. But in Egypt we have little contact with Americans on a personal level. To the Arab on the street, Americans are people who ride in polished buses from one hotel to another. They rarely walk upon our pavements or visit our shops. They live at the Hilton and go by bus to the Khan el-Khalili. They go in their bus to the Citadel and to the Pyramids. And they eat in European restaurants. Very few of us have the opportunity to speak with you."

Again that steady, candid gaze. It was a beguiling gesture, to say the least, but I was not going to succumb. "I am sure a little cultural exchange would be interesting, Mr. Rasheed, but all I'm interested in right now is to learn just what you know about Adele and this jackal business."

His face remained frozen in a half smile and did not alter in the least at my tone.

"I have a right to know," I said flatly.

Then Ahmed Rasheed looked at me squarely and said, "Trust me."

How simple! "Trust me," he said, as if that took care of everything. And was this a request or a command? Was he asking me or ordering me? Possibly it was a rhetorical statement, something one says but doesn't really mean.

"I can't," I replied.

We were silent again for what seemed a long moment. In the background I recognized the faintest cacophony of Egyptian music. It was a subliminal sound, adding just the slightest touch of flavor to this foreign setting.

"You will trust me in time," he said.

Whether I resented his self-assurance or whether I was still angry at John Treadwell's manipulation of me, I do not know. But when Ahmed Rasheed tried to draw me into his trust and convince me of his sincerity, I fought him.

"Tell me what's going on."

The smallest hint of a smile creased the corners of his eyes. "Is it so important to know? Is it not enough that I am working on it, that you are safe, and that we are all in the hands of Allah?"

I shook my head.

Ahmed continued to stare. What was it that was always there in his eyes. Mystery? Was I imagining that in the depths of that bewildering gaze there lay a nameless enigma? Or had I read too many novels, seen too many films?

He was a man, nothing more. And I had met many men, inside the hospital and out, and I had seen many eyes over the tops of surgical masks. But never before had I seen eyes like these, or rather, the puzzle behind them.

Suddenly, as if sensing my disquiet, he stood. "Asmahan will be here soon and we will eat. I hope you made my kitchen your kitchen while I was gone today."

He had taken a couple of steps away from me, I suppose to start getting things ready for dinner, when he stopped short and stared. His face folded into a frown and I followed the line of his gaze to the open newspaper on the table against the opposite wall. The front page with its photo of the sheet-covered body and the legs of policemen.

Without a word he went to the table, picked up the newspaper and, folding it, went off into the kitchen with it. He emerged a moment later without the paper but with a worried expression. "I am sorry that you saw that, Miss Harris. It was regrettably neglectful of me."

"It's all right," I murmured, wondering if it had really been accidental.

A moment later, and not a second too soon, Asmahan came through the front door carrying a full shopping bag. She started at once in rapid Arabic, talking all the way into the kitchen as Ahmed followed her, and keeping up the chatter as she unpacked her groceries. Listening to the two of them, recognizing a comfortable familiarity between them, I found myself half-wondering how long they had known each other and how soon they planned to be married.

I quickly put such idle thoughts out of my mind, however, when Ahmed returned to the living room with a bowl of oranges in his hands. "Asmahan will prepare a special meal for you. She is delighted to have you try her cooking, since she assumes you have never eaten Egyptian food."

"I haven't."

He sat opposite me, grinned knowingly and said, "You will have a treat."

He relaxed into the armchair and began to peel an orange, while I, still on the edge of the couch, wondered what was expected of me. When I started to rise, Ahmed gestured for me to remain seated. "You are our guest. You must not go into the kitchen."

"I should help . . ."

But he laughed. "Asmahan will be offended. Please, stay."

So I settled back into the couch and forced myself to relax a little. My mind wandered aimlessly as I stared blankly at the brown hands of Ahmed Rasheed as they peeled the orange. I thought of Rome, only days before and yet so distant now in my memory. I thought of John, or rather of the anger and disappointment he had caused me. I thought of Adele—somewhere in this country involved in God-knew-what. And I thought of Dr. Kellerman.

"Can we go out and make a phone call?" I asked suddenly.

Ahmed regarded me in momentary surprise, then seemed to give weighty consideration to my request. After a long, thoughtful moment he said, "Perhaps it is not wise, Miss Harris. It will mean leaving the flat, going out into the street, and standing in public for a length of time."

"But you insisted I was safe here!"

"Yes, here." He put the half-eaten orange on the table and leaned towards me, his eyes anxious. "And on this street you possibly are. But the telephone exchange is a short distance from here. Arnold Rossiter's men could be in the vicinity. And might they not watch the telephone stations for you? Might they not suspect you would try to telephone someone? I think it too risky."

The familiar conflict, which I was becoming used to, of trying to battle my emotional wants with logical reasoning, sprang up again. I knew he was right, but I wanted to make the call. "For God's sake, how many telephone exchanges are there in Cairo? Rossiter surely doesn't have a hundred men working for him!"

Ahmed stared pensively at me.

"It wouldn't take long to make the call. The chances of one of them spotting me out of all those people out there are practically nil."

Still the steady gaze.

"Well, what am I, Mr. Rasheed, your guest or your prisoner?"

He appeared to consider his words before speaking. "You are really neither, Miss Harris. You are here under my protection. Which is to say, the protection of the Egyptian government. Because of the seriousness of this problem, I must exercise great caution. I cannot let you make your phone call."

I bit my lower lip. For some reason, I was becoming desperate to talk to Dr. Kellerman, to tell him where I was, to hear his voice, to reach out to him . . .

"Please . . ."

Asmahan came into the room just then with an armful of plates and silverware. As if on cue, Ahmed rose to join her, and helped set a dinner table for the three of us while I remained on the couch, twisting my fingers in frustration.

The girl hurried back into the kitchen, leaving him at the table, watching me. Then an idea came to me.

"Mr. Rasheed." I sprang to my feet.

"Yes, Miss Harris?"

I stared back at him across the room, caught again in the strength of his gaze. I was going to say, "Would you make the phone call? Would you call Dr. Kellerman and tell him where I am, that I'm all right and what's happening?"

But the words never left my mouth. Staring at Ahmed Rasheed across the room, looking at his large dark eyes, his cocoa skin and his secretive expression, hearing his curious accent with the harsh Rs and nasal vowels, and remembering just exactly what my situation was, I suddenly realized the idea would not work.

"What is it, Miss Harris?"

I turned away from him, away from his stare. Dr. Kellerman would be bewildered, possibly shocked, and certainly alarmed. Getting a phone call from a mysterious Arab in Cairo who said he had Lydia in his flat and that she was all right . . .

"Nothing. Never mind." I swung around to face him and forced a smile. "Ma'alesh."

He smiled back. "You see?"

We returned to the couch and to the oranges and sat wordlessly until Asmahan, some time later, announced in Arabic that our dinner was ready.

I thoroughly enjoyed the meal. I had had no idea I was so hungry or that Egyptian food could be so delicious. And, as well, the company was delightful. All through dinner Asmahan kept up a light, jovial conversation just as matter-of-factly as if she understood English and I, Arabic. Ahmed sat between us translating and coaching me in repeating the names of everything we ate.

"Aysh baladi," he said, taking a round of flat bread and tearing off a piece. "This is how we eat *fool wa tahmeya,"* and he dipped it in the dish of spicy fried beans.

I did the same and had to repeat the Arabic until it sounded right. We also ate lentil soup, *shor-bet ahds*; a green salad, *sahlahtah khudrah*; shish kebab and fried vegetables; and lastly the pudding which Ahmed had told me about—*mehalabeyah.*

When I indicated to Asmahan that I had enjoyed the food and tried to thank her, Ahmed interjected with, "In Egypt when we have enjoyed a friend's meal, we say *haneyan.*"

So I looked at Asmahan and said, *"Haneyan."* To which she replied, *"Allah yeehun neehee."*

"Asmahan said to you, 'May God bring you happiness for wishing me this.' She is pleased you are pleased."

"Well, I'm glad she's glad . . . that I'm glad."

We all three laughed—Asmahan, too, as if she had understood, and then we rose from the table. When I attempted to help with the cleaning up, it was again patiently explained to me that as a guest I was to rest in the living room with a cup of tea. "It is Asmahan's honor that you have enjoyed the meal. She will not want you to come into the kitchen."

It was not long before Asmahan joined us for tea, and the ensuing hour was spent in very light and idle conversation, revolving mostly around American films and film stars. As we chatted, Ahmed again translating, I marveled at the ease with which I had adapted to this particular situation. So unlike my regular life, my private, antisocial, and orderly life. I sat with my feet up on the couch, drank foreign tea as if it were Coca-Cola, and laughed with these two Egyptians as if I had known them for years. It was only when, inadvertently, my elbow brushed against the hard spear of ivory still hidden beneath my shirt that I was sharply reminded of why I was here, the transiency of the moment, and the real danger I was in.

Because of this, because of constantly remembering the unpleasant reality of my situation, I was glad when Asmahan announced her departure. I needed to be alone again. The day had been too long and I felt a strong desire for solitude, for time in which to think about plans I was soon going to have to make for myself.

Ahmed helped Asmahan into her sweater and then donned his own jacket. "I will walk with her back to her house and then return at once."

"You needn't hurry," I said, understanding that they must want some time together and that I was interfering with their privacy.

"I will not hurry, Miss Harris, but I will not be gone long. Now, please, lock the door after we have gone."

I did as I was told, lingering by the door until their footsteps could no longer be heard. Then I went to the window and opened the shutters a crack. Ahmed and Asmahan appeared on the pavement below. They linked arms and, walking close together, joined the busy throng.

I returned to the couch and fell into an absent stare. It was nighttime in Cairo. The streets and squares were alive with traffic and strollers and partygoers, and all the thousands of people who stream from their houses after sunset seeking the excitement and thrill of Cairo at night. Street lights blazed everywhere. Monuments were floodlit. Store windows poured out bright lights and music. It was a city come to life, and Ahmed and Asmahan were part of it.

I thought of them now. She was a strikingly beautiful girl and he, I would not deny it, was a handsome man. I envied them. I envied their comfortableness together, their quiet affection and reliance upon one another. I envied them for what they had now and for what lay ahead of them. I was envious because I doubted that I would ever achieve the same.

As one reverie blended into another, as thoughts of other people gelled into reflection upon myself, a not too surprising revelation came to me.

I was changing.

It was nothing terribly substantial, just a vague intuition that had no sharp details or palpable form. Sitting on the periphery of my conscious thought, only a pale notion of it came to the surface. I sensed that I was changing, and yet I could not discern just how. As to why, of course, this was obvious. My comfortable life had been shaken, my sense of values jolted. All my perspectives had been altered, and I was now seeing things from different angles. Suddenly, over the last few days, nothing seemed the same any more. And as a result, other revelations became apparent.

For the hundredth time that day, I thought again of Dr. Kellerman. He stood before me in wrinkled surgical greens, a mask dangling down his chest, fatigue and strain etched on his face. Then I pictured him coming into an operating room, commanding instant respect by his mere presence. I saw his clear blue eyes smile at me over his mask; eyes that had beheld so much, that had tried to say so much, and that had hidden so much.

How odd it was to realize now, curled up on this stranger's couch, with foreign cooking odors and gaudy music enveloping me, how odd it was to realize only now that Dr. Kellerman was in love with me.

I jumped when the door opened and Ahmed Rasheed came in. He could not have been gone more than ten minutes, and I wondered how he could have left Asmahan so quickly.

"Would you like some tea, Miss Harris, or something more to eat?"

"Oh, no, thank you." I got to my feet and pressed a hand against my stomach to indicate how full I was. "I'm actually very tired and just want to go to bed."

"Of course. If there is anything you will wish, I shall be doing some work at my desk. You must not hesitate to ask."

"I won't. Thank you. *Shokran.*" I felt slightly uncomfortable as I left him standing in the living room and pushed open the bedroom door. And when I remembered that it was his bed I was to sleep in and that he himself would be spending the night in the next room, I felt even more awkward. It had also occurred to me to wonder what Asmahan must think of my taking up residence with her fiancé. And then I wondered just what he had told her about me, and how much.

I paused at the bedroom door. "Mr. Rasheed, how long will I have to stay here?"

"I do not know."

"Days? Weeks?"

"I sincerely hope not."

"And how long before you tell me *why* I'm staying here? Besides, I mean, the danger you say I'm in. I assume there's more to this."

He smiled engagingly. "Much more, Miss Harris. And I assure you, when I feel it is safe to tell you, then I will tell you."

"Thanks. Good night."

As I closed the door, he said, *"Tesbah allah kheir."*

I lay for a long time in the darkness, tired but unable to sleep. My mind was a mélange of thoughts. Primarily, just who was the man who sat the other side of the door, and just how far could I trust him? Oddly, the jackal didn't seem to interest him and yet, somehow, it was at the center of this mystery. Twice my living quarters had been searched for it; one man had been murdered for it and my sister was possibly in grave danger because of it. And yet Ahmed Rasheed seemed not to care about it.

Still, just in case his was a very good act, I put the jackal once again into the pillowcase for the night.

As I drowsed and felt myself drifting off, I strengthened one last time a resolve that I had made earlier that evening. Tomorrow, no matter what transpired, I was somehow going to get out and phone Dr. Kellerman.

CHAPTER 10

AHMED RASHEED WAS NOT THERE THE NEXT MORNING.
Feeling quite rested and a great deal more confident than in
the last few days, I was ready to start seriously evaluating my
situation and to consider some plans of my own. The first thing I did, after
taking a shower and hiding the jackal again under my shirt, was to take a
look at the desk my host had worked at until late into the night.

Expecting to find some revealing evidence as to his line of work, hoping
to discover the exact nature of his position with the government (if that had
been the truth), I was disappointed. Very little in the way of written or official
documentation was there and what there was was all in Arabic: much of it was
correspondence—freshly sealed letters ready to be mailed and open envelopes
of mail he had received. There were also several books, again not in English, a
catalogue of some sort, periodicals, and some newspaper clippings scattered
over the desk top. Half-written sheets of paper, hastily scratched notes, and
what appeared to be office memos of some sort were also strewn haphazardly
about, but these too were in Arabic and therefore unhelpful.

As I looked down at the clutter, I remembered a remark Dr. Kellerman had once made to me when he had visited my flat. "Lydia Harris, a neat and tidy desk is a sign of a sick mind." I smiled now. My own desk at home looked like a shop window display. This one looked lived-in.

But it told me nothing about the man who used it.

The thought had crossed my mind to really search the flat, to look for anything that would give me some insight into the identity of my "protector." It followed that, if I could learn just what his job was with the Egyptian government, then I would have an idea of what sort of mess Adele was in.

Yet I could not bring myself to do it. Curious as I was, desperate for any light on this mystery, it was not in my nature to invade someone's privacy. Peruse a desk top, yes, but I did not open drawers or touch a thing. I myself had had my flat searched. It was unthinkable that I should inflict the same injury on someone else. And lastly, the thought of being caught in the act by Mr. Rasheed was a considerable deterrent.

So I put this necessity at the bottom of my priorities, to be resorted to only in desperation. Right now, today, there was something more pressing.

I took a long look through the shutters, searching for anything or anyone that might be slightly suspicious. Like the fat man with Coke-bottle glasses. But there was nothing. The street was its usual peripatetic self, totally ignorant of this flat and the fugitive within.

This time I was not surprised when Asmahan came in. In fact, I openly welcomed her. Wearing a very pretty dress, high-heeled shoes, and a wide-brimmed sunhat, she entered with another bag full of food.

"Mees Harees," she said, kicking the door shut behind her. "*Sabah el-kheir.* Good evening."

"Good morning," I said.

She dropped the bag on the table and chattered on in Arabic. When she flung off her wide-brimmed hat and let her luxurious hair fall, I felt a small stab of envy. My own hair, shoulder length and parted in the middle, was an average brown and very straight. Asmahan's was a striking ebony black with blue highlights, and fell to her waist in thick, heavy waves. Ahmed Rasheed was a lucky man.

She continued her steady stream of Arabic as she unpacked the shopping bag, depositing on the table tins of fruit juice, a stack of chocolate bars, chewing gum, and a bakery-shop box full of sticky pastries, all of which, I imagined, were intended for me.

When the bag was empty and its cornucopia bounty spread on the table, she turned to me and asked with a delightful grin, "You like?"

"Yes I do. *Shokran*."

"*Affuan!* Now we have tea. Please sit."

I sat, and braced myself for another round of strong mint tea, which I was becoming accustomed to ingesting every few hours. While Asmahan busied herself in the kitchen, I worked on the idea which I had been formulating all morning. A great deal of its successful execution depended on how much Asmahan knew about my situation, and what Ahmed's instructions had been with regard to me. He had said she was there to keep me company and nothing more, and I wondered if this was true.

She joined me a few minutes later with the sweet tea and the pastries. A cup of good, black coffee would have gone well with either, but I couldn't ask for fear of upsetting her. As we ate and drank, I made some attempts at conversation. "How long have you and Ahmed known each other?"

Asmahan gave me a puzzled look, clearly not understanding. So I said simply, "You and Ahmed?"

Still she shook her head. Possibly she did not understand what I wanted to know or did not know how to express an answer, but I had thought my question clear.

"I wish you could speak English, or I Arabic."

She sipped her tea and smiled over the rim of her cup.

I thought a moment, wondering if I should take the chance. And deciding to go ahead and risk it, I simply came right out and said, "I would dearly like to make a telephone call."

"Telephone?" she said.

"Yes, you know." I mimed bringing a receiver to my ear and dialing a number.

"Ah, telephone!" she said suddenly. "*Aywa, aywa!*"

"But Ahmed doesn't have one. I wish there was somewhere I could go. . ."

"Mees Harees!" She impulsively took hold of my hand, her face alight with joy. Another rush of Arabic came from her mouth, out of which I caught the word telephone. Then she stood, went to the shutters, opened them and gestured down the street. "Telephone!" she said excitedly.

I felt suddenly pleased with myself. My guess had been right, Asmahan knew nothing of my real situation and Ahmed had given her no orders to keep me under lock and key.

"We go!" she said excitedly. "Mees Harees, we go, yes?"

Then I thought a little more. Apparently Mr. Rasheed had trusted me to be watchful of my own safety and had assumed I would not be so injudicious as to leave the flat on my own.

Well, I was about to be injudicious. None of my faceless, mysterious assailants could possibly know where I was. Ahmed himself had convinced me of that. And a harmless trip to the telephone exchange would not take long, it was not far, and it was high noon over Cairo. Out of millions of people, how could I possibly be spotted?

I joined Asmahan at the windows and looked down. A great throng of pedestrians moved like a river below us. Each with his own purpose, no one paying the slightest attention to this flat. I watched for some time, and again felt a confirmation of security. Ahmed Rasheed had been right. None of Rossiter's men knew where I was hiding. It would be so easy to hurry out, make the call, spend one reassuring minute with Dr. Kellerman and then dash back. It couldn't fail. I would be with Asmahan. No one would notice two girls out for a walk together. Especially . . . I turned around and eyed the wide-brimmed sun hat on the table . . . especially an Egyptian girl with a friend whose face was hidden.

My heart started to race. Of course it would work!

I became excited. In just a short while I would be talking to Dr. Kellerman. Hearing his voice, closing my eyes and imagining he was with me. "Can we go?" I said to Asmahan.

She was an emotional and excitable girl and was obviously influenced by my own sudden excitement. It must have seemed an adventure to her. "Aywa!" Then she said something in Arabic and laughed.

I took a moment to run into the bedroom—hurrying, for I didn't want her to suddenly change her mind for any reason—grabbed my bag, made sure the jackal was safe under my shirt and, at the last second, decided to put on a sweater. It would keep my white arms from being spotted in the swarthy crowd.

As we prepared to leave, I cast an admiring eye over Asmahan's hat, commented on how nice it was, and was glad when she offered it to me to wear. Asmahan touched a fingertip to my cheek, then pointed to her own face, indicating the difference in our complexions. Then she gestured upwards, drew a circle in the air and touched my cheek again. I am sure I was close in translating it to mean that since I would burn in the afternoon sun, I should be the one to wear the hat.

I paused before the mirror by the door. Little of my face showed, for I had also put on large sunglasses, which, together with the wide shadow cast by the hat's brim, helped to conceal much of my fairness and identity. Then I hoisted the strap of my handbag over my shoulder, gave one last fleeting consideration to what I was doing, decided to go ahead with it, and pulled open the door.

The real weight of what I was doing did not even occur to me as the two of us emerged into the bright sunlight below. I had invented this scheme for several reasons. One, the most important, was to communicate with Dr. Kellerman and assure him I was okay. Another was that I would have done anything to get out of that flat. It was an impossible test of nerve to remain cooped up as I was, constantly wondering where I was, at who's mercy, and for how long. A third, less conscious reason for getting out into the open was, I suppose, to prove something to myself. I needed to prove beyond a doubt that I was indeed safe at Mr. Rasheed's home and that I still had courage to face any challenge. I needed to know for certain that the murderers of John Treadwell were not, after all, watching me nearby, and that I was not losing my intrepid nature by hiding behind shuttered windows.

And so it was with a certain reckless bravado that I struck out into the city that afternoon, and because of the need to speak to Dr. Kellerman, because of the personal tests I was putting myself to, and because of the noise and security of the crowded pavement and the delicious feel of the hot sun. Because of all this, I gave no thought to the seriousness of my actions. I was overconfident.

My companion and I merged with the hundreds of other pedestrians who overflowed the pavement and dominated the street and reveled in our walk in the sun. I was surprised to find how close we were to the center of Cairo. The street we walked along, the one Ahmed lived on, was a main boulevard called Al Tahrir Street. Asmahan and I did not go far before we entered a hectic, clamorous and enormous traffic circle, Liberation Square, on the far side of which stood the Nile Hilton and the Egyptian Museum. To our left, unseen because of buildings between us, was the Shepherd's Hotel. Ahmed had not had far to take me that night.

I could not believe the sights my eyes saw, the sounds that overcame me, or the smells of this unbelievable city. When we first emerged into broad daylight, I had been on my guard and extremely apprehensive, studying each face that passed by, glancing back over my shoulder numerous times, listening for suspicious sounds. I did not know what I was looking for, but I was certain I would know it when I found it. And yet, as I felt the hot, bright sun on us and was overwhelmed by the energy of humanity around us, I gradually lost my wariness and relaxed into enjoying the excitement of this new experience.

The telephone exchange was four streets away and near Liberation Square. It was necessary for us to cross lanes of maniacal traffic, become pressed into the mobs standing on curbs, and pick our way over broken pavements. The people were fascinating, ranging from young men and women in familiar western dress, to old men in traditional long nightshirts, peasant women dressed entirely in black, devout Moslems with veils over their faces, donkey drivers, street urchins crying "baksheesh," Blacks, Semites, Orientals, and Anglos—all filling the noisy streets with their animation, loud talk, laughter, shouts and horn honking.

When we fell through the door of the exchange, I greeted the silence with welcome. It was a small store-front affair with large windows and a door that swung silently closed. It took us a minute to adjust our eyes—I did not remove my sunglasses—and accustom our ears to its quiet.

The doorless phone cubicles went all around the room and some formed an island in the center. Several were in use, people pressed as privately as possible into the small "booths," murmuring quietly and paying no attention to anyone else. A plain counter stood to our left, behind which three women sat at a switchboard. Slightly to the right of this desk, and against a short space of wall, was a vacant wooden bench.

Following Asmahan's lead, I went up to the counter and waited until a particularly obese woman in a flowery print dress rose to help us. Asmahan did all the talking, securing after a minute a slip of paper on which I was to write certain information.

"Do you speak English?" I said hopefully.

The woman nodded. She appeared bored. "You will give me the name of the person you call and also the telephone number. You will pay me for this now and wait until the call is finished. Then you will pay me for it all. Do you understand?"

"Yes, yes. Thank you." Picking up the stubby pencil she proffered, I held my hand suspended over the paper. Which number to give her?

Then it occurred to me. "Do you happen to know what time it is in Los Angeles?"

She glanced up at the clock on the wall, thought a moment, then said, "Ten o'clock in the night."

"Ten o'clock. Oh for God's sake. Well, that rules out the hospital." Knowing what odd hours Dr. Kellerman could sometimes keep, I decided to give her the number of his exchange. That way I would reach him no matter where he was.

When she informed me that a fee was to be paid prior to making the call, I became distressed. I had no Egyptian money. But Asmahan, immediately guessing my problem, withdrew some piastres out of her purse and thrust them at the woman. I thanked her as sincerely as I could and promised to pay her back.

"It will take a while to call America," said the obese woman, examining the number. "You will sit until I call you. Then you will go to a telephone. Do you understand?"

"Yes. Yes, thank you."

So we took our places on the wooden bench and folded our hands patiently. Asmahan and I waited an eternity, during which time I thought of absolutely nothing except hearing Dr. Kellerman's voice. Ahmed Rasheed did not enter my mind, nor Adele, nor the jackal, nor the death of John Treadwell, nor the danger I was in. I thought only of Dr. Kellerman and of the solace contact with him would bring me. When the obese woman behind the counter called me back, I jumped.

A note with a carefully written message on it was pushed at me along with the words, "This person cannot be located. They said you will try later."

I read her neat handwriting. Dr. Kellerman's answering service had said he could not be reached that evening and that a Dr. Thomas was covering his calls.

"Damn!" I muttered in disappointment. Since he had signed out to another surgeon, there would be no way of locating Dr. Kellerman. My only resort was to try his home. So I filled out a new slip, had Asmahan pay an additional fee, and retired back to the bench where we sat for the next fifteen minutes.

It seemed hours before she called my name again, and in that time I saw other people who had come in after us be directed to phone booths. They had been infinitely luckier than I, and were apparently going to remain so.

"There is no answer at this number," said the fat lady.

Absurdly I felt like saying, "Are you sure?" but realized it was no use. Dr. Kellerman just wasn't to be found, and didn't want to be disturbed. Which was why he had signed out to Dr. Thomas. Which was why no answer at his home. I was devastated.

I looked at Asmahan as if I could cry, and seeing the expression on my face, she patted my hand and said, *"Anah asif."*

"Yes, I'm sorry too." Damn, I had gotten my hopes up. "I want to try again later." To the woman I said, "How late are you open?"

"We close in one hour for three hours and open again at five. Then we close at ten o'clock."

"Good. We'll be back."

My mind was working fast. Asmahan and I could return in just under an hour and try again. By then it would be close to midnight in Los Angeles with a greater possibility of Dr. Kellerman being home. If not, then we would return at five and try again, hopefully before Ahmed Rasheed came home. I asked the woman to relay this plan to Asmahan in Arabic, who then nodded vigorously in agreement. Then she asked me a question.

The fat woman said, "She wants to know what you will do in the meantime?"

I shrugged my shoulders helplessly.

Asmahan spoke rapidly to the woman, using gestures and pointing over her shoulder. It was then translated for me. "Your friend would like to take you to the Mousky. She says you will walk there."

"How far is it?"

She heaved her fat shoulders. "Not far. But it is a long, long street."

"Well, *what* is the Mousky?"

"It is for shopping. You will see." And she turned away before we could make any further use of her.

I allowed Asmahan, with persuasive Arabic and a tug on my wrist, to draw me out of the telephone exchange and back into the street.

"I don't know . . ." I said hesitantly.

"Mees Harees. *Et nayn bahd idohre.*" She tapped her watch and then help up two fingers. "*Et nayn bahd idohre.* Telephone."

"You're sure we'll be back by two?"

"*Aywa! Aywa!*" Her head bobbed up and down as she linked her arm through mine. "Now we go Mousky. You see beautiful things. Come."

It wasn't only Asmahan who influenced me to strike off towards parts unknown, but also the bright sunlight, the crowded pavement, and a total feeling of security. When I happened to catch my reflection in store windows we passed, I saw that I was well disguised, that not even I recognized myself for an instant. It was good to be outside and walking and forgetting, if just for a moment, why I was here.

It was in the middle of the Mousky, half an hour later, that I lost Asmahan. One moment we were pressed together before the stall of a cloth merchant, fingering the fine linens and trying to breathe in the crowd, and in the next moment her arm slipped casually from mine. I paid no heed, thinking she had stepped away to look at something else, and was not aware of what had happened until I looked up to ask her something.

And I found myself completely alone.

At first I did not panic, and it was not until later that I became truly frightened, but when my initial look at the faces surrounding me did not produce Asmahan's, my heart skipped a beat. I remained calm and casual, staying in one spot, looking this way and that, expecting her to suddenly appear through the crowd with apologies. But she did not. Hundreds of people milled about me in this narrow market place, a great roar of deafening shouts and yells and calls made my head begin to ache.

And then I remembered the Domus Aurea.

After standing as long as I could on that spot, looking around and around, I finally decided to take a few steps in the direction I thought she went. There were dark faces and flashing eyes everywhere, but no Asmahan. My foot slid on a pile of donkey dung. My body was jostled by people hurrying to and fro about me. Suddenly, over loudspeakers everywhere, blared the muezzin's voice, startling me at first and then causing me to wince. It was a loud, piercing cry and came down upon me from every speaker and radio along the Mousky.

I smelt onions and coconut and rancid perfume. I felt a moldy animal brush along my back. My feet trod over the uneven cobblestones and slipped on rinds and oil and droppings. Dirty ragged little children tugged at my blouse, crying, "Baksheesh! Baksheesh!"

Asmahan had disappeared completely. Every woman in the bazaar had black hair. A few might have been her, but were not. And the more I searched, the farther I was carried from our original spot. How easy it was to be carried on the tide, like along a raging river, trying to grasp for protruding branches along the bank. Suddenly, the sun no longer felt heavenly and I regretted the rashness of my actions. It had taken us quite a walk to arrive at the Mousky, none of which I would be able to retrace on my own. And I did not remember the name of Ahmed's street. I would have to seek help soon, a taxi or a policeman, before something happened to me.

Then I remembered the jackal, that it was on my person, and that certain parties were in this city who would kill for its possession.

The biggest fear I had during my interminable wanderings through the Mousky was that I was going farther and farther from the center of Cairo. Yet I had no way of telling for sure. There was no way to see over the tops of all the heads, and even if I could, I doubted whether I would recognize any landmarks. Still, I did keep some measure of wit about me: I was certain of one thing—that it was far wiser to remain among the congestion of this insane market place than to attempt striking off along one of the many narrow streets and alleys that branched from it. Here, at least, I was relatively safe among the thousands of natives and peasants milling around me. But there, walking by myself down an unfamiliar street, I would be an easy target.

I also thought of something else. That if Ahmed Rasheed was to come looking for me, he would come to the Mousky bazaar, even though it was miles long and jammed with hundreds of people.

One thought rose above all others in my mind—above the fear of stumbling upon one of Rossiter's agents, of having to struggle here in this crowd with him, of having to fight for the jackal—and that was that the hour was growing late and that it would soon be dark, and then my troubles would really begin.

Then I saw the American tourists. There were about twelve of them clustered around the stall of a silversmith. That they were Americans was obvious from their dress, but even more so from their loud speech and mannerisms, which were what caught my attention. So I pushed against the tide and worked my way towards them in the firm belief that not only was there safety in numbers, but safety among one's own ilk as well.

A few were engaged in the expected haggling over some hand-wrought pieces of silver, while the others examined the wares and expressed their admiration to the three craftsmen behind the table. Three Arabs, who must have been grandfather, father and son, were all bent over their work, while a fourth, a female, discussed prices with the tourists.

"Ten Egyptian pounds!" one bombastic American blurted. "Ten Egyptian pounds for this?" he held a delicate silver cup in his beefy hands.

The Arab woman shrugged and spread her hands helplessly.

"For Chrissake, how the hell much is that in real money? Edna!" He swung around and shouted, "Edna!" in my face. Then, with an embarrassed grin he said, "Oh excuse me. Have you seen my wife?"

"No."

"Probably off spending money somewhere. Say, do you know how much ten Egyptian pounds is in money?"

"No, I don't. Excuse me, could you tell me . . ."

"Edna, for Chrissake, where are you?" The man was large and burly with meaty breath and a slight Southern accent. He swung his head this way and that looking for his wife.

"Excuse me, do you know which way is the Nile Hilton?"

He looked down at me. "The Hilton? Sure, it's that way," and he jerked his head to the left. "That's where we're staying. Where the hell is my wife? She has all the traveler's checks."

The others in the group, having decided to make purchases, were all now speaking up and demanding the Arab woman's attention. I was jostled about, elbowed, and had my ears shouted in.

"Could you be more precise, please? Just *where* is the Hilton?"

"Hah? Oh, that way." This time he thrust a thumb to the left. "I couldn't give you directions or anything. Took a damned bus here. Streets are crazy in this country. Why, are you lost?"

"Possibly."

"Where's your group?"

"I'm not with one."

"Then take a taxi." He looked around over the tops of heads. "If you can find one."

"I tried," I shouted. "I only got more lost. Isn't there a direct way to the Hilton?"

"You got me lady. I ain't no Ayrab. Why don't you call the Hilton? Maybe they'll send someone for you." Then he turned away from me and stretched his neck over the rest of the silver display.

"Well, I'm not staying at the Hilton. I don't think they'd . . ."

He turned back to me, somewhat annoyed. "Then where are you staying?"

"With . . . with friends."

"So call 'em. Or give a cab driver their address. Where the *hell* is Edna?" He rose on to his toes and gave another search. "There she is!" he shouted over the crowd. "Hey, Edna! I'm over here!" When he lifted his arm to wave, the odor of sweat wafted my face. "She didn't see me." He glanced down again at me, said, "Excuse me," and started to walk away.

I hesitated a moment, watching his broad back melt through the crowd, then said impulsively, "Wait a minute, please!"

He stopped and turned. His smile was impatient.

"Do you suppose I could get back to the Hilton with you and your wife? Would that be all right?"

He shrugged. "Don't see why not."

I was at once relieved. Somehow, once at the Hilton I knew I would be able to find my way back to Ahmed's place. "When does your bus leave?"

"Aw heck, I'm not waiting for that. This place gives me a headache. I'm getting us a cab, soon as I can get Edna away from the shops. We'll be glad to drop you at your friends. Where did you say they live?"

"I don't remember. The name of the street, that is. I'd know it if I saw it."

Just then someone bumped into me, causing me to fall against this bear of a tourist. He caught my arm and held it. "Watch it, little lady. You're no match for this crowd. We Americans have to stick together. Come on, let's get my wife and get out of here." He turned again into the tide and started to pull me with him, muttering as he did so, "Ten pounds for a piece of junk!"

It was around this time, as my compatriot dragged me along with an iron grip, that a chilling sensation swept over me. I don't know what caused it, or why a fresh fear should suddenly be triggered now, but as we pushed our way through the knot of American tourists, some intuition caused me to shiver and cast a quick glance over my shoulder.

The fat man with the thick glasses stood right behind me.

If it had not been for the firm hold my rescuer had of me, I might have fallen, for my legs suddenly gave way. I stumbled a little, leaned against his massive body, and managed, in a split-second, to contain myself and act calmly.

How the fat man with the Coke-bottle glasses found me, I did not know and did not care. The only thought that went through my head was, did he recognize me? With the sun hat and dark glasses, possibly I was anonymous. But no, this was false hope. It was far too much of a coincidence that, out of the hundreds of square miles of Cairo, and out of the millions of people it contained, the fat man should just happen to be standing behind me at that given moment. Yes, he knew it was me all right.

With a surge of strength I pressed forward and caught hold of my companion's shirt sleeve. "Where's your wife?" I said frantically.

"Right there, see her? Spending my money."

I looked wildly ahead. "Can we hurry, please?"

His grip on my arm tightened, until it almost hurt. "Don't worry, little lady," he said quietly.

What exactly happened next is a blur to me, for several unexpected things occurred all at once and too quickly. To our right a donkey cart suddenly turned over, and a thousand oranges rained upon us. I screamed and felt a body fall against me. The big tourist said, "Oh, shit," lost his hold of my arm, grappled for it again and missed when he was shoved out of the way. In terror, thinking of the fat man behind me, I reached out for Edna's husband, but an eruption of humanity split us completely apart. More chaos exploded, donkeys braying, a ceramic stall crashing to the ground, women screaming and men shouting. Next my hat flew off and my hair fell to my shoulders. Instinctively I held my arm tightly against the jackal that was stabbing my side. As I was carried along, farther and farther from the safe Americans, I knew that I was going to have to fight for my life.

I was knocked and shoved about, my feet stepped on, and my handbag wrenched about. I sought blindly for an exit, but there was none. As I tried to escape the fury of the crowd, and as I felt sure that any moment my legs were going to fail and I was going to go under, someone seized me from behind, both arms around my waist, and started to pull me back.

"No!" I said breathlessly. I tried to fight but was too weak. "Please, don't . . ." He was too strong for me, pinioning my arms and dragging me out of the center of the mob. There was nothing I could do. I cried out, but no one heard.

Propelled backwards, but still trying to fight, I saw that we had reached the periphery of the crowd and were aiming for a narrow alley.

"Please!" I cried, twisting in his grip.

Through my mind darted the frantic thought, no, not like this. It can't end like this! And I thought of Dr. Kellerman and tried desperately to shake myself free.

Suddenly, out of sight of the crowd, my assailant stopped and spun me around. I gaped incredulously into the furious eyes of Ahmed Rasheed.

"What . . .?"

"Don't talk. We must hurry." He took hold of my hand and together we dashed down the dark alley and away from the chaos of the Mousky. We ran over the cobblestones, darted around sleeping donkeys, startled napping beggars, and ran until we gasped for breath. When I started to stumble and fall back, with Ahmed dragging me along, the alley opened on to a sunlit street where a black-and-white taxi cab stood before us.

Without a word, Mr. Rasheed flung open the door, pushed me in, and climbed in behind. He spoke to the driver in Arabic and the car jolted off.

"Oh God!" I cried, burying my face in my hands. "Oh God, oh God!"

His arm rested lightly on my shoulders, but he didn't speak.

Tears streamed down my cheeks, tears of relief, tears of fright, and tears of exhaustion. My whole body trembled and shuddered. I flung my sunglasses to the floor, sobbed a little more, then took a deep breath and finally straightened up. I rubbed my fists into my eyes before looking at Mr. Rasheed. I was sorry I did.

Ahmed Rasheed, his arm still about my shoulders, was glaring at me with barely controlled fury. His eyes were afire with anger, bright and dilated like those of a fever victim. His lips formed a thin line. His whole face was set in rage.

"I'm sorry," I whispered.

"Do not speak now," he said evenly, and glanced at the cab driver. So I forced my mouth closed and tried to keep my body from trembling.

The taxi charged through the traffic without care or heed, jumped red lights, pulled out in front of people and allowed no courtesy to other drivers. In Egypt, the car horn seemed to have completely replaced brakes, so that no one stopped for *anything*; one simply blasted one's way through. I pressed my feet to the floor and held on to the back of the front seat as we bounced and jerked our way through crowded, narrow streets. My relief was immeasurable when we finally arrived at a familiar place, and for the one and only time the driver touched his brakes.

As we pulled up in front of Ahmed's flat and climbed out, myself badly shaken, I heard a high voice call my name. "Mees Harees!" Asmahan ran out on to the pavement and embraced me. Her speech was octaves higher than usual and came out in gasps and spurts. When she stood back from me I saw that her eyes were red-rimmed.

Before I could say a word, Ahmed Rasheed took hold of my arm and led me into the building. He paused only long enough to look up and down the street to see if anyone was lurking in the late afternoon shadows. Then we went up.

It was not until after we were all inside, the door locked and the shutters closed, that he finally turned on me. His eyes expressed the fury that his voice was trying to control. "What did you think you were doing, Miss Harris?"

I opened my mouth to speak, but all that came out was a barely audible whisper. "I'm sorry."

"Did you not have any idea of the danger you were in?"

"I didn't think . . ."

"Miss Harris," his voice grew louder, "you had no right to put yourself to such a risk. Or Asmahan. Or to cause me this worry."

I stared at him like a chastised child.

"I have gone to a lot of trouble to protect you. And then you do this. When I came home and Asmahan had said she had lost you, I could not believe it. I could not believe that you had done this thing. Was your phone call so important?"

I did not reply.

"When Asmahan said you were in the Mousky, *alone* in the Mousky, I became fearful. What is the word? Frantic? I did not know what to do! To find you in all those people, before someone else reached you . . ." His voice stopped suddenly but his eyes continued to convey his rage.

We stood for a long time, the three of us, in the darkening room. Asmahan was behind him, twisting her fingers and appearing to take the blame entirely upon herself. Ahmed was directly in front of me, less than four feet away, glowering and fuming and under great restraint. I could only look apologetically at them, totally lost for words.

His voice was steady, his words carefully chosen. "I did not tell Asmahan why you were here or that you were in danger. I told her only that you were our friend and a stranger to Cairo and in need of a place to stay. To have told her the truth would have been to cause her needless worry and concern. Even now, she does not know the full seriousness of what happened today. If I were to turn to her now and explain that you could have been murdered . . ."

"Wait. Wait, please. Don't be harsh with her. It was all my fault."

"I know this. I have not been angry with her. But you can see for yourself how she takes the blame. My worry and concern for you, when you were alone at the Mousky, surprised her. She kept assuring me you would find your way home. How could I tell her that it was possible you might never come back?"

"Mr. Rasheed . . ."

"Just what did you think you were doing, going out of the flat? And exposing Asmahan to that danger?"

"I thought it would be all right. You said I was safe . . ."

"Last night I said we would not go out yet."

"Mr. Rasheed . . ."

"Had you forgotten John Treadwell?"

"Now wait a minute!" Suddenly, I was angry. "I said I was sorry. I don't appreciate your standing there like some Lord High Executioner. How many times do I have to apologize? I feel badly, very badly about what happened! I know you were worried about Asmahan, and you're right, I shouldn't have taken her with me. I was risking my own neck and should have gone out on my own. But for God's sake, I feel terrible about it! And I feel sick and hurt all over!"

My last words hung heavily in the air as I realized my voice had gone high and shrill. I was trembling again. The light was rapidly leaving the room, but no one made a move to turn on a lamp. "It won't happen again," I murmured.

Ahmed Rasheed continued to stand unmoving before me, his eyes holding mine as if he wanted to tell me something but didn't know how.

For the last time I said, "I'm sorry," and there was bitterness in my voice.

Then, to my surprise, Ahmed stirred a little, released a heavy sigh, and said in a low voice, "I was worried about you."

I gazed back at him. Somewhere in the distance, through the lavender sunset and over the rooftops, began the wail of the muezzin. His cry penetrated the shutters and drifted about the room as if a gentle reminder of who and where we were. Far away street sounds were muffled, tinny Egyptian music was barely audible through the walls, and in the increasing gloom, I shivered involuntarily.

I don't know how long Ahmed and I stood staring at each other, but when Asmahan's voice broke the spell, I turned away. Next a light went on, and another, and then Asmahan hurried past us and into the kitchen. As I stood watching after her, I felt the hard gaze of Ahmed Rasheed on my back.

"Forgive me," he said quietly. "I have no right to be so angry with you."

I spun about.

"You can do as you wish," he said.

"I shouldn't have involved Asmahan. I'm sorry. And . . . and thank you for rescuing me. God, how stupid!"

He seemed to consider another thought and then, dismissing it, walked past me and joined Asmahan in the kitchen.

I wandered around the room a little, looking at this and touching that, before I sat down on the couch and tried to calm myself. That I had suffered a bad shock was obvious, for I still shook and felt weak. My arm was sore from where the big tourist had held me, and my heels were scraped where they had been trampled on in the scuffle. As I rubbed my painful spots and tried to deep-breathe myself to relaxation, I went back over the entire incident in my mind and found myself just as baffled.

Asmahan and Ahmed came quietly into the room, spread the cups and some cakes around the coffee table and sat down without a sound. While she poured the tea, Asmahan kept looking at me out of the corner of her eye. It made me uncomfortable. What on earth did she think of my involvement with her fiancé?

"Miss Harris," said Ahmed, who was seated next to me on the couch. "Tell me, did you see anyone suspicious in the bazaar? I mean, could you suppose you were being followed?"

"The fat man I told you about, with the thick glasses, was there."

He closed his eyes for a moment. "I see."

"But I don't know how long he was there. He must have just in that moment spotted me because I didn't notice him before that, and I guess I wandered for two hours before I ran into the tourists."

"Tourists?"

"A group of Americans. I tell you, after two hours of hearing nothing but Arabic and seeing only foreign faces, I was glad to run into them. You see, Mr. Rasheed, I *can* take care of myself after all. I was just about to be escorted back to the Hilton when all hell broke loose and you showed up . . ." I frowned, trying to reconstruct that phrenetic moment.

"Escorted by whom?"

"An American tourist and his wife. I figured I would be safe with them. So Fatso with the glasses wouldn't have got to me after all."

He considered my words. "An American tourist? What did his wife look like?"

"Edna? Well, I don't really know. I didn't actually see her. She was away from the group."

"Then how do you know she was there?"

"I beg your pardon?"

"And how did you know that this American with whom you were about to ride was indeed with that American group?"

"What?" I gave him an incredulous look. "Are you serious? Wait a minute, Mr. Rasheed." I forced a laugh. "I think you're being too melodramatic. Yes, granted, the fat man was there, but I was in the process of eluding him. I figured that making quick friends with a couple of American tourists was a good idea."

Without another word, Ahmed rose and crossed the room to where his jacket lay over the back of a chair. He reached into the inside pocket, drew something out, and returned to the couch.

"Tell me, Miss Harris," he said, showing me a photograph, "have you ever seen this man before?"

I stared in disbelief at the face of the man in the picture. It was Edna's husband, the big American tourist. "But this is . . ."

"This man, Miss Harris, is Arnold Rossiter."

A cup rattling in a saucer brought me back to reality. My head turned towards the sound, then my eyes focused on Asmahan's hands and the fog lifted. Somewhere nearby, a man's voice was saying, "Are you all right, Miss Harris?"

I looked at Ahmed Rasheed. My body shuddered again. "He had hold of me," I said, barely above a whisper. "Here," and I pointed to the red marks on my arm. "He had a strong grip on me and he was leading me away. God, he was hurting me, but I thought he wasn't aware of it. I thought he was just in a hurry to get to his wife and find a cab . . ." My voice faded away.

"You do see now why I was so worried about you. He is a very cunning man, Arnold Rossiter, and known to be an excellent actor. He has been reported in many guises—a priest, a shepherd, an airline pilot, and now a tourist. He is not American, he is British."

"Could have fooled me," I said flatly.

"And he did." Mr. Rasheed took the photo from me, regarded it for a moment, then put it on the table. "But you had no way of knowing. You were lost in a foreign city and willing to trust anyone who seemed honest. It is ironic, I think, that I am your only true friend, and yet you do not trust me."

I brought my head up sharply.

"However," he went on, "I do not believe we were followed here. We left the Mousky quickly enough and during a moment of confusion."

"Good God! Arnold Rossiter actually had hold of me! If that donkey cart hadn't turned over just then, you might never have been able . . ." I looked at Ahmed Rasheed. There was a cryptic expression on his face. "You?" I said, pointing stupidly at him. "Did you do that?"

"I had to, Miss Harris. I had searched the Mousky for half an hour when I sighted you. And when I saw that man who looked like Arnold Rossiter had a hold of you, a man who is very much larger than I, I knew that I must cause a distraction. The orange cart seemed likely."

"Oh God!" Suddenly I felt insanely like laughing.

"There was no other way, in such a short moment, to take you away from Mr. Rossiter. Confusion was the only reasonable solution."

"And it worked!"

"Yes." He finally smiled. "It did."

I shook my head in wonder. "I just can't believe it. If that was Rossiter, how did he devise to be in front of me in the Mousky? If he had followed me there, how did he manage to be ahead of me, join that group and be involved in a discussion about money just as I walked up? For that he would have had to know ahead of time that I was going to the Mousky, and he couldn't have known that because Asmahan and I only decided to go there at the last . . ." My hand flew to my mouth. "Of course, the woman at the telephone exchange. He could have found out from her. He followed me there, saw me leave . . . Oh wow." I shook my head again. "I guess I didn't do many bright things today."

Now Ahmed tried to force a little laughter and patted my hand reassuringly. "It is all right, Miss Harris. You are safe and that is all that matters."

When I saw him smile, I felt a little better. "How many times can a person say 'I'm sorry' in one day? You must think I'm a real dolt." I smiled back at him. "You risked a lot yourself to save me. Thank you."

With this he stood and, speaking to Asmahan in Arabic, went and picked up his jacket. "It is getting late. I will walk her home now and return soon. You will lock the door, yes?"

"Yes."

This time I didn't bother to look through the shutters to watch them go. I locked the door and returned to the couch where I thankfully drank the rest of my tea. I was incredibly tired by now and ached in every corner of my body. It would have been nice to soak in a hot bath right now, but Ahmed didn't have one, so I would have to settle for a long sleep.

But then, considering the events of the day, was I going to be able to sleep? I had had a bad moment in the Mousky, had come close to being kidnapped by a murderer, and, to top matters, never did get to talk to Dr. Kellerman.

My mind was a kaleidoscope of thoughts, of feelings, of confusion. I drew the jackal out from the waistband of my trousers and brought it up before my eyes. I studied the bizarre face, the ivory grin, the sly eyes, and pointed ears. What secrets did it hold, this ancient toy? Why was it so valuable, and why were such sinister people trying to gain possession of it?

I let it drop in my lap as my eyes fell to staring at the blank wall opposite. Other pictures flashed into my mind. The big American tourist with the Southern accent, and how secure I had felt in his care. The sheer fright of discovering Fatso standing right behind me. The terror I had felt when the cart had overturned and the crowd had stampeded. And I remembered the feel of Ahmed Rasheed's arms tightly about my waist.

Then I thought of him now, with Asmahan, perhaps kissing her.

Hearing his footsteps on the stairs, I secreted the jackal under my shirt again and gulped down the last of my tea. Closing and locking the door behind him Ahmed said hastily, "There is no one out there. Mr. Rossiter has no idea where you are at this moment, or with whom."

"Thank God."

He smiled. "*Inshallah.* Are you hungry, Miss Harris?"

"No, as a matter of fact, I'm not." I got to my feet and smoothed out my disarrayed clothing. "I feel lousy and just want to go to bed."

"Very well." He walked to the table and started to remove his jacket.

"Mr. Rasheed, who is Arnold Rossiter?"

He paused for just a moment, then finished removing his coat, draping it neatly over the chair. His shirt underneath was immaculately white, or possibly that was just in contrast to his dark skin.

"You aren't going to tell me, are you?"

"Not now, not yet."

"Well," I walked towards the bedroom door. "At any rate, I'm sorry for what I've put everyone through today. I assure you, I had no intention of getting involved in anything like this."

He was standing close to me, smiling faintly.

"And I'm really sorry about Asmahan. I woke up this morning with the singular idea of calling Dr. Kellerman; nothing else seemed important. I felt so safe and secure, overconfident I guess, and so certain that I wouldn't be recognized. I had no right to expose your fiancée to danger like that."

Mr. Rasheed's smile congealed into a puzzled frown. "Fiancée?"

"Yes. Like, you know, your girlfriend. Betrothed. Or whatever we say in English. Asmahan!"

"Yes, I know the word, Miss Harris. But Asmahan is not my fiancée."

"She isn't?"

"No," he said with a laugh. "She is my sister!"

CHAPTER 11

I LAY LIKE A MUMMY IN MY BED, STARING UP AT THE DARK ceiling as though it was a night sky and I was reading the stars. In my fanciful way I imagined I had been lying there for centuries waiting for my resurrection. But in truth I was only waiting for the dawn, which was probably the same thing.

My mind, despite the absolute silence of the night and the solitude of the darkness, was sharply awake and plagued with a thousand thoughts. In and out of my head floated a parade of faces: Arnold Rossiter, Ahmed Rasheed, John Treadwell, Asmahan, Dr. Kellerman. They all came to look at me, to rob me of rest and peace. And though I tried to fight them, to find respite from them, all I could do was relive over and over again the events of the previous day, just as I relived them now for the one hundredth time.

And when I came to the end, to Ahmed Rasheed's words, "She is my sister," I again felt that odd reaction inside me, the half-beat of my heart and the peculiar stab of joy. Indeed, it was this final moment of the day—not the hassle at the telephone exchange or my panic in the Mousky or my scrape with Rossiter—that came back most frequently to keep me from a peaceful sleep.

Why had I reacted so to his words? A feeling of relief and gladness. It had been so unexpected. I had been mildly taken aback to find myself reacting in such a way, indeed, reacting at all. Why should I care whether Asmahan was his fiancée or his sister? And why, I wondered as dawn started to seep through the window cracks, was I wondering about it now?

I pictured the man who fancied himself my protector. That he was quite different from any other man I had ever known was obvious. But there was something else. It was not my habit to be easily intrigued by anything foreign or novel. In fact, I tended to be more aloof, more suspicious of such things. No, there was a quality about the man sleeping in the next room that appealed to me. And in the end, I had to admit, I was becoming attracted to him.

The hour before dawn is the best time to think, for it is always the coolest, quietest and stillest time of the day. I lay comfortable and unharried. Behind me was a day that I was thankful to see gone, and before me lay a day that could hold promise and possibilities. It had been a full week since Adele called me from Rome, a full week since I had decided to join her, and God, it seemed an eternity. So much had happened to me in that brief time, and I knew that a great deal still lay ahead. Somehow I sensed that this odyssey was not going to end soon or here, but rather, I thought in the pale morning light, that it held much more in store for me.

I thought again of Ahmed Rasheed. And I thought of Dr. Kellerman. And I thought of the change that was taking place within me.

I waited until I heard the front door close before I decided to get up. My first act was to lock the door. Next I took a long shower, rummaged about in the kitchen for something to eat, made my own tea (I was beginning to crave for it), and then settled down to wait for Asmahan.

She never came.

The few books in Ahmed's flat that were in English were university textbooks, ranging from trigonometry to ancient history and political science. The ones that interested me, the ones with fascinating pictures and attractive covers, which appeared to be fiction, were all in Arabic.

I did not blame Asmahan for not coming or Ahmed for keeping her away. The situation had grown dangerous and Asmahan could be hurt by it. God only knew how much longer this would have to go on, and it was senseless to involve anyone else.

The day dragged mercilessly. Occasionally, when I heard footsteps on the stairs, my hopes rose that it was Ahmed coming home. But each time they disappeared through another doorway. Three times I heard the call of the muezzin and vaguely wondered if Ahmed, wherever he was, stopped what he was doing to kneel and pray toward Mecca.

I even attempted to write a letter to Dr. Kellerman. There was a good chance it would reach him before I reached a telephone, but then . . . what could I say? Dear Dr. Kellerman, you won't believe it, but right now I'm living with an Egyptian secret agent who is hiding me from a murderer, and the Cairo police were after me day before yesterday because they thought I killed the man I came with from Rome. And remember the jackal I showed you? It seems everyone is trying to get it from me. This secret agent, Ahmed Rasheed, thinks I might be murdered for it, and he doesn't want that to happen because he wants me to find my sister for some reason that he won't tell. Having a fine time, wish you were here.

The letter never went to press. Maybe soon I would be able to tell him about it in person.

When Ahmed finally came home, I was glad to see him. The ordeal at the Mousky had made me apprehensive, so that I had not been able to relax all day. I had paced a great deal, peeped through the shutters twice, and had entertained any number of plans I should start considering for myself.

I wondered how long this could go on. I was into my third day hiding in Rasheed's flat, with no change on the horizon. How was I going to find Adele this way, so inactive, so useless? And what, I found myself wondering over and over again, was Ahmed Rasheed really doing about the situation?

His usual suit was replaced this time by a sweater and slacks, giving him a casual, almost American look. He greeted me warmly, smiled freely, and appeared to be totally unconcerned about anything.

"Have you learned anything new, Mr. Rasheed?"

"Your sister has not been back to the Shepherd's Hotel." That didn't surprise me. I hadn't been thinking of that.

"Nothing else?"

Finally he turned from his tea-making. "Miss Harris, you will please go and sit down. First we will have tea. Then there is something I must tell you."

Unaccustomed as I was to deciphering his tone, I could not tell whether he was speaking gravely or simply politely. But recognizing the necessity of going along with him, I went back into the living room and waited patiently until he joined me, some minutes later, with the tea.

"All right." I got up and sat next to him on the couch. The faint scent of his aftershave reminded me of his bedroom. "What is it?"

As he poured the tea, he said, "What do you plan to say to your sister when you see her?"

"What do I plan to say? That's an odd thing to ask me. Why do you want to know?"

"You see, it is important, Miss Harris, that you are careful of what you say to her. You must remember that I am looking for her for a different reason than you."

"And you think I'll give you away?"

"I beg your pardon?"

"I mean . . . you're afraid I'll tell her about you?"

"Precisely."

"Well." I thought a moment. "I hadn't really given much thought to it. I intend to ask what the devil happened to her in Rome and why she wasn't at the Shepherd's Hotel like her letter said. I also want her to explain the jackal. Other than that . . . maybe talk about the past. Fill in the last four years . . ." I let my voice drift away as I pictured my capricious sister before me. The truth was, I had no idea what I was going to say to her. I was only interested in finding her.

"But when you speak with her, you will not tell her about me?"

"If you don't want me to. But I'd like to know why. I'm entitled to that much."

"Yes you are, and I will tell you soon."

"And besides, what if you find her first?"

He smiled again, laughing a little this time, and said with obvious delight, "Miss Harris, I *have* found her first."

The words were like a thunderbolt. "What!"

His laughter grew as he withdrew an envelope from his hip pocket. In it was the small, blurred photograph of a crowd of people. He held it up to my eyes.

There was no mistaking it—Adele's face was in the crowd.

"That's her! That's my sister!" You would think I had died and gone to heaven. "Where is she? When was this taken?"

"One moment, please, and I shall explain. Is this really your sister? Good. I had thought so, but waited for your final identification. This photo was taken by a man who works for me. Two days ago I sent him on a small journey up the Nile. You Americans have a word for this—a hunch. And so I went after this 'hunch' and was quite successful as you can see. The man I sent followed certain information I gave to him, and he searched the area exceedingly well. This photo was the result."

I was confused. "Up the Nile! Searched the 'area.' What are you talking about? Isn't my sister in Cairo?"

"Not at all. Yesterday morning, when this photo was taken, your sister was in the city of Luxor, five hundred miles south of here."

I sat back in disbelief. Once again my ignorance of the world was showing. That there was another city in Egypt surprised me. And that Adele would go there baffled me even more. "Mr. Rasheed, what is in Luxor that would take my sister there?"

"It is not the city itself that she is involved with but rather something nearby. In the desert."

"The desert." That sounded more like Adele. Sand dunes and camels and sheikhs on wild horses. "You say you're going to tell me what this is all about?"

"Soon, but first . . ."

"Well, first Mr. Rasheed, I want to go after my sister."

"Do you think that is wise, Miss Harris? It is not safe for you."

"I've come this far. Listen, do you know what I've gone through for that girl? You don't think a silly little murder threat is going to stop me, do you?"

To my surprise, he laughed again. These Arabs had an annoying habit of turning everything into a joke.

"Of course you will go to her. As soon as possible."

I eyed him suspiciously.

"I am going to Luxor myself, and I would not expect you to remain behind."

No, not an annoying little habit after all, but just an easier way of accepting the distasteful in life. Thinking of the noise and the dirt and the poverty of the streets, I recalled also the smiles and the greetings and the pleasantness of everyone I saw. Ahmed Rasheed was typical of all Cairenes, easy going, winsome and with a flair for laughter.

"When can we go?" I asked in a small voice.

"We will leave tomorrow, by plane. There is a flight at one in the afternoon."

My heart went into tachycardia and my palms grew cold and moist. All of a sudden Adele was no longer a myth, but alive and just within a plane's reach. All of a sudden I was terribly excited.

"Can't we leave tonight?"

"There are no flights to Luxor tonight. We missed the last one."

"Isn't there *anything*?"

He saw the anxiety in my eyes and, knowing how he adored his own sister, must have understood a little of my feelings. "There is a train, but . . ."

"What's the matter? Has it left?"

"Not yet. Not until eight o'clock, but . . ."

I looked at my watch. It was six. "We can make it!" I cried. "When will it get us to Luxor?"

"At eight o'clock in the morning, but . . ."

"Please, Mr. Rasheed." I impulsively seized his hand. "We might lose her. I missed her in Rome. I couldn't bear to lose her again."

His fingers closed tightly about my hand. "But, Miss Harris, it is a long train ride, and the plane is so much nicer."

"But it arrives hours sooner! Please!"

He acquiesced. "Very well. But we must hurry. I have to go out for a few minutes first and during this time you will pack your suitcase. When I return, we will leave at once."

We stood together, our hands still clasped, and he saw the excitement in my eyes. "Miss Harris, this is dangerous business. You must not have too many hopes, for I fear you will be disappointed."

"I can handle disappointments by now, Mr. Rasheed. I've had enough practice."

As soon as he left, I went into the bedroom and packed my few belongings with care. I entertained the thought of putting the jackal in my handbag or my suitcase, but ended by leaving it tucked in the waistband of my trousers, hidden under my blouse. We had grown attached to one another, that little animal and I, and I had become accustomed to the feel of its hardness against my side. Indeed, it was almost a welcome feeling, for it periodically reminded me of reality, brought everything back into perspective, and kept me from drifting too far.

I paused before the mirror to look at myself. The reflection was still the same as always, a poor imitation of my beautiful sister, a little faded for the wear, a young woman who had always been fearless and unafraid of challenges. I gazed back at myself, wondering what my future would be after tonight, wondering if I would ever stand at an operating table again.

And just as these things happen, a brief and unimportant moment from my past suddenly came to mind, for it was the perfect example of the irony of my life. It had been two years before when, in a department store, I had been drawn into a discussion about comfortable shoes. The saleswoman had asked me what I did for a living, and upon my reply she had exclaimed, "A surgical nurse! My, but you must see life as it really is!"

I had agreed with her then, but I did not agree now, for I suddenly saw the operating room as nothing more than a protective cloister, a monastery in which to hide.

Far in the background I faintly heard the call of the muezzin. There was a vaster world beyond the operating room than I had ever suspected, and it was beginning to dawn on me that possibly I had not been so fearless and unafraid as I had always thought. It seemed more of a truism to me now, as I was about to embark upon another journey—this time up the Nile—that I was nothing more than a runaway, a hermit that didn't want anything to do with life beyond my own tiny sphere.

Well, that protection was gone now and I was on my own for the first time in my life. Now I truly had to be fearless and unafraid for both my sake and my sister's. And for the first time in years I did not have a surgical mask to hide behind.

The station derives its name from a colossal statue of Rameses II that stands at the front, but I only got a glimpse of the pharaoh because of the poor light and because I was not interested at the time. Rameses Station was an enormous complex of buildings, platforms, and trains. At this hour of the evening, with so many arrivals and departures, the entire area was what you would call "jam-packed" and seething with every type of humanity possible. No one paid any attention to a well-dressed Arab and a young American woman at his arm as we battled our way through the mob and the noise. Like any train station, it was vast and echoey, magnifying every voice, every shout, every scuffle. Natives in their long *galabias* and white *khafiyehs* stood about with crates of chickens and bundles bound with string. Women dressed entirely in black, a common sight in Cairo, with their eyebrows shaved and their most peculiar perfume clogging the air, stood in groups and prattled loudly as barefooted children clung to their dresses. Many balanced luggage on their heads. Many eyed me with curiosity as I passed. I tried not to stare back, but my mind boggled.

Ahmed steered me into an annex that was a coffee shop of sorts, although it was a bleak area with wobbly unmatching tables and chairs and the air was stuffy with smoke. The room was filled with men, mostly countryside farmers or uniformed soldiers who all gave me casual attention as my Arab companion sat me down. I had to say "What?" to him many times because of the din. Then he brought me the usual tea and struck out again. In the one minute he was gone I panicked, looking around at the brown, grinning faces. Those who caught my eye spoke to me in Arabic or said, "Welcome in Cairo." These I was not even polite to, I just ignored them. Anxiously I scanned the faces for a familiar one—Fatso with the Coke-bottle glasses or Arnold Rossiter. But there was not one westerner in the crowd. Filling all the available tables and standing in between, they were all Arabs of one type or another.

Ahmed came back not a moment too soon. He had tickets in his hand.

"Why are you not drinking your tea?"

"I'm too excited, I guess."

"But you must drink."

I looked again around the coffee shop. The walls were faded and chipped. The floor plain cement. No decoration anywhere. Not a picture, not a plant, not even fixtures over the naked light bulbs. Just a mob of happy, laughing Arabs.

"Are we in?"

"Yes. I have the tickets. At night there is only one train to the south which goes all the way down to Aswan and it is second class. I have purchased compartments for us so that we will have more privacy. You will be able to sleep."

"Great. If I can. When do we leave?"

"In fifteen minutes. You must drink your tea and then we will board the train."

I looked around the room again, the smoke stinging my eyes, and thought what I really needed was a drink. Why were there never any bars anywhere?

Ahmed kept an eye on me as I drank. He was half-smiling, as though not at me but at something in his mind. Those beautiful eyes of his looked almost mesmerized. I could do nothing but stare back.

"You are ready? We can go now."

"I'm for that."

He carried both our bags and then insisted I take hold of his arm as before. In my other hand I balanced a bundle which he had brought home before we left—a package from Asmahan. Food, no doubt. Then we tried to maneuver through the mob. I looked for signs leading to the trains, but there were none. Little in the way of the written word was to be seen, although simple pictures and arrows had been painted on the walls. This was because the majority of the train riders were illiterate.

At one point, crossing that endless room, I came loose from Ahmed and got shoved back. A thousand apologies came from the peasant who had done it, and Ahmed replied laughingly in Arabic. Then he handed me his bag which was lighter than mine, and with a free arm took me firmly about the shoulders as we started off again.

Once at the tracks he released me and took the other bag again. As soon as we stopped he motioned to a young boy standing nearby. When the child came running up, dressed in rags and his eyes cloudy with trachoma, Ahmed said something in Arabic, dropped a coin in the urchin's hands, and walked away. As he did so the boy grinned and saluted him.

I watched in amazement as this boy of about ten moved the bags closer to me and stood at my side until we almost touched.

"Are you my bodyguard?" I asked him.

Grinning up at me he said, "Welcome in Cairo. It is pleased to be you."

"Thank you."

He bowed stiffly. "Henry Kissinger, Missy."

"Yes, Henry Kissinger to you too."

We did not wait long, for Ahmed was back in an instant with a night-shirted man at his heels. He gave the boy another coin, sent him on his way, then handed our tickets to the porter. Bowing to me and muttering something unintelligible, the man picked up our bags and dashed deftly into the crowd. Ahmed seized my hand and we followed.

We reached the train and apparently the right car, for the man clambered aboard and we behind. When the door numbers matched the ticket numbers, the porter took our bags in, dusted off the seats, straightened the cushions, and said a number of "good healths" in Arabic. Ahmed gave him a few coins and he was gone.

"You know, we could have done this ourselves and saved money."

He gave me an odd look. "Our country is very poor, Miss Harris, and I do not doubt it is very simple compared to America. Many Egyptians need work. When there is no work, we make work. That man will have many children to feed and will work many hours for a few coins. Only a few are lucky, like myself, and since we are, we must help others. It is Allah's law."

"Yes, well . . ." The sermon made me uncomfortable, so I turned my attention to the compartment. It was outrageously small, but it was clean, and for that I was thankful. The floor space was about two feet by four, and there was a cupboard, a sink, and bunk beds. Altogether it was quite cozy.

"You like this?"

"Very much. I shall sleep like a log."

We both sat on the seat, and Ahmed closed the door. With so much of the noise cut down, he was better able to talk. "I am in the compartment next door, but I will remain here until the train is out of Cairo and until your ticket is taken. The conductor might not speak English. Then I will leave you and you will lock the door. Do you understand this?"

"Yes, sir."

"If you need me, knock on this wall and I shall hear you." He rapped a knuckle on the wall by my bed. "I shall come at once."

"All right."

"In Luxor we will go to a hotel—I do not know which one—the New Winter Palace will be full I believe, but the Winter Palace and the Luxor Hotel will have rooms. I did not have time to telephone. But they are nice places."

"Anywhere would suit me."

He smiled politely and looked at me sideways. "I think not, Miss Harris. I think you find my country distasteful. Perhaps it is so to Americans. I do not know what your country is like, but it must be very rich and very clean."

I almost said, "it is," when I realized he was being sarcastic. So I said, "I'll be honest with you, Mr. Rasheed. Until my sister called from Rome I had never been out of the U.S. Then in Rome I was amazed by all that I saw. Now, in Egypt, I am shocked by all I see because I'm unprepared. Postcards never tell the whole story. You can't blame me for being stunned!"

"I do not blame you for anything."

"Yes you do! I'm only reacting naturally. If anyone is acting proud and offended, it's you, because I think you're ashamed of Egypt and you're trying to be something you're not. You treat those poor beggars as though they are very far beneath you, and it makes you feel good to throw them a few coins. You're pretending to be better than they. Don't accuse me of something you're guilty of yourself, Mr. Rasheed."

He regarded me in stunned silence. Outside, beyond my window, were muffled cries in Arabic. It was a circus out there. And here I sat inside with this man whom I hardly knew and who really had me at his mercy. Then I thought, what the heck am I doing here?

I heard Ahmed Rasheed say, "Perhaps you are right, Miss Harris. I will not argue with you."

Then I looked at him again, his nacreous eyes and dark skin. If Ahmed were wearing the white *khaffiyeh* and black rope he would be a desert sheikh, mysterious and romantic. Yet he was just Ahmed Rasheed, government official doing his job.

"I'm sorry. I'm just tense. Listen," I had Asmahan's package in my lap, "let's break bread, okay?"

"I beg your pardon?"

"Let's eat." I whipped off the string and was about to tear the paper when he stopped me.

"Paper is precious, Miss Harris."

"Yes it is. Now then, we have here . . ."

"*Bortuáhn.*" He held up an orange. "*Bortuáhn sukaree.* And this is *torta.* And the bread is *aysh baladi.*"

I laughed. "And I am *hungree.*"

He laughed with me and we proceeded to devour the food.

When the train started, I opened the curtain and looked out of the window, though I could see little in the darkness. I saw my own face looking back at me, and in the background I saw Ahmed Rasheed watching me.

A conductor of sorts soon came. He was a young man dressed casually in slacks and a sweater. The tickets were examined, rubber stamped, torn, initialled, hole-punched, clipped, and then handed back to us. He and Ahmed enjoyed a pleasant conversation in Arabic, and the man left.

"Must you go to your compartment now?"

"Not yet. That man took our tickets for our fare only. Another will come by and take our compartment tickets."

"When there is no work . . ."

He smiled at me. "You understand."

When the second conductor had come, performed his duties, had a little chat with Ahmed, and gone, Ahmed gave me instructions. "Now I shall go, Miss Harris. You will please lock the door. And do not forget the wall," he tapped it again, "if you need me."

"I won't. And thank you. *Shokran.*"

"*Affuan,* Miss Harris. *Tesbáhi allah kheir.*"

"Good night."

I immediately locked the door and curled up on the seat with a blanket around me. I was tired and bewildered and thankful for a few moments in which to gather my thoughts. Quite naturally they went to Adele.

What would I find? This was my biggest question. I had no idea what sort of situation my sister was in. No idea what had happened to her between that first telephone call in Rome and now somewhere in the Egyptian desert. Had she been kidnapped? Was she in league with a gang of criminals? Or was she just alone and touring about?

A number of pictures came to mind. First I saw my sister tied with ropes and imprisoned in a tent with her mouth gagged. Then I saw her free and flirty, shopping for clothes in Luxor without the slightest awareness of all this dirty business.

But then there was the photograph. Yes, it was indeed her, but the picture was too undefined, too blurred to tell where she was precisely or what she was doing. Standing amid a crowd of natives in skull caps and *galabias,* Adele had her arms akimbo and was peering off to a point right of the camera, a puzzled expression on her face. She was wearing what appeared to be khaki pants and blouse with high black boots and her hair was trussed up in a haphazard way.

Not exactly Adele, but that didn't say everything. She'd do anything for a lark. If that's all this was—a lark. Or maybe that is how it started out, but not at all how it was now.

I unfolded the seat and crawled into bed fully dressed. I had but one change of clothing left. In Luxor, I would have to do some laundry.

As I lay in the dark listening to the clickety-clack of the train and as I was rocked gently by the sway, I gave fleeting thought to the close call I had had in the Mousky. There was no doubt in my mind now, that if Ahmed Rasheed had not shown up at just that point, my life would have been most certainly next to worthless.

Then I pictured my Egyptian traveling companion. Just who was he? Where was he taking me? What was going to happen? At this point, I trusted him, even though I was still bitter about John Treadwell and determined to never again be such an easy victim of charm and good looks. I had to trust Ahmed, I had no choice. Once, he had saved my life, and possibly twice if one considered the incident at the Shepherd's. Yes, I had to trust him, put myself in his hands and be at his mercy.

But I still could not help wondering . . . just who was Ahmed Rasheed?

CHAPTER 12

I AWOKE SEVERAL TIMES DURING THE NIGHT AND LOOKED OUT but saw little. There was only the clickety-clack, the rhythmic sway of the train, and a blur beyond my window. I had difficulty sleeping, and when I did I was visited by bizarre dreams. The first glimmer of sunrise across the river was impetus enough for me to rise and prepare for the day ahead.

Donning slacks and a shirt I then unraveled the mechanics of the sink, managed to wash in it, and put my face back together. All things considered I was looking not half-bad.

After a bold trek to the toilet at the end of the car, a feat of maneuvering in itself, I tripped back to my compartment, locked the door, and lit a cigarette while waiting for the sun to come up. A few pieces of Asmahan's spicy cake found their way to my mouth as I sat with knees drawn to my chest. On the other side of the window, a strange and fascinating picture began to take shape. It was scenery I had never seen before. Each new ray of sun revealed another detail of the Egyptian countryside. And as it brightened in the early sun, the fertile Nile Valley emerged as an awesome, breathtaking panorama.

Our train was heading southward on the west bank, traveling at a speed of about fifty miles per hour. It was 5:30 a.m. when the sun rose fully and completely illuminated the scene. We made a brief stop at, a dilapidated station called Griga, and pushed forward again. By now I could see everything about me and marveled at all I saw.

There were cows and pastures and farms everywhere. A green so brilliant and refreshing that I felt exhilarated just seeing it. Oxen and camels, their ribs protruding, turned great waterwheels to irrigate the vegetation. Scrawny dogs scavenged in the fields. Sun-blackened peasants in white *galabias* were already up and toiling in the coolness of morning. Later on, I imagined, everything would stop for siesta at the hottest time of day.

The buildings we passed were simple, with holes that served as doors and windows. They were dirty and lopsided and stood clustered in the dust at the edge of the grassland. Towns and villages, if you could call them that, were no more than rows of mudbrick dwellings populated by leathery farmers and their veiled women who walked with enormous loads on their heads.

Fields and fields of sugarcane sped past me. More sugarcane, I thought, than must even be found in Hawaii. There were miles of it, this sweet stuff that fed people who drank sweet tea and ate sweet pastries. Then there were date palms, row upon row of them, and cotton fields and wheat fields, each squared off by dusty roads which must have marked the individual farms of the *fellahin* who worked them.

As the train clattered past the towns, hordes of youths and children ran to the tracks to wave and shout. They wore the long white nightshirts or, the younger ones, nothing. They were all brown and black and dirty and smiling. Dogs barked at the train whistle. Isolated cattle turned and ran, startled. This was another Egypt.

A sound incongruous with the clickety-clack made me look up. Someone was knocking at my door. I listened before saying, "Who is it?"

"Ahmed Rasheed. Did I wake you?"

"Not at all." I hastened to open the door and saw his smiling face. "*Sabah el kheir*," I said.

"*Sabah el kheir,* Miss Harris. Have you slept well?"

"What do you think?"

"I am going for tea. Will you come with me?"

"There's a dining car? Far out! Let me grab my bag."

We bumped and staggered our way back, making death-defying transfers between three cars, until we came to the diner. It was empty at this early hour, but the tables were all covered with clean cloths and the aroma of coffee filled the air. We took a table on the left side so that we rode by the Nile, with me facing the engine. We ordered tea and coffee from the white-coated waiter and then fell to staring at the passing view.

"Do you make this trip often, Mr. Rasheed?"

"Many times, but I always fly; it is faster. Sometimes I am in a hurry."

I looked at my hands. "Your job calls for that?"

"Yes it does. Miss Harris, I promised you that I would make an explanation. Now I shall do it." He paused when the waiter returned.

I said, "*Shokran,*" and the man said "*Affuan affuan!*" excitedly.

Smiling, Ahmed said, "They are not used to Americans who speak Arabic. You please them when you do."

"You were going to explain something, Mr. Rasheed," I said, watching him drop four sugar cubes into his tea. From a silver pot I poured my cup half full with coffee, then added hot milk. It was almost good this way.

"Yes, I shall. First I must tell you who I am. My work is at the Ministry of Culture, and I am an official of the Service of Antiquities."

"You are an archaeologist?"

"More or less, although not as you think. I do not dig. But I am an expert in ancient artifacts. I must be for my job."

"You work in the museum?"

"No, no. Please, Miss Harris, I shall tell you. You said you thought I was a policeman. In a way you are right, although I am more correctly a detective—an investigator." Now he reached into his coat pocket and withdrew a small leather wallet which he flipped open to reveal a badge and an identification card. Both were in Arabic only.

"What do you investigate?"

"The manufacture and illegal sale of false artifacts."

My eyes flew open. "*False* artifacts! My jackal!"

"But also in my job I must search for men who are illegally smuggling *genuine* artifacts out of Egypt."

"Then which am I involved in?"

"The second one, Miss Harris. Your jackal is indeed genuine and approximately three thousand years old. I have estimated it to come from the twentieth dynasty of our pharaohs."

"You've seen it?"

"When you were asleep in my flat after we left the Shepherd's Hotel."

I opened my mouth to say something but quickly closed it.

He went on: "Does the name Paul Jelks have a meaning for you?"

"No."

"He is a British archaeologist currently working in the desert near Luxor. We have been watching him for a while now."

"And he is the criminal you're after?"

"I do not know. But we are definitely interested in arresting Arnold Rossiter, whom we have been hunting for three years now, and he escapes us each time. He has murdered more than once as well as smuggled our precious artifacts out of Egypt. He must be stopped."

"Do you think he's working for Paul what's-his-name?"

"Jelks. We can only guess, although I do not think so. It started a few weeks ago when word reached my office that a young woman—your sister—was going to the antiquities dealers in the Khan el-Khalili and asking for the value of a certain ivory jackal. She did not want to sell it, but only wanted a price quoted, which is odd. It was almost as if she was tempting the sellers of registered antiquities to buy something other than the jackal. As though the jackal were only—how do you say—bait? Naturally my office was interested, all the more so since my sources indicated that it was genuine. Very few such fine pieces circulate at a given moment. She would not tell anyone where she had obtained it. So I asked about and eventually followed your sister's trail to Rome where she contacted John Treadwell at the Residence Palace Hotel. She showed him the jackal and they spoke a while. When I was planning to approach her, she suddenly disappeared and so did John Treadwell. In a few days, you, Miss Harris, arrived in Rome. Quite naturally I was curious about your position in this."

I nodded dumbly. "So what does all this mean?"

"I can only make you a theory, Miss Harris, but I believe it is close to the truth. Your sister must have become friends with Paul Jelks in Luxor and is working with him. Arnold Rossiter is after what Paul Jelks is trying to sell. And I believe you are caught in the middle."

"Well then, just what—if not the jackal—is Paul Jelks trying to sell?"

"We believe," he dropped his voice and looked around, "we believe it is the contents of a newly discovered tomb."

I thoughtfully stirred my coffee until it was cold. The clickety-clack sounded far away and distant. The green and yellow colors sped past my window ignored. I was trying to recall what I had read of ancient Egyptian tombs.

At Dr. Kellerman's house one evening after dinner we had adjourned to his den to sit for a while and play a few games of cards when he had been called to the hospital for an emergency. I had remained at his insistence and had, out of restlessness, browsed among his books. The one I chose to entertain me for the while had been brightly bound and full of glossy photos. The title had been *Tutankhamun*. Having only intended to glance through the volume to pass the time, I had become engrossed in the text—the story of a remarkable discovery in a place called the Valley of the Kings. And I remembered some interesting facts: how rare it was to come upon such a well-stocked tomb; how the treasures within had been valued as "priceless"; how the artifacts had filled in many blank pages of ancient Egyptian history; how the archaeologists involved had made great names for themselves; how the world had applauded their achievement.

I looked at Ahmed Rasheed in puzzlement. "I haven't heard of a tomb being discovered."

"But that is it, don't you see? This is a secret. No one knows of it at all. Indeed, I am not even certain this is what has happened."

"You mean a tomb might have been discovered and they have kept it to themselves?"

"We believe so."

"But why keep it a secret?"

"Possibly so the discoverer can sell the contents to a man like Arnold Rossiter and leave the country a far richer man than when he came."

"But Jelks could just as easily sell the antiquities himself, couldn't he? Why use Rossiter?"

"Because, Miss Harris, anything that is found in the Egyptian desert belongs to the Egyptian people. These days are not like the days of Howard Carter and William Petrie. In the past there was wholesale export of Egyptian treasures to the museums of the world, while our own country saw none, or very little, of it. Since then new laws have been made, and men like myself have been appointed to see that these laws are upheld. We do not want our heritage to be spirited away to a foreign country when we would proudly display it ourselves for our own people. When a tomb is excavated, it is done so under the protective eye of the Egyptian government. And whatever leaves our country is decided upon by the Service of Antiquities. Needless to say, there are unscrupulous men who will ignore these laws and try to steal our heritage for a great deal of money."

"My God." I shook my head. "You think Paul Jelks found a tomb like that of Tutankhamun and is trying to get the treasures out by smuggling?"

"Or at least sell them to a man like Rossiter who will then smuggle them out of Egypt, yes."

"And Adele? Where does she come in?"

Ahmed Rasheed shrugged. "I cannot say. Possibly she is not aware of what is happening. Possibly Dr. Jelks sent her to the Kahn el-Khalili to value the jackal by telling her that he had a small collection of the pieces to sell. I do not know."

"Then she went to John Treadwell for some reason, then called me for some reason, then disappeared for some reason after mailing the jackal to me . . . for some reason. Oh wow." I tasted the coffee. It was awful.

"This is only a theory, Miss Harris, but it is all we have right now."

"Well look, maybe Adele doesn't know this Jelks person. Maybe she found the jackal or bought it in Luxor."

"Then why did she go to Rome to see Mr. Treadwell?"

"What is Arnold Rossiter up to? Why didn't he just accept her deal in Rome and come to get the stuff? What happened?"

"We do not know. She showed the jackal to John Treadwell, possibly as proof of the great treasures that are still in the tomb, then vanished, and we do not know why. When you appeared in Rome with the jackal . . ."

I smiled weakly. "I know what you must have thought. I'm sorry I was so nasty to you, Mr. Rasheed. I just wish you had told me sooner."

"How could I? At first, in Rome, I did not trust you. I was not certain you were Adele Harris's sister, but simply a person working with Arnold Rossiter. I thought it was a disguise particularly since you were traveling with John Treadwell. But after his murder and after I brought you home, I began to believe you. And now I am certain you are telling the truth."

"Thanks." I sighed heavily and looked about me. A few more passengers had entered the dining car and were chatting happily. The train made a brief stop at a place called Denderah. My watch said seven o'clock.

"What will be our first stop in Luxor, Mr. Rasheed?"

"First, we must go to a hotel. Then I will talk with the two men I have working in Luxor. We will see if they have found your sister and can tell us where she is. If not, then I think we will do some research of our own in Luxor's bazaars."

"I'm nervous. Arnold Rossiter is bound to be there." I shook my head again. A train rattling up the Nile Valley was certainly a far cry from Santa Monica Hospital. "Tell me something, Mr. Rasheed. Why were they after my jackal as well as me? I mean, why search my room for it?"

"They must have thought it would give them a clue as to the whereabouts of the tomb. Certain climatic conditions can appear on ancient objects, giving away the region of burial. Or possibly the style of craftsmanship of the jackal would tell them the dynasty and therefore give a lead to the whereabouts of the tomb. Different dynasties used different burial areas. They are looking for the tomb, Miss Harris, not you or your sister. They are following you in order to find your sister who will then lead them to the tomb, they hope."

"And so do you."

"Yes."

"And once the tomb is found?"

"They would have no further use for you."

"But I could tell the authorities."

"Only if you were alive."

His words were no surprise. I had reached that conclusion already. If Arnold Rossiter found the tomb without me, then I could be "put out of the way" conveniently to prevent my going to the authorities. "Why did he kill John Treadwell?"

Again he shrugged. This is what annoyed me most, the tiny amount of positive information and the horrendous number of blank spaces.

We were going to have to fill them in fast.

I sat close to the window as we neared the station at Luxor. Ahmed was in his own compartment getting his things together so that I spent these last few minutes in deep thought. All of what he said I believed, including the most bizarre facts. Suddenly I had complete faith in him, and even looked to him for my own saving. He *had* to find Adele, and he *had* to keep us from the clutches of Rossiter. After all, that was his job.

The train slowed again. Up ahead a broken sign said *Kus* in English and, presumably, Arabic. The view from my window was not of a mudbrick station, but of the arid desert and bleached landscape. We were on the right bank now, on the eastern side of the Nile, having crossed over at Denderah. Luxor was on the east bank, and it was just minutes ahead. I gazed out with unblinking eyes. From this side of the compartment I saw only an orange, endless desert that stretched for miles. On the other side, I knew, were the familiar green fields and lush farm lands. But here was the Egyptian desert, populated by scorpions, cobras, vultures and wild jackals. An occasional brown weed popped up through the hard sand. A few cacti refused to give way to the intense heat and dryness. I stared blankly out, my mind a turmoil of thoughts.

Then my eyes began to focus. Unconsciously, while I meditated, they began to close in on the details of the landscape before me, but it was not for some minutes that my mind was aware of what my eyes were looking at.

Stretching for some yards away from the now slow-moving train were the bleaching skeletons of large animals. They were all intact and lying on their sides, the giant rib cages like white wrought-iron fences. I straightened when I realized what these things were, then my eyes moved quickly to other sights, objects I had not at first noticed. One was a starving cow, standing among the bones of her ancestors, her tail swishing slowly. Her head hung low and her breathing was labored. Not far from her lay the fresh body of a dead bull, on its side with two legs in the air. Opposite them lay the half-rotted corpse of another cow, dead for some days and alive with flies. More and more carcasses appeared among the whitened skeletons. Some of them were more decayed than others. Some were only slightly decomposed, others barely recognizable. Then, off to the side, a scrawny bull walked slowly to the area and stood when he was within its limits.

I sat up straight now and felt a jolt as the train started to speed up. My eyes glued to the cattle burial ground, I continued to gape until the area was completely out of sight. Then I sat back in my seat and stared ahead in bewilderment. On the outskirts of the little village of Kus in Upper Egypt was a burial ground to which cattle wandered when they were to die.

Ahmed Rasheed must have been standing in my doorway for some time before I noticed him. And when I did, I must have said something like, "I can't believe my eyes," because he came back with a secretive smile and the words: "You have not yet seen the Valley of the Kings."

The New Winter Palace was like any modern hotel in the United States with the exception that the view from its balconies was unlike any other in the world. We had been fortunate in finding two rooms available upon our arrival, although I secretly believe Ahmed's influence had something to do with it. I left my passport at the desk and went up in the lift with Ahmed and our brightly dressed porter. He grinned and bobbed up and down and said, "Henry Kissinger." Again fortunate in our circumstances, we were able to get two rooms adjoining, so Ahmed Rasheed was no more than a tap on the wall away. I liked the room at once. It was bright and airy and had the very latest in plumbing. The bath was new and clean and the crisp towels were lettered with "Upper Egypt Hotels Co." And the view, the view! It took my breath away! Several floors up, we overlooked the powder blue Nile River and could see the well-preserved Temple of Luxor to our right. On the left stood the brown Winter Palace, formerly *the* place to stay when visiting Luxor, now the hotel to go to when the New Winter was full. The town of Luxor itself stretched behind us to the desert and up and down the Nile a few miles. Here the river remains unbridged, as it was when the ancients lived on this bank, with the other side relegated to the dead. On the western bank stood some of the greatest ancient monuments in the world.

I stood with Ahmed Rasheed on that balcony like someone who had just been awakened after a long sleep. I could not speak for a long time, but lingered instead over the green palm trees and lush banks of the river and listened to the clop-clop of the horse carriages below. Hardly any motor traffic disturbed us here. Everyone was either a pedestrian or went by horse or donkey. Directly below was the beautifully landscaped garden of the hotel itself, then there was the paved road, then the Nile itself. On the river floated the ever present *feluccas,* their triangular sails silhouetted against a morning sun. A large river boat was moored below, one that carries tourists who have both the time and money on leisurely two-week cruises from Cairo to Aswan. And two large ferry boats sat moored together, awaiting visitors to the Valley of the Kings.

Everywhere I looked were sights that delighted me. For a while, standing there with a cool breeze refreshing me and with Ahmed Rasheed speaking softly about the things we saw, I was able to forget the work that was ahead of us.

Then he reminded me. "On that side are the most famous sites in Egypt. Hatshepsut's Temple, the Colossus of Memnon, the Valley of the Queens, and the Valley of the Kings . . ."

"Is that where Paul Jelks is?"

"That is where he is supposed to be, where he received permission to be. We will find his camp there, anyway."

"And Adele, too?"

"I hope so."

"And that damned tomb?"

He dipped his head to the side.

"Why didn't you come here in the first place?"

"I would have if you had not appeared. First, I had to follow Adele to Rome and question her there. And when she disappeared I was making different plans for my search. But then you arrived, in the company of John Treadwell, and I was sure I could follow you to your sister. As it was, however, I found her first through my two agents here."

"And I've been following you to my sister."

"As it happens, yes."

"Have you ever met this Paul Jelks?"

"Only once. Dr. Jelks came to my office to apply for his permit to work here."

"But if he was excavating with your knowledge and approval, how could he expect to keep his find a secret?"

"He was not supposed to be excavating at all; there was no permit issued for this. He was given permission to photograph in the already discovered tombs. Some have not been fully documented and the wall paintings may deteriorate with the changing climatic conditions brought about by the High Dam at Aswan."

"How could he dig without your knowing of it?"

"It is a big desert. We cannot be in all places at all times. He could not dig in the Valley itself, but elsewhere, yes, it is possible."

"Wow," I said for the hundredth time that morning. I glanced over at the magnificent Luxor Temple and imagined all the work that had gone into its excavation and restoration. I remembered the many months and hardships of Howard Carter before he came, by accident, upon Tutankhamun's tomb. Then I thought of Paul Jelks, British Egyptologist, and my sister, Adele, digging for a tomb in the vast expanse of the desert.

"I wish I had come here before now. And for another reason. I could love it."

"I hope you do. It is unfortunate that politics keeps many people away. And our wars frighten them. Since June 1967 our tourism has dropped. And then there was the Ramadhan War. Americans do not wish to come here."

"The Ramadhan War?"

"It was in October."

"You mean the Yom Kippur War."

"Is that what you call it?" He gave me a look of surprise. "The Yom Kippur War?" Then he gradually smiled. "I see . . . "

"But I had always thought Americans were disliked over here. Yet, I never found that. In Cairo, people were friendly towards me, especially when they learned I was American."

"Some may be jealous of your country's money, or its power. But people are the same all over, I think," he laughed flippantly. "It is a beautiful day, let us not talk of such serious things. And also, I must start my work. I must speak with my two agents here before we do anything else. You may wish to rest—I know you could not have slept well on the train, if only because you are anxious to find your sister, as indeed I am. So I want you to remain in this room while I am gone."

"All right," I said reluctantly.

"I will come back after I have spoken to my men. Then we will have lunch and discuss a plan that I have."

"Certainly," I said without enthusiasm. "But why can't I look for my sister now? God, she might even be in the lobby of this hotel!"

"It would not be safe. Instead of you finding your sister, Mr. Rossiter may find you. And then I would be looking for you both."

"Yes, I see. Of course, we'll do as you say."

"It is best, I know. We must not rush now and spoil everything."

I walked him to the door and locked it after him. Then I went back to the balcony and stood for a long time.

I had taken a good shower and washed my hair by the time he returned. It was noon and getting warm, so I closed the curtains to keep the heat out. Ahmed knocked distinctly on the door and I let him in. "Well?"

"It is not good, I am afraid." He sat down in the chair and I on the bed opposite.

"What do you mean? What did you find out?"

"The photograph was taken three days ago. They have not seen your sister since."

"Didn't they go out to the camp?"

"No, I told them not to. When we approach Paul Jelks, I must be the one to do it. I know all the facts. My men could make a mistake and all could be lost. They did as they were told, and they did well to photograph your sister in the crowd and not be noticed themselves. Then they lost your sister's trail and she has not been seen since."

"At least you hope your men were not noticed."

"True."

"Then my sister must be at the camp," I insisted.

"I would like to think so."

My face fell. He raised his eyes to me and I didn't like what I saw. "I cannot give you false hope, Miss Harris."

"What are you thinking?"

"That Arnold Rossiter might have gotten here first."

"Then we must go to the camp at once! Now!"

"We would not be wise to go there now. It is best to go early in the morning. Believe me, I know best."

"Did your men learn anything about Jelks?"

"Only that he is doing his job in the Valley of the Kings, though his progress is slower than expected. A young American woman comes into the town once a week for supplies. Sometimes she stays overnight in this hotel."

"Adele. So she *is* working with him. She must have gone back to the camp."

"I hope so."

"So do I."

We were silent for a moment, then he broke in with, "I am hungry, Miss Harris. Will you come down with me?"

"I'm not hungry, but I'll join you."

The dining room was quite large and filled with hungry tourists. We found a small table by the wall and several waiters attended to us. The tea was delicious and the atmosphere relaxing. Somewhere in the back of my mind was the thought that someday I would have to come back to Egypt as a casual tourist.

After he had finished eating and we were sitting quietly over our tea, I said in a low voice, "What's this plan you wanted to discuss?"

"Ah yes." Ahmed leaned back in his chair and glanced about. The dining room was by now nearly empty, and those few patrons still about were far from us. The waiters also were beyond hearing. So he leaned forward and said, "Everything that I have told you so far, Miss Harris, is theory only. There are no facts. But frequently in my work all we have are theories. It was upon rumor alone that I began the investigation, and it was upon the most fragile evidence that I continued it. That is to say, following a young American girl to Rome who possessed an artifact of unknown origin and who then contacted the agent of an internationally known art smuggler—all this is what you would call hypothetical." He pronounced it, "Hypothetical."

"And it is only a theory that our source is Paul Jelks. He could be innocent, although we can think of no other likely suspect. We know where he is camped. Were we to go now, and demand a search or ask incriminating questions, we might find nothing and put him on the alert so that we would never learn the truth. If it is not Jelks, then whoever it is could hear of our questioning and thus find a way to elude us. You see, Miss Harris, it is delicate work for we are dealing with crafty people. They are not stupid, and neither must we be."

"Then what are we going to do?"

He looked around again and leaned a little closer. "I must have more certain proof before I go to Paul Jelks. If there is any way that I can know for certain it is he, then I will waste no more time in approaching him. If I were to find that it is indeed Paul Jelks who is offering artifacts for sale, then I can go to his camp and by my authority confiscate all that he holds. And then question him until he reveals the whereabouts of the tomb."

"If there is a tomb."

Ahmed inclined his head a little.

"Well, how do you get this proof then?"

"Perhaps not proof, Miss Harris, but possibly only a clue to tell me that my theories are correct, and for this reason I have devised a plan. But it requires your help."

"You must be kidding. I'll be glad to help."

"And," his voice was somber, "it is dangerous."

"So? I haven't been in danger so far?"

He smiled and relaxed by visible degrees. "Very well then. This is my plan. My agents have been to all the dealers of antiquities in Luxor, and very few would admit to having seen a jackal in the possession of a young American girl. There are reasons for this. One could be that very few were indeed the only ones she visited, but I doubt this, for it would not make sense for her not to have gone to all of them. Another reason for so few admitting to it would be these dealers' wariness of government officials. These men must be careful to protect their licences. They fear that if they were . . . how do you say it . . . implicated in illegal dealings, they could lose their licences. And so, when questioned by government agents they are . . . mouth-closed."

"Closemouthed."

"Yes, and they will not tell us if they have seen this American girl with the jackal. Possibly some have even offered to take the tomb contents, and grew afraid when my men came by to question them. There are many ifs here, Miss Harris."

"So what's your plan?"

"I had thought that if the same American girl were to return to those dealers with her jackal and pretend to offer more, perhaps she would find them willing to talk to her."

"Adele? But how?"

"No, Miss Harris. I mean you."

We went over it and over it for the next hour until we were both satisfied. I was not afraid. If Ahmed's plan worked then I would find my sister. And that was all that mattered.

I was simply to go to the shops of the licensed antiquities dealers, dangle the jackal before them like bait, and wait for one to make a slip. It was risky, but worth it.

"We cannot go now, for the shops are closed and do not reopen until four. It is now two o'clock. Shall we walk for a little while before starting our work?"

We stepped out of the New Winter Palace Hotel into a quiet afternoon of warm breezes and floral scents. Like Cairo, Rome, like so many other cities in the hotter climates, Luxor went to sleep between one o'clock and four to pass through the warmest part of the day. It was a custom I found pleasant and, anxious though I was to get on with finding Adele, I welcomed the chance to slow down after a string of hectic days.

Al Nil Street ran parallel with the river and led from below the hotel northward to as far as anyone wanted to walk, although we went only a short distance. Ahmed and I did not speak much, keeping to ourselves and our private thoughts. I could not guess what was going on in his mind, but in mine were the same unanswered questions. This evening, in the shops of the dealers, what was I going to learn about the jackal and my sister?

We circled Luxor Temple, on the other side of which was a city park where we were assailed by urchins crying, "Baksheesh, baksheesh!" Ahmed gave them some coins and sent them away. We continued along Al Nil Street until we came to the Savoy Hotel.

The temperature was slowing us down. Ahmed found a stone bench that we could sit on, shaded by a tree, and look out over the Nile. It was a peaceful moment, watching the *feluccas* glide gracefully over the river and listening to the water lap gently against the grass. I was at peace sitting there and felt almost serene. Luxor was a beautiful town—quiet and picturesque, and it made me sad to think that such circumstances had brought me here. Domus Aurea and John Treadwell were far away from us, as if they had only happened in a dream.

And Adele was somewhere nearby. She was either in the town or across the river in that wasteland of sand. Or she had gone on somewhere else. But I was tired of this mystery and of the hectic pace I had had to keep up. I would have liked to stay here for a month and sit by the Nile every day, just dreaming. It would have been so easy with someone like Ahmed Rasheed.

Horses clopped behind us carrying pairs of tourists up to the Karnak

Temple. I turned occasionally to glance over my shoulder at them, each carriage different, each gaily decorated according to the owner's taste.

Out of nowhere Ahmed said to me, "Will you ride one?"

"I beg your pardon?"

"A carriage. You are watching them. We can ride to Karnak and back. Or around Luxor. Will you like that?"

"All right, that would be very nice."

It was not long before an empty carriage trotted by and Ahmed waved him down. Helping me in first he told the driver to go to Karnak Temple, then he settled back with me and proceeded to give me a bit of Egyptian history.

But I was not listening. I was miles away and worlds apart from what he was trying to tell me. My mind was drifting, it was soaring over that powder blue river and looking down on the world below. Whoever Lydia Harris once was, she had changed. She had changed such a great deal in these past ten days that it was hard to remember what she was once like.

No, more than changing . . . it was almost as if I was *awakening.*

Then I thought of Dr. Kellerman. I thought of the many times he had asked me to call him by his first name, and yet I had never been able to. What was it about our relationship that seemed so extraordinary to me now? How clear it was all of a sudden, how easy to recognize what passed between us. I knew now that Dr. Kellerman loved me and had been, in his awkward way, reaching out to me. And yet I had been blind to it.

No, that was not true. I had only thought I had been blind to his offer of love, but in reality I had only been fooling myself by pretending not to see his reaching out. I had lied to myself, convinced myself it was not there, and had shied from the affection he was trying to give me. Why? Why had I refused to recognize the tender emotion Dr. Kellerman had been offering?

Perhaps I will never know. But what I know now and realized that day in the carriage with Ahmed Rasheed was that all my life I had avoided falling in love with any man. One could speculate on it, of course, and theorize, but the fact remained that I had turned my back on love.

How ironic that I had always thought myself a courageous woman, bravely facing any challenge and meeting it head-on. That first aortic aneurysm with Dr. Kellerman, my first brain tumor, and a host of other challenges I had all my life gone out of my way to face and to fight and to overcome. But, in the end, I wasn't brave, nor did I face real challenges, for the biggest challenge of all was falling in love, and this I shied away from.

As my eyes strayed over the scenery around us, I casually studied the man at my side. All my life, objects and things had been my strength, and I had shunned people and avoided involvements. But I was changing now. I had first noticed it in Cairo and felt it growing within me. A strength, possibly even a courage I had never before known.

Ahmed was staring off to the roadside, his intense eyes involved in lost thought. I wondered what he must think of me, what was going to happen to us after this was all over.

He is so foreign, I thought to myself, and we are worlds apart. Is it possible to fall in love with this enigmatic man?

"The Avenue of Rams," I heard a voice say.

I looked at Ahmed. "What?"

"You asked me what those statues are."

"I did?"

"They are crouching rams that lead to the pylons of Karnak Temple. Great pharaonic processions once moved between these animals. They are gods."

I continued to stare at Ahmed Rasheed. "I should read all about this," I heard myself say. "There is so much to it."

He laughed softly. "You have not been listening to me."

"What do you mean?"

"It is in your eyes. But you are polite. You must not think of your sister now . . ."

"I wasn't thinking of her. Really I wasn't. I was thinking . . . of someone back home."

"I see. A friend?"

"Well, yes. He's a very good friend. And he's the only one who knows why I came here. I tried to call him from Cairo . . ."

"And he works at your hospital?"

"You might say that. He's a surgeon."

"I see," said Ahmed Rasheed again, although I didn't think he did.

I thought again of Dr. Kellerman, and I thought of this swarthy man next to me who spoke with a strange, nasal accent and was so alien to me. Was it possible to love two men at once?

Ahmed was watching my face closely. When he asked, "Why are you not married?" I was not terribly surprised.

And when I replied with a shrug, he did not seem surprised.

"Why aren't you?" I asked in return.

"I was once."

"Oh . . ."

"My wife died four years ago of something you call diabetes. It was very fast. She could not be saved."

"Diabetes! God, I'm sorry." To my modern way of thinking, people did not die of that disease these days. There were drugs, treatments. But then again, people still died of polio and smallpox, and *that's* hard to believe. "I didn't mean to be nosy . . ."

"But I asked you first." He was smiling again. "We must know something about each other if we are to be friends. Now you know all about me."

"It's that simple?"

"That simple."

I sank back into the carriage and closed my eyes. In my mind I saw Ahmed Rasheed pouring sugar into his tea. Then I opened my eyes and looked at him. So he was both naïve and worldly at the same time. Like all Egyptians, he had the innocence of a child and the guile of the Semites.

"It is getting late," he said, looking at his watch.

"Yes, it is," I murmured.

But they were two different kinds of love. The one for Dr. Kellerman, so tender and quiet, had always been there, like a gentle whisper behind my heart. But my new feelings for Ahmed Rasheed were confused, exciting, arousing sleeping passions. Was this possible?

"Now, we will go back to the hotel and, from there, we will go to the bazaar. Miss Harris, you are certain of this?"

I looked into those wide, clear eyes. Now I trusted him, felt safe with him, was excited by him, and falling in love with him . . .

"I'm not afraid."

CHAPTER 13

I felt a little odd about having the jackal once again in my handbag—so long had I carried it under my blouse. I had felt secure and confident with it so intimately cached, but now, out of its secret hiding place and in the open, almost defenseless, I felt ill at ease. And to have to display it, as bait, made me apprehensive.

"There are many shops in Luxor which sell registered antiquities, and we cannot go to all of them. However, I have made a list of those we suspect Paul Jelks might attempt dealing with. They are men who have large businesses and handle large amounts of merchandise. Now, are you certain of what you are to do?"

"Yes. It's not hard. All I do is go into the shop and browse around to see if anyone mistakenly recognizes me as Adele. If not, I approach the dealer with the jackal and get his reaction. If still nothing, then I ask him if he remembers it. From there I play it by ear."

"Excellent. You know I cannot come inside with you, but must remain outside, unseen."

"Yes, I know that."

He paused to regard me. Then, to my surprise, he took hold of my hand and, squeezing it tightly, said, "Lydia, you run a great risk doing this. You may change your mind if you wish. You do not have to do it."

But I shook my head. "I'm just as anxious to end all this as you. Maybe more."

"Very well then. We will begin."

The best and most expensive shops are found near the New Winter Palace, so this is where we started. The first, located in a complex of souvenir, clothing and jewelry shops was the establishment of Mohammed Rageb, licensed dealer in antiquities. The sign above the door, lettered in gold, gave his government licence number.

It was a spacious, well-lit shop with large glass windows on two sides and modern lighting fixtures in the ceiling, and room to move among the displays of furniture and statuary. As the owner was engaged with another customer, I browsed through his merchandise keeping a constant eye on the front door. If anyone suddenly walked in, I wanted to be ready.

"Good afternoon, madam," said the Arab, seeing me. The other customers walked out, so I was alone with him in the shop.

"Hello."

"What can I help you with?" He came close, smelling strongly of potatoes and onions.

"Well, I'm not sure . . ." I turned toward him in order to give him a good look at my face. He did not visibly react as if he recognized me.

"Perhaps madam is interested in jewelry. Please step this way." He indicated a long glass counter along one wall and walked toward it.

I carefully picked my way through the fragile antiquities: large statues of pharaohs and queens; giant vases of ancient design; delicate tables inlaid with ivory. Every item displayed a tag attesting to its authenticity and a registration number given it by the government.

The Arab hurried behind the counter and at once started to withdraw trays of jewelry. None of it could have been newer than a thousand years old.

His pudgy hands picked up a large heavy piece of gold, fashioned into the shape of a vulture and inlaid with semiprecious stones. "This pectoral is nineteenth dynasty, Thebes," he said with onion breath. "Take it, madam, and look closely. You might believe that the exquisite inlay of the wings and body are of lapis lazuli, or carnelian or felspar. But you see, they are not. These are ancient glass, and so well done that even experts have difficulty telling the difference. The ancient Egyptians attempted to make imitations of gemstones with glass, and you see that their glass was not like ours. See how it lacks shine, not like modern glass at all, because of a lower proportion of silica and lime. Now run your finger over it, madam. Tiny bubbles of air near the surface give the glass the same texture as the stone it is imitating. Very clever, our ancestors."

"Yes, well . . ." I put the pectoral down.

"I have some amethyst pieces of the Middle Kingdom," he said hurriedly. "Quarried in the Aswan district. Or perhaps madam is interested in something later. This necklace is made of beryl and dates from Hellenistic times."

"No thank you, I don't think so."

"Would madam like some tea perhaps. I was just about to . . ."

"I'm in something of a hurry, Mr. Rageb, so I'll come to the point. I would like you to look at something for me."

"Very well."

Keeping my hands steady, I drew out the bundle from my bag, unwrapped the jackal and laid it on the counter between two trays of jewelry. I watched the Arab's face closely for any untoward reaction—there was none.

He stared down at it, picked it up to examine it, then said, "What is it you wish to know?"

So Adele had not been to him. "Its age and possibly the area of origin."

"Ah, madam, how can I say? This piece of ivory is part of a set. I can tell you nothing about it unless I see the others. Or possibly the game box it came in. Do you have that?"

"No."

"Of course not. Ivory is more durable than ebony. The game pieces survive the centuries, but the boxes on which they were played do not. The few that there are, museums have."

"Would you know where I could purchase such a game box, or possibly the rest of the set?"

He shook his head sadly. "Nothing would give me greater pleasure, madam, than to be able to sell such items to you."

"Well, thank you anyway." I quickly rewrapped the jackal, stuffed it in my bag and hurried out.

Ahmed was standing across the street, under a tree on the grassy river bank. "Nothing there," I said as I joined him. "Not the slightest recognition. He wasn't even interested in where I got it."

"Then we must go on."

I went into three more shops near the New Winter Palace, all as fruitless as Rageb's, so that Ahmed and I ended by standing once again on the lush river bank, out of view.

"Now we must go into town. In the bazaar there are shops that Adele might have gone to. It would seem she avoided those near the hotels."

I turned my eye to the street that branched off Al Nil and wound its way behind Luxor Temple. It went into the heart of Luxor and led to a busy market place that I knew would be not unlike the Mousky. I was disappointed that we hadn't turned up anything so far, but I didn't voice this to Ahmed.

Then I turned to look at the river. The sun was setting behind the cliffs on the other side, turning palm trees into silhouettes, transforming the sky into lavender and the water into obsidian blue. Very soon it would be dark.

"Let's go," I said.

It was difficult to walk slowly into town, for I was anxious, but we knew the necessity of not drawing attention to ourselves, and so blended in with all the other pedestrians who were now filling the streets.

It was exactly like the Mousky and, when I saw it, my heart began to race. Although shorter in length, the Luxor market place was no less formidable than its Cairo counterpart, for it was just as crowded, just as noisy and just as overwhelming. Here is where I truly began to feel nervous.

The first shop was off a small alley and had a very unpretentious exterior. I had to push my way around a donkey in order to get to the door, and once inside was unimpressed with the interior. Barely larger than a walk-in cupboard, the shop of Ramesh Gupta displayed very little in the way of statuary or ancient furniture, but sported instead a few shelves of books, jewelry and some watercolors of the Nile. There was no counter, just an old wooden desk scattered with papers.

Mr. Gupta was an Indian in a turban and spotless business suit, who came barely up to my shoulders, and who spoke in a high, sing-songy voice. *"Bonjour, madame,"* he said, rising.

"Hello."

"Ah, British?"

"American."

"Ah." He bowed a little from the waist. "Can I pour you some tea, please?"

"No thank you."

A large pot and several cups took up most of the desk top, and the stuffy air was clogged with the aroma of mint tea.

"What can Ramesh Gupta do for you?"

I looked at his face, at his eyes, and saw nothing more than politeness to a new customer. I looked around the tiny shop, at the sparse stock and lack of light, and wondered why Ahmed had sent me in here.

"Do you wish to buy something, madam? All my antiquities are genuine and registered with the government. Let me show you . . ."

He reached for an enormous book that hung out over a shelf above the desk and let it fall with a thud. It fell open to a pair of pages that might have come from the Manhattan telephone directory. Thousands of items were listed in the Gupta catalogue, each with a description, age, registration number and cost. All in small print.

So that was why I was here. This dealer was bigger than all the others.

"I'm interested in having you look at something."

"Of course." His smile remained fixed, his face anxious to please.

But when I unwrapped the jackal and placed it on the desk, his expression changed. First he frowned, then, as if remembering, his smile returned. "Ah, the lady with the jackal. You still have not found a purchaser then?"

My heart started to pound. "I was hoping you could help me."

"But, madam," he said apologetically, genially, "I told you before that I do not handle such things. I deal only with the government. You must understand this. I am an honest man. And I must warn you that two days ago two officials from the Department of Antiquities were in here asking me questions. But I said nothing, of course."

"I appreciate it, thank you. Maybe you could tell me who . . ."

"But I told you before, I will have nothing to do with this. I cannot even give you the names of dealers who will help you, for the government is harsh with criminals. I want to keep my licence, madam."

I stood for a moment to consider my next move. He had still said nothing that would implicate Jelks, although now there was no doubt that Adele was involved in illegal activities. Nor did this Indian indicate how much he knew. Had Adele mentioned a tomb to him?

Ramesh Gupta himself supplied me with the answer. "You should take my advice, madam, the advice I gave you last time. A handful of artifacts is no large offense. Take them to the Egyptian authorities. It is far better to lose value on them than lose your freedom."

I thanked him and joined Ahmed outside down the alley, in a recess where we could not be seen. After I recounted it all to him, word for word, he said, "So it would seem your sister moved cautiously, indicating perhaps that she had only a few illegal items to sell of which the jackal was one. I would guess, therefore, that if she came upon a dealer who, unlike Gupta, offered to take her few artifacts, then she would tell him about the tomb."

"And about Jelks."

"Yes. So far we have virtually nothing. We must continue."

"Yes, I guess . . ."

"Are you all right?" His eyes expressed concern. In the darkness of the shadow where we stood, with twilight removing all light from the alley,

Ahmed took hold of my hand and squeezed it tightly. We stood close to one another, almost touching.

"I'm all right."

"Rossiter could be out there," he said quietly, indicating the busy market place which we could hear but not see.

"I know."

"Lydia, we can go back to the hotel now and try another plan. Perhaps we should just go out to the camp of Paul Jelks and trust our luck that he is the one."

"No," I said quickly. "Suppose he isn't? Or suppose he is and you aren't sure. You wouldn't arrest him, would you? Not when you were in doubt. And that would spoil it all. I'll keep going to the shops until someone slips. Once we know it's Jelks, we're home safe."

"Home safe?"

"Ahmed . . . don't change your plan of attack because of me. I can take care of myself."

I looked long into his eyes, felt his nearness, my hand in his, and then I felt his strength and my own strength. Eleven days ago I would not have been so bold. But today I was different. I was going to face hell and high water—and possibly even Arnold Rossiter—to get my sister back.

The next two shops produced nothing. It was evening when I joined Ahmed again, and my apprehension was mounting. Possibly it was just my imagination, or the effects of being jostled about in the crowded bazaar— the frightening memory of the Mousky was starting to obsess me—but I was beginning to feel nervous. Somehow, things were going too smoothly, too uneventfully.

Finally we arrived at the shop of S. Khouri, licensed dealer in genuine antiquities. It was in the bazaar itself, and had a large window displaying ancient statuary, pedestals, and vases. Ahmed gave me a word of encouragement, then stepped back into the crowd and at once disappeared. I quickly pushed open the door.

It was a musty little shop, filled to the eaves with brass ornaments, tapestries, sculptures, books, and paintings. Its only light came from two fixtures hanging from the ceiling, so that it was difficult to see anything very well and the dimness made the shop seem all the more cramped and crowded.

I made my way down the narrow passage towards the glass counter and had to take care not to bump the little tables which displayed delicate statuary.

As the door of the shop swung closed, temple bells on a string announced my arrival, immediately after which the proprietor emerged from behind a beaded curtain. He was a weasel of a man with sleek eyes and a pointed face. His black hair was slicked down like a helmet and reflected the feeble light from above. As I approached him I kept an eye on his face, watching for the slightest sign of recognition. There was none.

He smiled, clasped his hands and said smoothly, "Good evening, madam."

"How do you do." I stepped up to him so that only the counter stood between us and still his face betrayed no recognition. He was all smiles and congeniality.

"Madam is interested in antiquities?"

"In a way, yes." I glanced around. There was a thick smell of incense in the air. I had the feeling of being closed in, confined. "I would like you to look at something."

"Certainly."

My hands were clammy as I put my bag on the counter, but I managed to keep them from shaking as I laid the bundle down, neatly spread out the handkerchief, and exposed the jackal.

The man's ferret face did not change. "Exquisite," he said, and picked it up with one hand. "Lovely piece. Not at all damaged."

I watched him as he examined it and got the odd feeling that he was restraining himself, that he had rehearsed. It was an absurd notion, of course, for there was no reason why I should think this. Mr. Khouri smiled politely and displayed mild interest like all the rest. And yet . . . there was something different about him. Something that wasn't there with the others, a vague premonition I hadn't felt with the other dealers.

"Where did you find this lovely piece?" I heard him ask.

Then I saw the cluttered walls loom over me, felt the heavy shadows in all corners, and was suddenly overwhelmed with the sensation of being trapped.

"I have others . . ." I said uncertainly.

He continued the silky smile. "I am sure you do. But let me see this in better light." The Arab stepped around the counter to get under the overhead light, and as he did so I thought I saw movement behind the beaded curtain.

Mr. Khouri came behind me, turning the jackal over and over in his hands, and stood facing the counter so that I had to turn around. "This appears genuine," he said. "New Kingdom, I would guess." Then he lifted his narrow eyes to me. "What else do you have?"

I swallowed hard and decided to take the gamble. "I told you the last time I was here."

His grin stretched. "Of course you did. I do not know why you pretended not to have been here before, but that does not matter. I knew you would come back." He looked down at the jackal, tapped it thoughtfully against his palm and then said, "But I told you then that I would not deal through you, madam, but will speak only directly to your employer."

My heart began to race again. So, Adele was working for someone.

"And with such a great amount of merchandise to offer," said the oily Mr. Khouri, "I doubted anyone else in Luxor or Cairo would touch it. Only I can handle such a quantity."

I swallowed hard. So it seemed there *was* a tomb. "If you are interested," I said boldly, "then you'll deal through me."

But he shook his head and held out the jackal, which I took from him. "I am sorry, madam. I cannot risk that. Please tell Dr. Jelks that we must meet together privately or not at all."

I held my breath. My heart pounded wildly. He had said the name Jelks. . .

In the next instant I heard a sound behind me and, spinning round, found myself looking straight into a pair of Coke-bottle glasses.

⁓❈⁓

"Good evening," said the fat man. "Perhaps I can help you?"

I released a gasp and swung back around. Mr. Khouri was gone.

"Allow me to introduce myself. I am Karl Schweitzer."

I turned back to face him. He had a sloppy, half smile on his face and his eyes were grotesquely large behind the thick lenses.

"It is possible I can help you," he said, speaking with a German accent.

My mind raced. I knew that Ahmed was across the street and unable to see inside the shop, and that he would not be able to hear if I cried out. The antiquities dealer had disappeared—either by force or because he was in league with this man. And so that left me alone in this tiny, jumbled shop with the man who had murdered John Treadwell.

"How do you wish to help me, Mr. Schweitzer?" I asked in a constrained voice. I inched my foot back and felt it come against an obstruction. To my left was the counter and before me was Fatso. That meant my only exit was to the right, down a narrow path through obstacles and a long way to the door.

"I sometimes deal in antiquities." He pointed to the jackal in my hand. "I understand you have something to sell?"

"Well . . ." I stalled for time to weigh up the situation. It was possible Schweitzer was not aware that I knew who he was. It was possible he was thinking of trying some charade to lure me away. Anything was possible. And I was in no mood for games. I wanted this over, I wanted my sister back, and I wanted the nightmare to end. It wouldn't end with pretence and lies and acting and tricks. It was going to end with blunt honesty and maybe even a fight.

I was willing to risk it. So I said, "I know who you are, Mr. Schweitzer."

The smile froze on his face. "You do?"

"You were in the Domus Aurea with me."

He did not say a word, did not make a move.

"And I saw you with John before he was murdered."

Schweitzer nodded slowly. "I see . . ."

My fingers curled around the head of the jackal, his long muzzle and pointed ears digging into my hand. I held it tightly, like a dagger, ready to strike.

"Then we need not waste time," he said softly.

We regarded one another in the darkness, both of us guarded, on the alert.

"We can be of help to each other," he said warily.

"How?" My body began to tremble.

Within a split-second, he made a lightening move and brought out a gun from under his jacket. It was pointed at my breast, inches away. "I want you to come with me," he said softly.

I stared in disbelief at the gun. "Where to?"

"Surely you must know where. If you know who I am, as you say, then you must know where we will go."

"We can talk here," I said evenly. My pounding heart deafened my ears.

"I think not, fräulein. Please be peaceful. We do not want trouble."

I decided not to waste any more time deliberating. If Schweitzer could surprise me, then I could surprise him. So without thinking about what I was doing, I suddenly brought my left hand up under his arm, dashing it upwards, and with my right hand struck blindly out. The stem of the jackal found a home as the gun flew through the air and Schweitzer seized his stabbed shoulder, startled.

Then I spun round and scrambled towards the door. I stumbled over tables, pushed statues out of my way, and climbed frantically through the jumble until I reached the door. Flinging it open, I dashed headlong into the crowd, not looking and not caring, until I felt Ahmed Rasheed's arms about me and his body against mine.

"Lydia!"

"Quick . . ." I gasped. "Run."

We pushed blindly through the crowd, with no one paying us the slightest heed, until we found a quiet doorway away from the lights and people.

My words came out sporadically in sobs as I stood in Ahmed's protective embrace. He said, "What happened?" several times before he pried the jackal loose from my hand and saw that it was covered with blood.

"My God!" he whispered. "Lydia, what happened?"

"The fat man . . ." I managed to say. "He had a gun."

"Don't talk." We wasted no time in leaving the area of the bazaar, taking dark and deserted streets in our flight. We hurried down narrow alleys, over slippery cobblestones and down empty avenues. Ahmed knew the way well, guiding me without hesitation away from lights and people, but always in the general direction of the hotel.

When we finally neared the New Winter Palace and were once again among the usual pedestrians, he took me off to the side to look at me. My face was as white as flour, and I had blood on my blouse.

"Do you wish to go up to your room now?" he asked.

"Yes."

"There will be people in the lobby . . ."

"I don't care, I want to go up. Now."

"Very well."

We ran through the garden and up the steps to the main doors where, thankfully, the doorman was engaged with a taxi driver and did not see us. We pushed open the glass doors ourselves and hurried across the lobby to the lifts. We were fortunate in having one open up as soon as we reached it and in having the doors close behind us as we stepped in. Ahmed and I rose up alone in the lift.

Once inside my room, I slumped on to one of the twin beds, feeling terribly weak. Ahmed closed the curtains and double-locked the door, and then sat next to me and opened out his hand to look at the jackal. Blood from its shaft was on his fingers.

"Can you tell me now what happened?"

"Yes." I took a deep breath and related to him the entire incident in Khouri's shop, including my feelings of being trapped and the movement behind the curtain.

"So . . ." he said after a period of silence. "The fat man, Schweitzer, was there before you arrived. That would mean he either knew you were going to be there or that he had dealings with Mr. Khouri."

"How could he have known I was going there?"

"From one of the other dealers, perhaps, who might have told him you were going from shop to shop. By logic he would have assumed you would eventually visit Khouri—a well-known antiquities dealer."

I pondered this. Then I shuddered. "God, I actually stabbed him." I could not shake the memory of how the jackal felt as it sank into his fleshy shoulder.

Without a word, Ahmed rose and went into the bathroom. I heard the sound of running water. When he came back a minute later, sitting again next to me on the bed, both his hands and the jackal were clean.

Then I looked at my own hands—red with blood. "That isn't what bothers me, Ahmed. God knows, I'm used to blood. I've seen it spurt out of an artery and actually hit the ceiling. Once, I was even up to my ankles in it. But this is different."

"I know," he said softly.

"I mean . . . I actually *stabbed* him." I shuddered again and Ahmed put his arm around my shoulders, drawing me against him.

"You were trying to save your own life," he said gently. "And I feel responsible for what happened."

"It's not your fault at all. God knows I went into it with my eyes open. And I suppose I would do it again. I don't know. But there was no other way. From the very beginning, I've had to deal with danger. Tonight was no different. I suppose Adele would have done the same for me." I released a sigh and shook my head. "Good God! An ivory jackal against a gun. I must have been out of my mind."

"But it worked, did it not?"

"Yes . . . it did." I pictured the gun, inches away from my heart, I pictured the fat ringers holding it, and I tried to reconstruct my thoughts at just that precise moment. But I could not, because there were none. I had acted impulsively—some survival instinct had taken over. "And what if I hadn't been so quick?"

"You must not think about these things."

"And if I hadn't stabbed him, he might not have let go of the gun. He might have just regained his balance and shot me." I took the jackal from Ahmed's hand and looked at it. "Looks harmless, doesn't it? And yet it's been the cause of absolutely everything that's happened these last—what, eleven days? It's brought me to the other side of the world. It's nearly got me killed. And it's also saved my life."

I turned it slowly between my fingers. Ahmed's arm held me closely,

Then I thought, it's also changed me, and brought me to this moment.

"At least," said Ahmed in a low voice, "we accomplished what we wanted. We now know it is indeed Paul Jelks and that tomorrow I can go to his camp in an official capacity."

I did not look at him but kept my eyes on the jackal.

"Now there will be no doubt in my mind when I approach him," he went on, "that I am correct, and I will feel confident in pursuing my plan. I must thank you for this, Miss Harris."

"Yes, of course."

I drew myself away from his arm and got to my feet. I was no longer shaken. I felt strong now. What had happened to me an hour before might have happened a year before, for all the effect it still had on me. Right now, there was something else . . .

I went into the bathroom, washed my hands and the jackal, and came back into the room to sit on the bed opposite Ahmed Rasheed. I looked straight at him.

"Why did you just now call me Miss Harris?"

He stared at me, unanswering.

"Earlier, I was Lydia."

"Yes, I know." His eyes continued to hold mine. I felt my heart begin to race again, but this time for a different reason.

Once again Dr. Kellerman came into my mind, and I recognized the gentle, tender affection I had for him. It was a mixture of devotion and need, it went very deep and had been there for a long time.

But this other—this electricity and fire that I felt for Ahmed—it was an exciting love, a passionate one.

"Miss Harris . . . Lydia," he said, and seemed for the first time to be uncertain of himself. "I have never before known an American woman. We come from different worlds, you and I. Your religion is not mine. Your politics are not mine. Our customs are vastly different. We . . ." he spread his hands, "are vastly different."

"And who," I said quietly, "are you trying to convince? You or me?"

For the first time, he averted his eyes. I sensed a struggle within him. And as we continued to sit in silence, I thought back to that night at the

Shepherd's Hotel, when John had put me to bed, taken me in his arms, and we had kissed. I remembered how hungry those kisses had been and how they had aroused passions.

I looked at the silent man before me. I did not need to be kissed or even touched to be excited by him. Just his nearness ignited me.

"We will go out early tomorrow, and it is late now. You should sleep, Lydia."

"Yes, I suppose I should."

"But I will not leave you, for it is not safe."

I impulsively got to my feet, picked my bag up off the floor, replaced the jackal inside its handkerchief, and drew back the bedspread. My companion remained just as he was.

As I kicked off my shoes and started to get into bed, Ahmed suddenly stood and took hold of my arm. "Lydia, you must understand something."

I couldn't avoid his eyes. They seemed to be saying things his words could not.

"I feel it too," he said softly, uneasily. "But it cannot be. We met by accident, and soon you will return to your world. The reason that brought you here will no longer exist, and then you will leave. You have your hospital and your surgeon who waits for you, and I have my work with the government. We both have duties and obligations. What has happened between us, we could not help it, for it happened by accident. But it can never be. Tomorrow we will go out to the desert and, I hope, you will find your sister. Then you will both go back to the world you belong in."

"I know where I belong," I whispered.

His grip tightened on my arm. I would have given anything at that moment to have him acquiesce, to give in and take me in his arms and kiss me. But I did not want to be the one to cause him to do it. If Ahmed triumphed over his conflict, if he realized how meaningless were his words, and if he were to decide that cultures and worlds and religions meant nothing, then I wanted the decision to come from him—not from me. He had to find the answer within himself.

"Lydia, if it is the will of Allah, then it will come. But I think it is not, for I know that we will soon part and never see each other again. What has happened between us, and what is happening now, was never meant to be."

I pulled my arm away from him. As if in a dream I drew back the bed-covers and slid beneath them. I heard my mind say, this is what anaesthesia must be like.

Someone turned out a light, plunging the room into total darkness. There was not a sound. Luxor was asleep. The hotel was still and quiet. As I lay on my bed staring at the blackness, I heard someone lie down on the other bed. I heard a sigh and then I felt my body drift far away into bottom-less sleep.

I awoke with a start. For an instant, I thought I had only closed my eyes. Then, finding myself on my side instead of on my back, I knew that I had been asleep, but I had no idea for how long.

The room was still utterly dark. I listened for sounds, for movement, for breathing. There were none.

"Ahmed?" I whispered.

There was no need to turn on a light, for I already knew he was not there. I climbed out of bed and went directly to the window. Drawing the curtains open, I let fresh moonlight fall into the room and across the two empty beds.

Perplexed, I walked softly to the door, put my ear to it and listened. There was the vaguest sound on the other side. Almost like people talking. But quietly, as if not wanting to be heard.

I inched the door open only enough for me to see out with one eye, and saw Ahmed standing in the hall murmuring privately with someone I could not see. He was leaning against the wall and had his hands thrust casually in his pockets. He seemed relaxed, at ease, as if he was merely passing the time. And when he laughed softly, I wondered who his unseen companion was.

So I twisted my body and pressed the other eye against the crack, and got a good look at the person with whom Ahmed chatted so familiarly.

It was the man who wore Coke-bottle glasses, Karl Schweitzer.

CHAPTER 14

I WAS AMAZED HOW, IN AN ATAVISTIC WAY, I SLEPT HEAVILY through the rest of the night. I suppose it was some sort of ancestral defense mechanism that enabled me to sleep and to escape, for a while, from the traumas of the night before. First the strain of the bazaar, then facing a loaded gun and stabbing a man, and then learning that Ahmed was friendly with Schweitzer . . . These all had amounted to a bit more than I cared to face at that moment and so, after quietly closing the door on the two men in the hall, I had gone promptly and deeply to sleep.

In the morning, however, I felt little refreshed. And when I awoke I was glad Ahmed wasn't there, for I needed a cold shower and time to think. After both, when I was clean and my mind more organized, I could arrive at no other conclusion than that Ahmed Rasheed and Karl Schweitzer were on close terms.

I stood before the mirror and combed out my damp hair. What else could this mean but that Ahmed was not the government official he said he was, or that he was a crooked one? Either was bad. I knew Schweitzer had knocked me down in the Domus Aurea and that he had killed John. What, then, did that say for his friend Ahmed?

I felt not unlike the way I had felt upon learning the truth about John Treadwell: bitter, frustrated and most of all angry. Once again, I had been played for a fool by someone, and I wondered bitterly how many times in my life this was going to happen before I learned a lesson.

Standing on the balcony to let my hair dry, I saw the long crisp shadows cast by the early morning sun and wondered what impossibilities this day was going to bring. All I knew was, I wanted to find my sister and take her back to the sane and normal world.

Ahmed had to knock several times before he finally let himself in. I was still on the balcony when he joined me, saying, "I was not certain if you would be awake. How are you this morning, Lydia?"

"As well as can be expected." I kept my eyes ahead. "And you?"

"Very fine. I was able to sleep well." He also took a moment to look out at the river, and I half-hoped this would be the time he would tell me about his encounter with Schweitzer. I could have asked, but I wanted him to volunteer it. Which he did not.

Ahmed waited for me to say something more, and when I didn't, he went on, "The first ferry across the river leaves soon. The next one after that is an hour later. Will you want to go on the first one or will you want breakfast?"

"I'm not hungry," I said.

"Very well." He turned away from me and went back into the room. When I looked down I saw that my hands clutched the rail so fiercely that my knuckles were white.

I was trying to make a decision. Should I confront him with it or not? Should I just plunge into it, blurt it out and get it over with, or should I continue to play along?

Then I turned to look at him, and when I saw his beautiful face and engaging smile, my heart went out to him. No, I thought sadly. He'll only lie to me anyway and nothing would be accomplished. We might as well continue the charade a while longer. At least until I find Adele.

The morning sun stabbed our eyes as it rose over the New Winter Palace. The ferry was going to take us to the west, to the land of the dead, to that realm where Amon-Ra sailed each morning in his sun boat. Ahmed and I were the only two on the ferry at this hour, which was fine with me. I was in no mood for a crowd.

Because of the swiftness of the current, we had to work our way upstream in order to go downstream, so the trip was a long one. As the boat chugged its way towards the opposite landing stage, I watched my companion as he stood at the rail. The northerly breeze swept his face and ruffled his hair. In profile he was a striking man with a large nose and eyes like an eagle. I liked to look at Ahmed Rasheed, although now I was both sad and angry. In a way, I wished I had not seen him last night with Schweitzer. I wished I had not learned the truth, for then I could continue to trust him blindly and love him.

Now, of course, it could never be the same.

There were several taxis waiting when we arrived, so we had no trouble hiring one. We settled the price at one Egyptian pound before leaving, with the understanding that the driver was ours until noon. After that the price would go up.

Ahmed and I sat in the back as the cab bumped and rattled over the uneven road, leaving a cloud of dust behind. We drove through farmland and mudbrick villages with the brown cliffs ahead of us. I only half-listened when he made occasional comments on places we passed.

"This small village to our right was built in 1955 by your Mr. Cecil B. de Mille for the film of *The Ten Commandments*. After the film was finished and everyone left Egypt, the local peasants moved into this 'movie' town and made it their own. That is why it is so different from any other village in Egypt."

We passed sugarcane fields and had to stop occasionally for camels crossing. As with the train, children in long *galabias* waved and shouted as we passed.

Presently we drove past two seated figures on the right side of the road, and Ahmed said, "These are the Colossus of Memnon, giant statues who once guarded the entrance to a temple that is no longer in existence. One of the statues was said to sing to the rising sun years ago and was therefore considered to contain the spirit of the king. However, it was earthquake damage that created cracks in the statue through which wind would whistle."

I gazed blankly out at them.

"You are very quiet this morning, Lydia."

"Yes, I suppose I am."

"I can understand. And I hope for your sake that this is all over very soon."

No, you don't understand, I thought angrily. And yes, the sooner it's over the better. I shut my eyes tightly. Oh, Ahmed Rasheed, why did you have to betray me?

The cab lurched and jolted over the long dusty road. The day was beginning to grow warm. Eventually we came upon the Temple of Hatshepsut, or Deir el Bahri, and I strained my neck to take a look as we passed. The straight lines and tiers of columns set into the orange cliff impressed me more than I could say. When I would have rolled down the window for a better look Ahmed said, "It is best to keep the sand out. It will dry your throat and lungs. The air here is very dry and dusty, which is why everything is so well preserved. It was not so much the mummifying process as the desert air that saved the kings and queens of Egypt for us to look at today."

"That temple is unbelievable," I had to say. "Can you go inside?"

"Yes, except for the top level, which is currently being reconstructed by a group of Polish archaeologists. The middle level was rebuilt by the Americans, and the first, the French. You see that the treasures of Egypt are really the treasures of all mankind."

After Deir el Bahri we swung back towards the Nile and traveled along a very dusty, very bumpy road. As we passed a government rest house,

Ahmed offered me the chance to stop for tea, but I shook my head. The Valley of the Kings was close, too close, and I was in a hurry.

The sheer cliffs were on our left all the time as we followed the road that curved around them. The Valley of the Kings was on the other side of these monsters and the road was long and difficult. In the growing heat I wondered how Howard Carter ever did it.

"Haven't all the tombs been discovered now?" I asked after a while. "I mean, are there any left unsearched for?"

"Surprisingly, Lydia, there are many things yet hidden in Egypt's sand. But my country is too poor to spend money on archaeology, for it is costly, and other nations are too involved with more immediate economic spending. Yes, there must be many tombs, many temples yet unexcavated. However, you must remember that it is uncommon to find a tomb perfectly intact. Such tombs as those of Tutankhamun and Queen Hetepheres are very rare indeed."

"Why is that?"

"Tomb robbers."

"Can't they be stopped?"

He laughed. "I meant the tomb robbers of pharaonic times. Unfortunately, too few pharaohs ever enjoyed their treasures in the afterlife, no matter what lengths they went to in hiding their burial places. Priests could be bribed."

"Then what happened to bring Tutankhamun through?"

"We do not know. You Americans will call it 'blind luck.' But to find a tomb that is not empty, that is full of the treasures it contained at the hour of burial, Lydia, this is monumental!"

I stared out at the desert around us, for we had long since left the farms behind, and tried to imagine all the kings and queens yet hidden beneath the sand. Then my eyes flew open. "My jackal!"

"Yes?"

"My little jackal has probably come from just such a tomb. That must be what Adele meant on the phone about its 'explaining everything.'"

"Now you see the importance of all this. The secrecy. The need to learn the truth."

"My God . . ." I picked up my bag and clutched it to my chest. The jackal was in there. A little piece of ivory that might just be the first treasure to come from a brand new tomb—a tomb no one knew existed and that still contained all the king's possessions. My mind reeled with wild imaginings.

"If there is indeed such a tomb, Lydia, then we will be instrumental in the most astounding discovery since Tutankhamun! Pages upon pages of Egyptian history will be filled in. Newsmen from all over the world will come and tell our story. Thousands of visitors will arrive each day, just as they did back then. Tourists will bring their money and this will help my country. I cannot emphasize the importance of what we might be involved in. And that is why, Lydia, we must not let a man like Arnold Rossiter get to the tomb before we do."

When he said this, I leaned my forehead against the window and closed my eyes. How could this be? my mind cried. How could he sound so sincere, so devoted, and yet be in league with Schweitzer and Rossiter, the very man he so convincingly condemned . . .

My heart was racing as we approached the valley, and up ahead, in a recess among the cliffs, I saw a cluster of white tents.

"Where are the tombs?" I asked, looking frantically about.

"They are farther down the road. A fence and a gate mark the entrance to the burial area. This is for the protection of the tombs. Dr. Jelks's camp is over there. You can see it."

"Is he the only archaeologist here?"

"At the Valley of the Kings, yes. There is a French group near Deir el Bahri, and some Americans are working to restore a tomb in the Valley of the Queens."

I sat forward with my hands on the front seat. As the camp came closer to us in a veil of dust, my eyes darted excitedly about for the familiar shape of Adele. I had come so far, so far . . .

I was out of the cab before it came to a complete stop, and Ahmed was right behind me. Our motor had attracted the attention of those in the camp, so that a small welcoming party came out to greet us. They were all men.

"Hullo!" called out the tallest. "What can we do for you?"

"Is Dr. Jelks here?"

"Not at the moment. I'm his assistant, Dr. Wilbur Ames. Can I be of help?"

"My name is Ahmed Rasheed. I work for the Service of Antiquities." The man's expression remained unchanged. "When do you expect Dr. Jelks?"

"Shortly. He'll break for siesta soon. Been working in Seti's tomb since dawn. Come inside for some tea, won't you?"

Dr. Ames turned and we followed him and the others to the compound. My heart was thumping in my ears. I expected any moment to hear Adele's voice shout, "Liddie! Liddie!"

But no shout came as we were led through the Land Rovers and into the largest tent, which served as a mess hall. A picnic table and benches took up one side, while on the other stood fairly sophisticated cooking equipment. Our hosts sat on one side of the table, we opposite. A young girl, no more than sixteen, with wispy blonde hair, poured us tea.

"My daughter," explained Dr. Ames, casting me a curious glance. "Rosalie wants to be an Egyptologist like her daft old dad. So tell me, Mr. Rasheed, to what do we owe this surprise?"

"I prefer to wait for Dr. Jelks to return. However, you can tell me please if Miss Harris is here."

"Adele?"

My heart positively exploded.

"It's funny you should ask. We've been wondering where she's got to. She hasn't been in camp since last night."

"Oh God!" I said, seizing Ahmed's hand. "That can't be!"

Dr. Ames gave me a startled look. Ahmed said to him, "This is Adele's sister, Lydia, and she has come from Los Angeles to be with her."

"How do you do. Yes, I thought you looked familiar. Very like your sister. Adele has been with us a few weeks now; most delightful creature and a wonderful companion for Rosalie."

"Then where *is* she?"

"We don't know. She was with us last evening and then took one of the Land Rovers to Luxor. Or so she said. She hasn't returned."

"Haven't you looked for her?" I felt sick.

"No. Adele often goes into Luxor to spend the night at a hotel. She thinks our quarters are too primitive and once in a while she desires a bath and real bed, as she puts it."

"When does she usually come back?" asked Ahmed, holding my hand in both of his.

"That's the odd part. Usually by sunrise, so she can help Paul with his work. Great little assistant, your sister."

"Well it's nearly eleven now!" I cried.

"Yes, but she could be shopping."

I turned to Ahmed. "Something awful has happened. I just know it!"

"I say, what's this all about?"

Wilbur Ames was being remarkably calm, considering he was keeping a tomb discovery a secret and was dealing with smugglers. That is, *if* such a tomb existed and *if* Rossiter was who Ahmed said he was.

I retrieved my hand and watched Ahmed out of the corner of my eye. Schweitzer was in Luxor last night and Adele disappeared last night, and I saw Ahmed with Schweitzer last night. What a coincidence.

I left my tea untouched and sat and watched. Ahmed explained only briefly that a letter from Adele had brought me to Luxor.

"She will show up some time today, Miss Harris, I'm sure of it. And she will be thrilled to bits to have you here. As much as she feels about Paul, camping is not your sister's forte."

"Feels about Paul? What do you mean?"

"Oh, you didn't know? I thought she might have mentioned it in her letter. Your sister is in love with Dr. Jelks."

My eyes flickered to Ahmed.

"In fact, they're engaged to be married."

So that was it. Adele was involved more deeply in this than I thought. This crooked Egyptologist Paul Jelks had my innocent sister fencing his stolen treasures. I did not look too favorably upon Wilbur Ames. In the coolness of the tent, with light from outside barely illuminating anything, I felt my mind moving very rapidly. It was going to be difficult, if not impossible, to get Adele away from all this. I even doubted if she could be persuaded after I told her about Rossiter.

I was going to ask another question when the light suddenly went out and a shadow filled the doorway.

"Hullo," said another cheerful voice. "Is Adele back yet?"

"Oh, Paul. We have guests. I would like for you to meet Adele's sister, Lydia Harris."

A bright-faced young man strode towards me and seized my hand. "How good to meet you! I've heard a lot about you."

"And this," Dr. Ames continued, "is Ahmed Rasheed from the Service of Antiquities."

Paul Jelks's face did not change, but his handshake immediately went limp. "How do you do? What can I do for you?"

"I am making a routine inspection of the area. How is your work coming along?"

"Fine! Just fine!"

He took great strides to the gas burner where he poured himself some tea. Dr. Jelks was just the sort Adele would go for—tall, muscular, handsome and blond. He was no more than thirty-five, with a red face and calloused hands. His flaxen hair was cut unusually short and a faint moustache could be seen under his nose. As he sat next to me and grinned Cheshire-cat style, I wished he looked a little more sinister.

"So what brings you here, my dear Lydia?"

"Adele wrote me to join her."

"Did she indeed? She never told me that. And where is my wayward fiancée now? Mooching about the dress shops no doubt." Then he suddenly shouted out some rather excellent sounding Arabic, which brought a man's head round the open door to whom he gave snappy orders.

"I've sent him to Luxor to fetch Adele. She'll have wanted to meet you first, of course."

I heard an engine start and then tires crunch over the sand. I assumed, of course, that this is what he told the man, but not understanding Arabic I had no way of knowing for sure.

"Well, Mr. Rasheed, would you care to step into my dark room? I can show you the fruits of my labors. Remarkable murals, those Setis. And now that summer is passed and November nearly upon us, we can expect cooler days. God, that blasted heat is a bugger!"

Dr. Ames spoke next. "Can we show you about the camp?" So far the other men were mute. "You're welcome to inspect anything you wish." Very accommodating, the two of them.

"No thank you, Dr. Ames. That will not be necessary. Actually, I would like to talk to you two alone, if I may. The four of us?"

Jelks and his associates exchanged glances. "Certainly, Mr. Rasheed. I hope we haven't violated any rules."

"Not yet."

The others reluctantly left the tent and Rosalie with them. I had no idea what Ahmed was planning. Dr. Jelks took a seat next to Wilbur Ames so that we faced one another across the table, as though teamed up.

"May I ask you something, Dr. Jelks?"

"Fire away."

To my surprise, Ahmed opened my bag and retrieved the handkerchief. Unraveling this, he dropped the jackal on the table, and as he did so, the other two men jerked back as if it was a snake.

"What is this?" asked Dr. Jelks, his voice no longer composed.

"I was hoping you could tell me. Can you?"

"I can try." Dr. Jelks picked it up and revolved it before his eyes, inspecting every inch of it. "The light's not so good in here, but I'd say it's around eighteenth, nineteenth dynasty maybe. Lovely piece."

"That is not what I am asking you, Dr. Jelks. I was hoping you could tell me where it came from."

Paul raised his eyebrows. "Came from? D'you mean the source of the ivory?"

"You know what I mean, Dr. Jelks. Evasiveness will do you no good. I want to know the location of the tomb."

"How should I know? This could have come from . . ."

"Dr. Jelks," said Ahmed evenly. "If you have excavated a new tomb, I should like very much to know about it."

"A new tomb? Don't be silly. You'd certainly know at once . . ."

"Then I will tell you how I came by this jackal. Miss Adele Harris sent it in a package to her sister."

"Adele?"

"From Rome, in fact."

"Rome?" Paul Jelks began to falter. He glanced at Wilbur Ames and then away again.

"You did know she was in Rome almost two weeks ago, didn't you?"

"Yes, as a matter of fact, I knew she had gone there for a few days. She wanted some new clothes and . . ."

"Dr. Jelks, do you know an Arnold Rossiter?"

Now both men became uneasy. The questions Ahmed fired at them were breaking their façades. Their practised calm was crumbling.

"Arnold Rossiter is in Luxor, Dr. Jelks, and I do not think he is far behind me. Now, I would like to know the location of that tomb so that I can put policemen about it. Otherwise, harm will come to a lot of people and the valuable artifacts inside will fall into ruthless hands."

"Mr. Rasheed . . ." Paul Jelks rose shakily.

"As an Egyptologist, Dr. Jelks, you must have some sense of ethics about what you are doing." Ahmed slammed his fist on the table. "You cannot possibly *truly* want Rossiter to take the contents of that tomb!"

I was amazed at the sudden force of the man. Previously so quiet and easy going, Ahmed Rasheed now displayed a passion and power so furious that he frightened me.

"Tell me where the tomb is!"

"All right!" shouted Jelks. "All right, I'll tell you!" He sat down again and put his head in his hands. "It's too late, Wilbur, I've got to tell them. We never should have tried it, it's not our kind of game. I knew Rossiter would catch up sooner or later. We've got to tell them everything."

As Paul Jelks began to tell us his extraordinary tale, I watched Ahmed in amazement. He had a faint smile of triumph on his lips. And because he had won his victory, I was proud of him. But at the same time, something disturbed me, gnawed at me.

How had he known Rossiter was in Luxor?

CHAPTER 15

$\mathcal{D}$R. PAUL JELKS TOLD US THE MOST PHENOMENAL STORY.
"My original intentions in Egypt were only to photograph the
tombs and to work on translations of the hieroglyphics in hopes
of clarifying certain obscure passages. Since I'm spending my own money,
I could not afford to dig anyway, and decided to satisfy myself with routine
academic work. I was not here for long, however, when a rather interesting
matter came to my attention.

"As is the case for any foreigner visiting this region, I was at once be-
sieged by the local natives with the usual bogus artifacts and tales of hidden
tombs—all for a price, of course. We were still setting up camp, in fact, when
they began to come by like vultures, each one with a proposition more fantastic than the last. However, as an Egyptologist and having gone through
this many times before, I gave no credence to anything I was approached
with. Until one evening.

"Mark Spencer, my photographer and engineer, and I were disturbed
at a game of cards by an old woman who came into the camp claiming to

have a gift for us. My Arab guards tried to send her away, but when the commotion drew my attention, I went out. The 'gift' she had for me was most intriguing. Wrapped in a mat of reeds and bound by a string was part of a goatskin scroll upon which had been painted hieroglyphics. This was the first of its kind I had seen, and I was curious to inspect the expertise of the forgery. Careful scrutiny under a lamp revealed such excellent work that I had to ask the old woman who had done it, and she said simply, the angels. Suspecting that she would not reveal the source I asked what money she wanted for it. Now this was the surprising part—she didn't want to sell, but *give* the scroll to me. In fact, she was most insistent that I take it and refused even one piastre. Seeing that she was frightened for some reason, I questioned her until she finally broke down and told me that the scroll had a curse on it, and that the curse was upon her family and would be so until it was returned to where it came from.

"Well, with nothing to lose and with an interesting forgery to gain, and, of course, to give the superstitious old thing peace of mind, I took the blasted scroll from her and she disappeared into the night." Paul Jelks noisily gulped down the last of his tea. "I say, rather reminiscent of the Tel-el-Amarna tablets, don't you think?"

"Please go on," said Ahmed.

"Anyway, as I said, I was here with a small crew and with the intention only to copy funeral texts from the tombs, so I gave no thoughts to the scroll for a few days. Then, one night, when Mark and everyone was asleep, I took the damned thing out and gave it a good look. To my genuine shock, the thing was not a forgery but the real article.

"I sat up for hours studying and inspecting it. Then I sent a piece to a lab in London for carbon dating, and the skin and ink came back positive. Three thousand years old."

He paused to wipe his forehead. It was getting hot in the tent. "Needless to say, I was shocked. You yourself know, Mr. Rasheed, how few and far between such scrolls are, and this one was put right on my doorstep. Perfectly preserved and quite legible, the text was an architect's notes to the building of a royal tomb."

"Do you still have the scroll?"

"Yes. I'll show it to you."

"Go on with your story."

"So I quite naturally translated the writing, and you can imagine my excitement when I realized what I was reading. Not only did it detail the layout of the tomb, but pinpointed its whereabouts as well. The fact that it was genuine and that it located a tomb where there wasn't one before was enough for me to try a daring experiment. I took Mark and one Arab with me, following the directions on the scroll, and during the night so that we were not seen, we dug with shovels at the indicated site."

We all hung upon his words.

"And?"

"And by morning we had uncovered a stone step. Mr. Rasheed, you can appreciate the momentousness of this! The chances of my coming across that scroll are one in ten million, and yet I did! Who knows where the old woman's family got it? And who cares? Obviously they had kept it for generations, centuries even, locked away somewhere, because they thought it was religious or magic or something. And then sickness by chance hits them. They blame the mysterious goatskin that belongs to angels. They know who to take it to—take it to a foreigner who robs tombs and who will know where to put it back. Take it to a foreigner, who it doesn't matter is cursed forever afterwards."

He poured another cup of tea and gulped it all down at once. "Then I sent for Wilbur. I needed both his help and money. And we hired more men. They're trustworthy, especially where money is concerned. Vast amounts of money."

"And is what you found in the tomb valuable, Dr. Jelks?"

He leaned forward and whispered, "More valuable than the treasure of Tutankhamun!"

Ahmed Rasheed closed his eyes. "Allah be praised."

"Then I met Adele in Luxor. She was traveling with a group. God, I fell in love with her at once. I brought her back to the camp and she decided to stay. Before too long I had to tell her about the tomb, and she was positively thrilled."

"That's Adele, all right."

"I'm sorry, Lydia, that she isn't here. You've come a long way."

Now I recounted to him what I had been through to find her—first Rome, then Cairo—but I left out John Treadwell and Arnold Rossiter. I didn't know how much Ahmed wanted me to reveal.

"I say, that *is* a bit of trouble! I'm sorry she wasn't in Rome to greet you, particularly after sending you the jackal and calling you."

"Was she at the Residence Palace, Dr. Jelks?"

"Call me Paul, please, since we'll be related some day. Yes, she stayed at the Residence Palace Hotel, but I had her register under a different name in case anyone should be following her."

"So that's why she wasn't on the records! And at the Shepherd's Hotel, too? That explains it." I also imagined Rossiter must have somehow intercepted my overseas cable and had one of his own men take my phone call.

Ahmed spoke next. "Now tell me please, Dr. Jelks, how you managed to get involved with Arnold Rossiter."

"That was a bit of bad luck, I must say. Wilbur and I were interested only in selling a few pieces from the tomb to cover expenses, and then to apply for an excavation permit and make the discovery look real. As you say, Mr. Rasheed, we have our ethics. As Egyptologists, we are not interested in the monetary value of the treasures, but in the valuable history the tomb can give us. When I told Adele what we were up to, she insisted she be the one to find us a buyer. Adele is innocent of all this, Mr. Rasheed. You must believe me! If I had known . . . anyway, it seemed such a lark to her and so terribly harmless, I told her to go to Cairo and to be discreet about finding a buyer for a small collection—mentioning nothing about a tomb. However, Adele's feet are not always on the ground and she is not terribly pragmatic. It seems someone in the Khan al-Khalili suggested she see John Treadwell in Rome and that he would give her a good price.

"Terribly pleased with herself, and thinking she was making a good deal for me, she delivered herself right into the web of Arnold Rossiter. John Treadwell was nice at first, but when Adele refused to give him any more information, he got nasty. She let it slip about 'a tomb' and that was the start of it all. Rossiter had her removed from Rome at night and taken to a villa outside Naples where he intended to interrogate her for the tomb's location, or if that didn't work, to hold her ransom for the tomb's contents—which I would have given him.

"However, Adele's not as daft as they say and she managed to escape back to Rome where Mark Spencer, who I'd sent after her, found her and brought her back to Cairo. She had intended to wait there for you, but then happened to see Rossiter at the Hilton and became afraid. Adele knew somehow that you'd find her down here."

"Unfortunately," said Ahmed, "so did Rossiter."

"Yes, well, I hadn't intended for it to get this mucky. It was all so innocent, really."

"It is a dangerous situation now, Dr. Jelks. Already one man has been murdered . . ."

"What?"

"John Treadwell, a few days ago."

"But what ever for?"

"Who knows? A falling out perhaps, a disagreement. Or possibly Mr. Treadwell had plans of his own. We will never know. But the danger is now imminent."

I was watching Ahmed Rasheed. When he happened to turn and look at me I asked quietly, "How do you know Rossiter is here?"

A veiled expression came over his face. "Miss Harris . . ."

"Oh what does that matter!" said Paul. "If that bugger is here, then we'd better get to the tomb. I hope to God that I haven't bungled the greatest discovery in the history of archaeology!"

He stood abruptly and Ames with him. "Frankly, I'm glad it's over. I'm not cut out for this sort of thing. Mr. Rasheed, would you care to go to the tomb now?"

"Very much, thank you."

I got up and moved as if in a dream. The air was stifling, the light dim. When Ahmed touched my arm I recoiled.

There was something about all this I didn't like. Something was wrong.

"You know, the Valley of the Kings is perhaps the most legendary spot on earth." Paul Jelks kept up a running commentary as we bumped in the Land-Rover along wretched dirt roads. Mark Spencer drove, with Paul next to him. I sat in the backseat, my mouth full of dust, between Dr. Ames and Ahmed Rasheed. "It's been a popular spot of romance for centuries. The Greeks and Romans began the original graffiti here, and medieval monks made homes of deserted tombs. The Age of Enlightenment brought philosophers, and Victorian archaeologists found it a Disneyland. And yet the greatest discoveries were made in our century, and are yet to come."

I closed my eyes and coughed. We were all sweating badly and smelled of it. Although I had wanted to remain at camp and await Adele, Ahmed felt better for some reason having me along. I wasn't too pleased about it.

"For thousands of years ancient Egyptians built tombs with funerary chapels over them, or near by, so the soul could have easy access to them. However, the chapel was also a marker for the location of the tomb. As long as the chapel had to be near the tomb, the tomb was always found and consequently robbed.

"In the eighteenth dynasty, however, this tradition was finally broken. From then on all tombs were buried on this side of the mountain, instead of on the eastern side where you find Hatshepsut and the Ramesseum, and the chapels were done away with. Hence, the tombs were harder to find."

I don't know who he was talking to, because Mark Spencer, Wilbur Ames, and Ahmed Rasheed already knew all this—and I wasn't listening. Yet he continued.

"Unfortunately not even this worked, since heavy concealment and elaborate mazes and booby traps still did not stop the grave robbers from stripping most of the tombs bare, so that after the twentieth dynasty no more pharaohs were buried here. There are many tombs in the Valley of the Kings, and almost all of them were barren when discovered—except for Tutankhamun's and mine."

His voice drifted away on the wind. Whether he still spoke or not, I didn't know. And I didn't care. We were entering a zone of agelessness, where time had stopped still, where what was yesterday is still today and will be tomorrow. The air was thick with flies. They were noisy and fat and bold. The dust was a plague, the heat unbearable. As the vehicle went into four-wheel drive and ground its way up a steep path, I thought I was going to scream.

"Of course, Mr. Rasheed," said Paul over his shoulder, "this will be my first visit by day. We always did our work at night."

I had no idea where we were going, but wanted the journey to end soon. As I looked back I saw the valley dropping away behind us, its little black mouths that were tomb entrances getting smaller and smaller.

"That pyramid-shaped peak is the highest in the Theban hills, Lydia, and was called the Peak of the West, where it was believed dwelt the dreaded serpent goddess Meresger, or 'lover of silence.' All these hills about us are sacred and mystical."

To me they were barren and endless. Not even the poorest stick of growth showed anywhere, just heaps and heaps of rubble piled against sheer, ragged cliffs beneath a blazing sun. When the Land Rover bounced over a spar and started racing downwards, I let out a cry.

"This is rough terrain, Lydia, and probably the reason King Tetef chose it for his tomb. There are no *wadis* here or mountain passes. To reach it you have to be an expert climber and a superhuman to boot. God only knows how they managed it."

Mark added, "God only knows how they managed the Pyramids, too."

"True. Those Egyptians were an inventive lot. When it came to a man's afterlife, no pains were spared. And concealment of the tomb was top priority. Even Tutankhamun's tomb, so brilliantly hidden beneath another king's tomb, was bound to be found by accident. But my tomb, Tetef's tomb, would never have been stumbled upon in a thousand years. And that is why he is one of the few lucky ones to have survived centuries of tomb robbers. He and his possessions are intact."

We drove through a narrow ravine no wider than the car itself and then came to a halt.

"You mean the king is still in the tomb?" I asked.

"Yes. Took us weeks to open the final door, but we found his body a few days ago."

It was impossible to stand with any grace in the area. Wedged as we were in a V-shaped gorge between two peaks and with a sloping wall of sand before us, I could not imagine anyone finding the entrance.

"Yet we did," said Paul, reading my mind. "Following the directions on the scroll to a letter we dug at the exact spot."

"Then where is it?" I asked, squinting because the sun was so bright.

"Come this way."

We had to trudge single file behind Paul Jelks, sand coming up to our ankles and filling our shoes. At the junction of the walls of sand and the narrow floor of the gorge, Paul dropped to his knees and began tearing at the earth like a puppy. Within seconds he had cleared off a broad wooden door, perfectly concealed beneath sand and undetectable even close to. Then he lifted this "door," improvised from wooden crates, and revealed a tunnel of steps going deep into the mountain side.

"Watch your step, Lydia. These stairs are badly uneven. I've got my torch."

Down the three of us went, leaving Mark and Dr. Ames behind. As we descended I had a strange feeling.

"Take a careful look, Mr. Rasheed, for you are seeing what no human eyes have seen for three thousand years. And unlike Tutankhamun's tomb, which showed evidence of robbery attempts, this tomb was untouched and looked exactly as it did the day the priests sealed it."

"I never would have thought . . ." began Ahmed, but he did not finish his sentence.

A foul odor met us at the bottom where we stood in an empty antechamber. Paul's light moved over the walls and spotlighted paintings of fantastic creatures and mystical writings. His voice echoed. "Of course it's not clean. We couldn't take the proper care we would have if this had been a legit excavation. We dumped all the dirt outside to use as camouflage. Now you'll notice," he crossed to the other side of the room, "that this is a very simple floor plan. So certain was Tetef that his place of hiding would never be found, that he didn't bother to build elaborate trap doors and pits such as you find in other tombs. He must have reasoned that, if the tombs were better hidden, then outrageous traps wouldn't be necessary; so he set out proving to his ancestors the mistakes they had made. And it worked."

We walked down a sloping passage that went on endlessly into the darkness. About halfway along, Paul stopped and listened. "Did you hear someone call me?"

"No."

"That's funny, I could have sworn . . ." He handed Ahmed the flashlight. "Take this and go on ahead. I'm going back to see what they want. Won't be a minute." And he hurried back up the ramp.

I looked at Ahmed in the darkness, his face barely illuminated by the flashlight. He stood very close to me, breathing softly. "After you, Lydia."

I turned my back on him and walked forward. That ticklish feeling was increasing, as though something was about to happen.

We entered a second room, and this was full of astounding treasures, very much like the things I had seen in Dr. Kellerman's books. They were the personal belongings of the gods. Bed posts in the shape of lions, bolts of linens and silks, jars of wonderful fragrances, ebony coffers containing fabulous jewelry, the mummy of a cat. They were all marvelous to behold.

"Look Lydia!" said Ahmed all of a sudden.

I spun about. His flashlight was shining upon a square wooden box with holes in its surface and a cluster of game pieces at its side. "This is where my jackal came from! It's part of this set!" I squatted down and looked closely at them, then smiled up at Ahmed. His face was hidden in the darkness.

"Would you like to see the king?"

"What?" I stood stiffly. The stench in the air was getting to me. There must have been very little oxygen. "No . . . I don't think so."

"You are not afraid of a mummy, are you?" He took hold of my hand.

"Of course not."

"He is in here. This is a privilege granted to very few, Lydia, to see the king as he really was. Shall we pay a visit to the man who gave you the jackal?"

We trod carefully between the fragile treasures and came to another doorway. It was narrow and set in a wall at least five feet thick. Next to it was a huge square stone that showed evidence of prying and chipping. A crowbar lay on the floor.

"Do not touch this stone, Lydia, for it is attached to a trigger mechanism that will swing it back into place. Now please, after you."

He held the flashlight so that it illuminated the interior of the little room, and I trustingly followed the beam. When I saw the granite sarcophagus I asked, "What's this?" At the same moment, the light suddenly went out and I heard a whooshing sound.

When I turned, I could not see the door any more. Nor could I see the wall. Nor even my hand in front of my face.

Ahmed had rolled the stone back into place.

Stupidly I said, "Wait a minute," and listened. "Come on now. That really didn't happen!" I stepped forward with my hands out and pushed on the stone. Of course, it didn't move. "Ahmed? Ahmed? Hey!"

My face was pressed against the rough wall. "Come on now, let me out! Somebody!" I screamed at the top of my lungs, but I knew it was of no use. The thickness of that door meant that nothing could get in or out—no light, no sound, no air.

No air!

I spun about again and pressed myself flat against the wall. With my eyes at their widest I still could not see—I was as sightless as if I were truly blind. It was a blackness beyond imagination. A fearful darkness that was everywhere at once, surrounding me, and had no defined limits.

"Oh God," I whimpered. "Oh God, no!"

Then I sank down to the floor and curled my feet under me. I tried not to cry, but the tears came with great sobs. Knowing that I must conserve oxygen I tried to hold back, but could not.

Only one thought was in my mind now: Ahmed Rasheed had sealed me in this tomb.

After a moment, my crying subsided and I felt my sorrow replaced by anger. So he was in with Rossiter then! Maybe he wasn't even a government official, or possibly a crooked one. And where was Adele? Had he and Fatso "taken care" of her last night?

Every manner of expletives reeled within my mind at this point. Indignation over having been played for a fool, *twice*. And fury that I had so foolishly, so easily walked into his trap.

And just how would he explain this to Paul Jelks?

Paul Jelks.

I gawked ahead of myself. His words echoed in my ears: "It took us weeks to get that last door open."

Weeks!

"But I don't have weeks!" I said aloud. "I barely have hours!"

Then I stopped talking and tried to do some clear thinking. What a fool I had been to tell Ahmed that no one knew where I was, not even Dr. Kellerman. And Paul Jelks was afraid of jail, so he would have to go along with Rasheed.

God, I was angry!

And God, I was frightened . . .

The darkness was overpowering. It was like a blanket, suffocating. It scared me. All alone in that tomb.

But no, not alone. I had company.

Tetef was with me.

When I came to, I had no idea of how long I had been unconscious, but I knew I was going to have a harder and harder time staying awake. The air was becoming thin. In my initial tantrum I had overexerted myself, causing me to faint. Now, if I was to survive for any time at all, I would have to keep very still and breathe as little as possible.

Then I thought of the person in the tomb with me, trapped like myself, unable to escape. King Tetef. His body lay a few feet from me. His shriveled corpse, lying mute after centuries of undisturbed sleep, was just a short distance in front of my eyes, yet I couldn't see it. Was he angry at my intrusion? Had his ancient sense of the inviolable burial chamber been offended? What measure of retribution might the mystical old pharaoh, so rudely snapped back from the peaceful realm of the dead, send down on me for crimes I never committed?

Oh, Lydia! cried my mind. Get hold of yourself!

When the tears started to come again I desperately fought them back. I knew what it was that upset me so terribly now. It was not the fact of being trapped in the tomb that was so devastating, but that it was Ahmed who had put me there.

They say that when a person is dying, his life flashes before his eyes. I can see now where that concept had its genesis, for, as I felt my lungs labor for air and my body grow weak with asphyxia, I reflected on my life and pondered the incredible turn of events that had brought me to this final hour.

A nurse dedicated to humanity and to saving lives, I had never before felt love for anyone. Bitter with the loss of my parents and brother, I had even driven my remaining sister away from me, shutting my heart to a world full of love and promise. Dr. Kellerman had not been able to find the key, but John Treadwell had managed to unlock the door. And yet it took a stranger with enigmatic eyes to open it all the way.

And now he had betrayed me.

It was difficult to tell if my eyes were open or closed, for it all looked the same. I was lying on my back, gasping and thinking about poor old Tetef in his sarcophagus. Well, he might have escaped tomb robbers for three thousand years, but he wouldn't any more. They had found him after all, to rob him of his immortality.

But no . . . that was not true either. For through the work of men like Carter and Jelks, the names and lives of pharaohs are brought to life for all the world to marvel at. In the living, they will be remembered, and that is true immortality.

My philosophical mood drifted as I felt myself gradually lose my grasp on life. It would not be long, I knew, before I was dead and, in a strangely ironical way, I was sorry to die for only one reason. Suddenly it was all clear to me.

Two loves, I had said to myself in the past few days, both very real in me and yet each so different. Dr. Kellerman and Ahmed Rasheed. My mind had wrestled with that dichotomy: which to choose, for choose I had to.

But now, in these last few minutes of my life—indeed as I teetered on the precipice of oblivion—it was all very clear to me. Nothing to cloud my judgement or sway my opinion. I needed only to look into my heart to see which of the two I most regretted leaving, and then I knew whom I would have chosen had I lived.

I labored in my breathing as I pictured him standing before me, and I managed to smile. Of course, it didn't do me any good now to discover which of the two loves I would have chosen, but it was there all the same. And in my last moments of life, he was all I thought about.

I was roused out of my stupor by a sound. Deliriously, I thought it was the spirit of Tetef rising up to get me. Then I heard another sound. And another. A clinking. A scratching. A scraping.

Someone was trying to get in!

I tried to call out but had no strength. I simply lay like a rag doll, waiting for the sounds to get louder and closer.

Suddenly a tiny beam of light broke through. Then voices. There was a great smash and a rainfall of rubble. More light.

Someone next to me, on his knees, taking me in his arms. "Lydia," he said softly.

"Ahmed. Oh God."

"Come on," said Paul Jelks. "Let's get her out. She needs air."

Then I felt myself lifted by two strong arms and manipulated through the doorway. The outer room smelt of smoke from the dynamite blast. I was hurried away and up the ramp. Light stabbed my eyes. Sunlight. And fresh air washed over my face.

"Allah be praised, you're alive!"

"How long . . ."

"You were in there three hours, Lydia."

"Three . . ." I squinted and covered my eyes. Ahmed placed me gently on the ground, and I felt my body begin to stir back to life.

Now Paul Jelks was at my side. "Poor girl! I must say you've suffered a hell of a lot. There, there, it's all right now. We'll get you back to camp."

I took my hand away from my eyes and found Ahmed gazing down at me. "What happened in there? The door . . ."

"Arnold Rossiter is what happened."

"Rossiter!"

"He followed us here, Lydia, and had his men hold Mark and Dr. Ames at gunpoint. Then he had them call Paul back out of the tomb. When you and I were inside, he closed the door on you and held a gun to my ribs."

"Come on," said Jelks. "Let's get her back to the camp. She's suffered a shock."

"I'm all right . . ."

Ahmed braced me as we walked to the Land Rover and then helped me into the backseat. As we crunched our way up the slope, I caught sight of three uniformed men standing guard at the entrance of the tomb.

"Who are they?" I asked, bewildered. "And how did you . . ."

Ahmed laughed softly and looked down at me with tenderness. "It was Karl Schweitzer who saved us all."

"What . . ."

"You were wrong in your theory of who he was, Lydia, and I only found out last night the truth of his identity. He wasn't looking for Paul Jelks at all, but for Rossiter."

"I don't understand."

"Karl Schweitzer works for the Museum of West Berlin and has been looking for Arnold Rossiter for many months in connection with some stolen masterpieces. He had thought you were working for Rossiter because you were traveling with John Treadwell, Rossiter's man."

"How ironic!"

Ahmed grinned. "It is interesting that Schweitzer was equally as surprised to find you in Khouri's shop as you were to see him. He had been questioning the man for any clues as to the whereabouts of Rossiter, when all of a sudden you appeared. If you worked for Rossiter, as he thought, why were you going to the shops trying to sell this jackal? It made no sense to him, but he was going to try to arrest you anyway."

"But he killed John Treadwell."

"No, that would be Rossiter's act. Karl Schweitzer left John alive and only heard about the murder later."

"I must have missed Rossiter by seconds . . ."

"And in the Domus Aurea, he was following you, yes, but he was not the one to hit you. It had been one of the others, another of Rossiter's agents."

"I don't believe it."

"I can assure you it is all true. When I questioned him last night he showed me . . ."

"Last night! Ahmed, why didn't you tell me?"

"You did not ask me."

I stared at him in amazement and then, suddenly tired, sank back into the security of his arms. I let the car lull me into a peaceful state. My head fell on to Ahmed's shoulder, my eyes closed for only a moment. When, in the next instant, his hand was on my chin and he was kissing me, it seemed so right, so natural. And when I put my arms about his neck and kissed him back, I forgot the others in the car. He held me tightly, as if never to let me go, and when I buried my face in his neck and felt the vehicle come to a slow stop, I remembered the revelation I had had in those last few seconds before being saved, and the decision I had made.

Then I raised my head and looked out of the window. Through the clouds of settling dust I saw Paul Jelks's camp and could make out the forms of several people, most of them in uniform.

I jumped down to the sand and kept myself steady as I gazed at the men who stood a few feet from me. Two of them had been the central villains of my long nightmare; two phantoms who had made my blood run cold and the sight of whom had made me quake with fear.

One was Rossiter (looking only slightly different from the American tourist in the Mousky) and the other was Karl Schweitzer. When I saw his bandaged shoulder and the sling supporting his arm, I felt suddenly, insanely, like laughing.

Ahmed and I approached them. He murmured something to one of the uniformed policemen. The man nodded. We stood in long afternoon shadows, our mouths and throats dry and our clothes covered with grit. And I found myself wondering what to say at a time like this.

I was given no further chance to consider this, however, when the sound of another vehicle crunching over the sand made me spin round. It was another Land Rover, and it contained four people.

Suddenly realizing who they might be, I grew excited. I took a step toward the car and held my breath. Both doors opened. From the passenger side stepped two uniformed men and a young woman dressed in khaki. She glanced over all the faces just once and, spotting me, suddenly cried out, "Liddie!" and ran towards me.

My sister and I fell into a tight embrace, each of us babbling incoherently, tears welling in our eyes. Then, with her hands clasped to my arms, Adele stepped back to regard me, her face a sunburst of smiles.

"Oh Liddie, Liddie," she said over and over again, shaking her head. "Who would have thought? Out here in the middle of the desert? My God!"

I smiled back and blinked the tears from my eyes. The emotional shock, however, of finally seeing my sister after all these years began to subside quickly when I got a closer look at her. In the initial minutes of being reunited with Adele, I had not noticed how much she had changed. But standing here with her now, the dying desert sun casting a dusky glow on our faces, I saw with alarm that my sister had somehow, in these four years, altered a great deal from the last time I had seen her. There were lines about her face and mouth, shadows under her eyes. Her cheeks were hollow, her hair drawn severely back in an unflattering knot. No, it could not have been just the years that had changed Adele, for there was something more than age in her face now; there was a trace of harshness, a hint of cruelty around the eyes and mouth.

As I continued to stare at her with my smile frozen to my face, Adele tossed back her head and looked around at the others gathered about us. Then I saw her gaze settle upon someone who stood behind me, and I heard my sister say flatly, "Hello, Arnold."

Ahmed spoke now, and it was to the officer who had driven Adele's Land

Rover. The two men conversed briefly, then Ahmed turned to me, saying, "They picked your sister up at Luxor Airport. She was preparing to leave."

"Preparing to leave?" I repeated.

Adele gave Ahmed a twisted smile. "I saw those two agents of yours take my picture a few days ago. I knew it was only a matter of time before you and the police would catch up with me. I went to Luxor last night on the usual pretext of wanting to spend the night at the hotel, and while I was there I did some looking around. When I saw the fat creep," she jerked her head towards Schweitzer, "I realized that the time had come."

"Where were you going?" I asked, totally confused.

"Anywhere, dear sister, far away from this godforsaken country."

I was stunned. How could this be my sister Adele? How could she have changed so? And, more important, *why?*

Ahmed's voice was quiet and calm. "Tell us, please, why you were going to leave Luxor."

Adele looked from him to me, then to Paul Jelks to Schweitzer, and lastly to Rossiter. Her eyes were quick and agitated, calculating. All around us an empty wind blew, carrying a fine mist of dry sand into our faces. The wind sounded lonely and hollow, whistling over the vast desert as it had done for centuries. I was struck in that instant with a vision of an ancient funerary procession, solemnly bearing the coffin of Pharaoh Tetef to his final inviolable resting place.

But then the vision faded and I saw my sister suddenly throw up her hands in surrender. "Why not!" she said flippantly. "What do I have to gain now by keeping silent? You want to know why I was leaving Luxor? I'll tell you."

Her eyes rested on me at last and held my gaze as she said, "I was running away from the police."

"But why? Dr. Jelks's crime is not so great! Adele . . ."

Her lips broke into a twisted smile. "Not because of Jelks! Oh, Liddie, I'm not that stupid. You mean you really don't know? You haven't guessed by now?"

I slowly shook my head.

Adele finally turned away to look at the man she planned to marry, and she said to him, "I double-crossed you, Paul."

Jelks stared back at my sister as if he were in a trance. Everyone else stood still and silent. No one moved. Adele continued to speak. "I was in it for the money, Paul, and that's all. In Rome, I met Arnold Rossiter and he made me an offer I couldn't refuse. For a while, anyway, he and I were partners."

Believing and yet disbelieving the incredible words my sister spoke, I managed to murmur, "Then why did you call me?"

"Because my 'partnership' went bad, Rossiter got rough with me, and I got scared. I couldn't come running back to Paul, not after I had planned to cheat him out of his tomb. I needed someone on my side, someone I could trust. And you were the last resort, Liddie. I couldn't tell you that on the phone, but I thought maybe sending the jackal to you would bring you to Rome and that somehow the two of us could get me out of my mess. I guess I miscalculated."

"But in Cairo . . ."

"Yes, I knew you were in Cairo. But God, Liddie, when I saw you and John Treadwell in the dining room at the Shepherd's Hotel, I couldn't believe it. Seeing you two together could only mean that somehow Rossiter had bought you, too. And there went my chances of getting out of this mess. And as well, I was shocked to see Treadwell in Cairo. I didn't think he would have the nerve to set foot in Egypt, not with his reputation with the police. But there he was, Rossiter's right-hand man, and with my sister no less. I didn't know what to do. So I took the opportunity to approach John when he was alone. You see, I was afraid he would tell Paul everything, and that would forever ruin my chances to cash in on the tomb."

"You approached John?"

"I more than approached him, Liddie. John threatened me. He got nasty with me. So I killed him."

"You . . ."

"I came back to the Shepherd's a little while later to find you, but you had gone. You had disappeared and no one knew where. Now I was completely alone and completely scared. My only chance rested with Paul. So I came back at once to the camp and told him the tale about Rossiter threatening me." Adele smiled sweetly at Paul Jelks. "Sorry, sweetheart. I was using you all along. Money was all I wanted."

Now Paul Jelks spoke at last, and his voice was distant, detached. "If you had married me, you would have had money and anything you wanted."

"Oh yes!" she cried with sudden bitterness. "And live the rest of my life in some godforsaken desert. Do you really think I loved you? You were just a novelty, something to *amuse* me at first. I was just about ready to move on when you told me about the tomb."

"Adele . . ." I whispered.

"Yes, Paul, you mentioned countless riches and fame because of that tomb, so I told you I loved you so I could cash in on it. Then you told me it would take *years* to excavate it fully and that the money would come much later. Well, I didn't want 'later' and I didn't want 'years,' so when you told me to take the jackal and try to find a buyer, I came up with a little plan of my own. My opportunity knocked with Rossiter in Rome, offering me half the deal when all the tomb contents were sold. It worked fine for a few days, but then Rossiter got pushy."

Adele stepped past me as if I weren't even there, strode up to Arnold Rossiter and spat at him. "You fool!" she screamed. "When I wouldn't tell you the location of the tomb, you decided to use force. And that's when I got scared and called my sister. Come on, Rossiter, don't you know you can catch more flies with honey than with vinegar. If only you had continued to romance me, to be nice and polite as you were at first, I would have brought you here in time! Then I never would have called Liddie, and you and I could have got rid of Jelks and had the tomb to ourselves!"

To my great surprise, Adele suddenly flew at Rossiter. "You blew it, you pig!" The police were upon her in an instant, pulling her off Rossiter and handcuffing her wrists.

Ahmed, standing very close to me, said quietly, "They will take her back to Cairo . . ."

But I shook my head. Then I watched them as they walked my sister back to the Land Rover. I stood in silence as I saw her start to climb in, then stop, look back at me, give me a small wave, and finally get into the car. The motor started with a rude roar, breaking the desert silence. I continued to stand absolutely still as other vehicles now started their motors; policemen bearing away Arnold Rossiter and Paul Jelks, Karl Schweitzer to nurse his throbbing shoulder, the rest of Jelks's crew under police escort. After they'd all gone in clouds of sand, only Ahmed and I remained at the deserted camp, which was now growing cold and dark in the late twilight.

He said again, "They will take her to Cairo. She will have a trial. But I cannot say . . ."

"I know," I said with a dead voice. "She is guilty of murdering one man, of deceiving others, and of committing crimes against the Egyptian government. What can I say? She is my sister. She called me to come and help her. Guilty or not, she deserves to have me nearby."

I felt Ahmed's arm go about my shoulders. I felt his reassuring warmth and nearness, and I knew that there were other, more important reasons for remaining in Egypt.

Then I heard him whisper softly, "If it is the will of Allah . . ."

FROM
THE DIVINING
A NOVEL BY BARBARA WOOD
NOW AVAILABLE

1

SHE CAME SEEKING ANSWERS.

Nineteen-year-old Ulrika had awoken that morning with the feeling that something was wrong. The feeling had grown while she had bathed and dressed, and her slaves had bound up her hair and tied sandals to her feet, and brought her a breakfast of wheat porridge and goat's milk. When the inexplicable uneasiness did not go away, she decided to visit the Street of Fortune-Tellers, where seers and mystics, astrologers and soothsayers promised solutions to life's mysteries.

Now, as she was carried through the noisy streets of Rome in a curtained chair, she wondered what had caused her uneasiness. Yesterday, everything had been fine. She had visited friends, browsed in bookshops, spent time at her loom—the typical day of a young woman of her class and breeding. But then she had had a strange dream . . .

Just past the midnight hour, Ulrika had dreamed that she gotten out of bed, crossed to her window, climbed out, and landed barefoot in snow. In the dream, tall pines grew all around her, instead of the fruit trees behind her villa, a forest instead of an orchard, and clouds whispered across the face of a winter moon. She saw tracks—big paw prints in the snow, leading into the woods. Ulrika followed them, feeling moonlight brush her bare shoulders. She came upon a large, shaggy wolf with golden eyes. She sat down in the snow and he came to lie beside her, putting his head in her lap. The night was pure, as pure as the wolf's eyes gazing up at her, and she could feel the steady beat of his mighty heart beneath his ribs. The golden eyes blinked and seemed to say: Here is trust, here is love, here is home.

Ulrika had awoken disoriented. And then she had wondered: Why did I dream of a wolf? Wulf was my father's name. He died long ago in faraway Persia.

Is the dream a sign? But a sign of what?

Her slaves brought the chair to a halt, and Ulrika stepped down, a tall girl wearing a long gown of pale pink silk, with a matching stole that draped over her head and shoulders in proper maidenly modesty, hiding tawny hair and a graceful neck. She carried herself with a poise and confidence that concealed a growing anxiety.

The Street of Fortune-Tellers was a narrow alley obscured by the shadow of crowded tenement buildings. The tents and stalls of the psychics, augers, seers, and soothsayers looked promising, painted in bright colors, festooned with glittering objects, each one brighter than the next. Business was booming for purveyors of good-luck charms, magic relics, and amulets.

As Ulrika entered the lane, desperate to know the meaning of the wolf dream, hawkers called to her from tents and booths, claiming to be "genuine Chaldeans," to have direct channels to the future, to possess the Third Eye. She went first to the bird-reader, who kept crates of pigeons whose entrails he read for a few pennies. His hands caked with blood, he assured Ulrika that she would find a husband before the year was out. She went next to the stall of the smoke-reader, who declared that the incense predicted five healthy children for Ulrika.

She continued on until, three quarters along the crowded lane, she came upon a person of humble appearance, sitting only on a frayed mat, with no shade or booth or tent. The seer sat cross-legged in a long white robe that had known better days, long bony hands resting on bony knees. The head was bowed, showing a crown of hair that was blacker than jet, parted in the middle and streaming over the shoulders and back. Ulrika did not know why she would choose so impoverished a soothsayer—perhaps on some level she felt this one might be more interested in truth than in money—but she came to a halt before the curious person, and waited.

After a moment, the fortune-teller lifted her head, and Ulrika was startled by the unusual aspect of the face, which was long and narrow, all bone and yellow skin, framed by the streaming black hair. Mournful black eyes beneath highly arched brows looked up at Ulrika. The woman almost did not look human, and she was ageless. Was she twenty or eighty? A brown and black spotted cat lay curled asleep next to the fortune-teller. Ulrika recognized the breed as an Egyptian Mau, said to be the most ancient of cat breeds, possibly even the progenitor from which all cats had sprung.

Ulrika brought her attention back to the fortune-teller's swimming black eyes filled with sadness and wisdom.

"You have a question," the fortune-teller said in perfect Latin, eyes peering steadily from deep sockets.

The sounds of the alley faded. Ulrika was captured by the black Egyptian eyes, while the brown cat snoozed obliviously.

"You want to ask me about a wolf," the Egyptian said in a voice that sounded older than the Nile.

"It was in a dream, Wise One. Was it a sign?"

"A sign of what? Tell me your question."

"I do not know where I belong, Wise One. My mother is Roman, my father German. I was born in Persia and have spent most of my life roaming with my mother, for she followed a quest. Everywhere we went, I felt like an outsider. I am worried, Wise One, that if I do not know where I belong, I will never know who I am. Was the wolf dream a sign that I belong in the Rhineland with my father's people? Is it time for me to leave Rome?"

"There are signs all about you, daughter. The gods guide us everywhere, every moment."

"You speak in riddles, Wise One. Can you at least tell me my future?"

"There will be a man," the fortune-teller said, "who will offer you a key. Take it."

"A key? To what?"

"You will know when the time comes . . ."

CPSIA information can be obtained
at www.ICGtesting.com
Printed in the USA
JSHW021122220323
39321JS00001B/176